A Mother's Journey

A Mother's Journey

JUNE HAMPSON

First published in Great Britain in 2012 by Orion Books,
an imprint of The Orion Publishing Group Ltd
Orion House, 5 Upper Saint Martin's Lane
London WC2H 9EA

An Hachette UK Company

1 3 5 7 9 10 8 6 4 2

ISBN (Hardback) 978 1 4091 3369 8
ISBN (Trade Paperback) 978 1 4091 3370 4

www.orionbooks.co.uk

I have trod the upward and the downward slope;
I have endured and done in the days before;
I have longed for all, and bid farewell to hope;
And I have lived and loved, and closed the door.

Robert Louis Stevenson

Acknowledgements

I am indebted to Natalie Braine and that grand team at Orion. Also to Geoffrey Boxall who came up with the idea.

Prologue

1962

'There's a bloke gonna come in any minute an' I ain't in Gosport an' you don't know me, Bert, got it?'

'You, the top prossie in Gosport, don't want to see a bloke?'

Bert was frying bacon at the gas stove, forking it over so it cooked evenly. He stopped smiling when Vera desperately cut in with, '*Please, Bert. I'm not here!*'

Vera didn't dare stay any longer in the near-deserted caff. She flew back up the wooden stairs to her room at the top of the lodging house adjoining the caff and peeked out of the window.

She shivered violently as the man's broad-shouldered body strode purposefully along the brightly lit pavement towards the caff.

It was obvious he'd come from the ferry. Suppose she'd been on her regular pitch there near the taxi rank? Suppose he'd seen her?

She dropped the net curtain back in place and looked down at the floor.

Her mackerel-coloured cat wound himself in a figure of eight around her feet encased in high-heeled mules. His fur was softer than the slippers' marabou trim.

'If I 'adn't let you in, Kibbles, an' looked out the window, I'd never 'ave spotted 'im.' Despite her soft words her heart was hammering. She tried to put the man out of her mind and concentrate on the cat she loved fiercely.

She bent down and picked up the weighty feline, who immediately began filling the room with his throaty purr.

'That man ruined my life. And I hoped I'd never see 'im again,' she whispered.

Yet her first thought had been to go down and give him a mouthful, scratch his eyes out maybe. She was after all a Gosport girl and Gosport girls don't take wrongs lightly. But Bert wouldn't thank her for causing a ruckus in his caff and she wasn't going to brawl in the street like some common tart.

Her heart still hadn't stopped its fluttering and she realised she was too upset to behave rationally. She needed time to think.

Still carrying the cat she walked to the wooden draining board and set Kibbles down in front of a saucer filled to the brim with sardines. Another saucer held his milk. He began to eat as she watched him.

This room was her refuge.

At the top of the building, it looked down to North Street and along North Cross Street and over Murphy's hardware shop where you could buy anything from a nail to a rose bush. Then the view swept across to the ferry pontoon where squat boats transferred passengers across the strip of murky, smelly Solent water to Portsmouth.

Vera took a deep breath in an attempt to calm her nerves.

She was trying hard not to think of Alfred below in the caff quite possibly interrogating Bert. She didn't want to think about what had happened that fateful day of the party but it all came back to her as vividly as if it was happening now.

Vera's skirt was pushed up. She couldn't move. His bulk had her pinned to the scullery floor and she could feel the strange slippery heat of him. Grunting sounds came from him as he fumbled and tore one handed at her clothes. She was on the floor inches away from the grease-stained gas oven, its smell of years of burned fat sickening her. She wanted to scream but his other hand now completely covered her mouth. And then he pushed into her and was moving inside her and it hurt.

She had been only fourteen.

Now she was thirty-five and Alfred Lovell, the man who'd caused so much pain in her life and who she'd never thought she'd see again, was downstairs.

What had brought him back to Gosport?

The only way to find out was to go down and listen.

She kicked off her hard-soled mules and opened her door. She stepped out and began creeping past the other rented rooms and back down the stairs.

Crouching on a step where she was sure she couldn't be seen, Vera hugged her nylon-clad knees close to her body. She prayed no one would need to use the lavatory and chance upon her sitting there and call out to her by name.

Even from the stairway she was aware of his almost forgotten spicy aftershave wafting up towards her.

Her body clenched as she heard his voice.

'I need to talk to Vera.'

Vera leaned forward and could just make out those broad shoulders, the strong neck and the glossy dark moustache, now threaded with grey, above full lips. His suntan only added to his good looks.

His piercing blue eyes were searching Bert's face for answers. Bert was wiping plates, making each dish glitter with cleanliness.

Silently she willed Bert to tell Alfred nothing.

'She's not 'ere tonight.' *Bless you, Bert*, she thought.

'Later on? Will she return later?'

Bert moved an overflowing glass ashtray to the other side of the Formica table. It was a studied movement, like he was thinking hard.

Vera counted just three customers. It was well past twelve and, even though the summer evening had been warm, Gosport had closed down for the night.

'Dunno.' Bert now began the laborious business of rolling up his shirt sleeves. 'What d'you want to know for? An' what's your name?'

'Alfred Lovell.' The man shifted his bulk from one foot to the other. Vera could sense his impatience. She remembered he had always been like that, irritated when things didn't go his way.

'Does she live here?' He tapped one foot on the wooden floor. 'If not, give me her address. I've heard you and she are pals.'

'Do I look like I come up the Solent in a bucket? If I am her pal I can't just give out her details, can I? That's supposing I knows 'em.' Bert hooked his thumbs into his braces and met Alfred's glare unblinkingly.

'I've come halfway around the world to see Vera, from Australia, to be exact. Not seen her for years, see? Though that's between me and her and has nothing to do with you.'

'That's as may be. Or you might just be stringing me a line, an' I *do* like to look out for our Vera. Very well thought of is our Vera. I'd be a mug to take you at your word, wouldn't I? Anyway, she's not 'ere.'

Vera held her breath as Alfred leaned closer to Bert. What if Alfred turned nasty? After all, he'd hurt her, hadn't he?

4

But he pulled back and Vera breathed a silent sigh of relief.

It wasn't that Bert couldn't take care of himself. He'd been a bit of a gangster in his former days so was well used to dealing with slippery customers. But the younger man had the advantage of physical fitness.

'Tell you what, mate. Why don't you jot your address down 'ere?' Bert fished in his greasy white apron pocket and pulled out a small stained notebook. He slid it along the table. Attached to the spiral binder by a piece of grubby string was a stub of pencil.

Alfred Lovell wrote on the pad and passed it back to Bert. Vera could still feel the tension in the air.

'If I don't hear from her in a week, I'll be back.'

And then his voice went quiet so Vera had to strain her ears to listen. 'When you see her, tell her Jen's dead.'

Vera heard the main door's bell chime its tinny sound as he made his way out.

Still Vera crouched there. So his wife, Jennifer, was dead was she? Alfred Lovell had lost his meal ticket. Vera, frightened the man might return, was too scared to move.

But he'd gone. The man who was constantly in her dreams and caused her to wake up crying and sweating had left.

Vera measured every man by Alfred Lovell and once more he was back in her life.

She held on to the banister and shakily pulled herself into an upright position. A cloud of her favourite perfume, Californian Poppy, rose with her and she breathed it deeply as though its scent could comfort her.

When she reached the bottom stair she fluffed up the ruffles on her red silk blouse and ran her fingers around the wide black plastic belt at the waist of her tight black skirt.

'He's left then?'

Bert was sitting at the table. He looked up at her voice. He'd lit a Woodbine and was scrutinising the address on the piece of paper. A fug of cigarette smoke hung around him.

'You're shivering,' he said. 'You ain't in command of yourself, are you?' Vera shook her head. Bert had done his best always to look out for her. He was a true friend in every way. Sometimes he knew her better than she knew herself.

'He's gone out the door but not out of your life.' Bert held out the paper with the address and Vera took it from him as though it was contaminated.

'Thank you for lying for me,' she said quietly.

'I didn't so much lie as bend the truth. I could tell by the cut of his clothes and his suntan that he wasn't a john. Anyway, you ain't never brought a john back to the caff in all the time you've lived here. Couldn't for the life of me see you starting now.' He took a deep pull on his cigarette then stubbed it out in the ashtray. 'Gosport's favourite prostitute you might be but when I sensed you hiding at the top of the stairs . . .'

'Do you think he knew I was there?' Vera asked worriedly. 'No.'

She sat down at the table. The caff was empty now. Bert got up and went over to the main door and slid the bolt along and turned the sign to closed.

'I'll clear up in the mornin'.' He walked to the now silent jukebox and pulled out its electric plug. 'Let's get out of this goldfish bowl,' Bert said with a wave towards the glass windows. 'Never know who's outside looking in.'

He turned off the lights so there was only the thin gleam from the streetlamp illuminating the stairs.

He held open the door from the caff that led into the hallway.

'Who's this Jen what's dead now? And what does this bloke mean to you? You want to talk about it, Vera?'

Vera stood up and felt the tears rise with her. She knew she was tough, and she'd held her secrets close all these years. But she so badly needed to confide in someone.

Using the back of her hand she wiped away tears as she went out into the hall.

In the big kitchen he pulled out a chair and Vera sat down. She watched him light the gas. The flames leaped up red and orange and blue until Bert finished filling the kettle and set it down, flattening them.

He pulled out a chair next to her and took one of her hands in his.

'Come on, love, no arguments. I'll make a cuppa an' you can tell me all about it.'

Chapter 1

1941

'If your ol' man didn't pour it down 'is throat so much in the Alma your mum'd be able to afford a sofa like that.' One look at Tim's stricken face told Vera she'd put her foot in it again. Why didn't she think before she opened her big mouth? She felt for his hand which stuck out of his short dirty jumper sleeve. 'I'm sorry.'

'Doesn't matter.' He looked down at her and smiled, but Vera could tell by the sadness in his eyes that her words had hurt him. He was a head taller than she was. She'd hardly grown an inch since the war started, so Vera decided that, at fourteen, five foot three inches was all she was ever going to be. Tim was the same age but his height and lanky frame made him look much older. He always had a book of some sort crammed into his back pocket. Today it was *Farewell, My Lovely* by Raymond Chandler.

He had his gas mask in a cardboard box slung over one shoulder. Vera had already thrown her gas mask in the hallway. She hated carrying it everywhere like they were supposed to do. The mask smelled of the same stuff the dentist put over her face to make her go to sleep to have a tooth extracted.

Tim waved a hand towards a cart and horse and the two brawny blokes unloading.

'Bet whoever that lot belongs to was bombed out, like we was, Vera. Gosport's gettin' it bad now. The armament depot down Weevil Lane, the submarine base at Haslar and of course Portsmouth and the warships means we don't stand a chance.'

'Well, we must think we stand some chance of survival else we'd be billeted out in the country, wouldn't we? We'd be evacuees.'

'I wish we could have been evacuated. But I refused when I found out it was only us kids. I wasn't goin' to leave my mum alone with that devil.' His hand slipped from her palm and fell to his side. Vera knew that too many hidings from his father had robbed him of his confidence. Sometimes at nights he and his mum walked the streets waiting for his dad to calm down after a day's propping up the bar.

Vera tried to change the subject. 'They got good stuff, ain't they?' She grinned at Tim, who was eyeing the two moquette armchairs now being carried from the cart and into number fifteen, right opposite Vera's house. He brushed his overlong blond hair back from his forehead and it promptly fell back again.

Vera put her hands on her hips, hips that she'd suddenly acquired along with a very full bust. Sometimes as she walked along Gosport High Street she quite liked the attention of the boys and their wolf whistles but other times she felt shy and wanted to hide and wished she was flat-chested like most of her school friends.

'The Last Time I Saw Paris' blared out from the passage of Vera's house. Tim raised an eyebrow.

'Our Patsy's home early from work,' Vera explained. 'She likes that song. Reckons she's goin' to Paris one day.'

'She'll 'ave to turn the wireless off when your mum gets back from church.'

'Not Patsy. She's eighteen now an' my mum don't go on at her so much now she's earning. We needs her wages. Patsy got the wireless off one of her boyfriends. She likes the BBC Forces Programme. All the same I'll warn her when Mum comes so she can turn it down.'

Vera glanced up at Tim. She liked him best of all the boys in the street and he was the only one she confided in about her mum's strictness.

Vera shivered in the early evening chill. Soon it would be dark. Tim said he never felt the cold, despite not having a coat. It was well known down the street that his mother sold their clothing coupons because she needed money more than clothes. Vera didn't care how he was dressed, she just liked being with him.

Tim Saunders and his family had arrived in the street a year ago. They'd been bombed out of their house in Bedford Street and, Tim had told her, it was a stroke of luck they hadn't perished. He and his mum had gone to the Criterion Picture House to see *Fantasia*. His dad had been drinking in the Barley Mow.

The previous night his mum had gone through his dad's trouser pockets when he was snoring in bed and extracted as much money as she'd dared without him becoming suspicious when he woke. If she hadn't they'd never have gone to the pictures.

Tim said he'd always think of the Walt Disney picture as his favourite film.

All along the street, women in flowered wraparound pinafores were standing gossiping at their doorsteps. The hum of voices floated on the air. The neighbours' steps were either cardinal red or whitened to a snowy brightness. Vera marvelled that even after a raid and all the dust that floated through the air the steps were the first thing to show signs of normality again.

The women's eyes never left the cart and its ever decreasing pile of furniture.

'Done your homework?' Tim asked.

Vera knew Tim always did his homework at school because once, in a fit of temper, his dad had torn up his exercise books.

'Don't 'ave any tonight.' She glanced up at Tim. 'Do you like being at the Grammar?' she asked suddenly.

She was surprised when he answered, 'Yes. It's all right.'

It wasn't really a mixed school, for the girls didn't have many lessons with the boys. Only French and geography. And at break times she spied Tim alone, reading. He was always alone.

'What you want to do when you leave?' Vera asked.

His face became gloomy but there was a far-away look in his eyes. 'I want to travel. Maybe write about foreign countries.' He sighed. 'Not a hope. I'm not staying on at school. Someone's got to bring in some money.' He smiled at her. 'What about you?'

'I want to be me own boss. I don't want to be answerable to anyone. I don't ever want to eat Spam again as long as I live!'

Tim laughed, then said, 'Vera, that's a tall order. Wouldn't it be better to get married an' let your husband earn the wages?'

'What like *my* dad and like *your* dad?'

Tim was silent.

'We 'ave got the vote, you know. Women can do what they like. We're working on farms, in factories, drivin' lorries, in the forces. Showin' the world that women can do jobs same as blokes.'

'You'll definitely 'ave to stay on at school to change the world, Vera.'

'This war is already doin' that but I *do* want to go on to university. Though I can't expect my mum and Patsy to go on working to keep me.'

'Your mum's just come round the corner.'

Vera's heart missed a beat.

'Patsy! Mum's comin'!' Vera immediately heard the music lowered to a more sedate level.

The endless backwards and forwards of the men unloading was forgotten as Vera watched her mother stride along the pavement. Small and slight, her black raincoat tightly belted, she was, as usual, in a world of her own. Vera knew she would smell of carbolic soap. She would be wearing no jewellery or make-up and she wouldn't smile at her neighbours. Her plain black low-heeled court shoes, freshly mended with Blakeys' heel tips, could now be heard. A few wisps escaped from the tight knot of hair pinned back from her face.

The other children ran to meet their parents if they spotted them walking up the street. Not Vera. She had been chastised too many times for 'making a show'. Vera could see the usual Woodbine cigarette tightly clamped in her mouth.

'Hello, Mum.' Vera let her smile drop for her mother wasn't looking at her.

'I want you in in five minutes for your tea.' Her mother's voice was throaty due to all the fags. Vera hoped she wouldn't have a cigarette dangling on her lip when she put the final touches to the evening meal. Vera got fed up with picking bits of grey ash out of the food.

Vera's mother was totally ignoring the movement across the road. She wouldn't lower herself to stare out of her own doorway but later Vera knew she'd want every single detail.

'I've peeled the potatoes. What's for tea?' Vera suddenly realised she was hungry.

'Spam and spuds.'

Vera's mum had crossed the step into the open doorway.

'You know I don't like Spam,' Vera protested. 'Why can't we have chops?'

'I have to queue for them, and one tiny chop each is sometimes all I can get hold of. Anyway, you eat meat too quickly. You could at least taste it before you swallow it whole. If you realised four ounces of butter, one of cheese and an egg is all you're allowed per week you wouldn't moan about the food so much that God provides.'

'But you always buy that awful tinned meat stuff an' I hate it.'

The hand was so quick that Vera never saw it coming but the sting around her cheek and ear made her head swim.

'There's a war on. Think yourself lucky you got something to eat! There's plenty of people who are starving. The good Lord provides food and you dare to say you don't like it? I spend my life on my knees cleaning other people's houses so I can keep you and your ungrateful sister! Get to bed!'

'But, Mrs—' Tim had moved quickly towards Vera but her mother was faster and, pushing him aside with her other hand, dragged Vera inside. The front door slammed. The key, hanging from the letterbox, on its string, jangled noisily against the wood.

Patsy's white face was staring out from behind the living-room door.

Vera ran up the thirteen narrow uncarpeted steps to her bedroom.

'How many times have I told you not to hang around with that drunk's spawn?' her mother shouted up at her.

Vera pulled her bedroom door closed behind her. She was shaking. Once again opening her big mouth had got her into trouble. She crawled on to the bed and covered herself with the feather quilt.

She lay there until she'd stopped shivering and felt calm enough to get out of bed.

Her room was at the back of the house and the window looked across the narrow gardens. Vera pulled back the net curtain and stared beyond the flat roof of the scullery to the lavatory at the bottom of their yard.

She needed to pee but didn't want to risk coming into contact with her mother, who might not have calmed down yet.

Vera didn't like the lavatory. Not even in the daytime. Spiders as big as her fists lurked there.

Patsy had threaded newspaper on a string for the three of them to wipe themselves with. Vera wasn't keen on the *Daily Mirror* as it left black print on her skin. She vowed when she grew up she'd have nothing but Izal paper in her lavatory, and no spiders.

Her bedroom was the only place she felt really safe. There was a double iron bedstead, a chest of drawers facing the bed with a brown oval-framed mirror perched on top, a green-painted trunk in the corner on the floor and her gramophone on a chair near the bed.

Not that she had many records as the gramophone was a present from Patsy. Some bloke had given it to her and Patsy didn't refuse it, knowing Vera would like it. Patsy had a Decca wind-up gramophone that was much nicer. Another man had given her that. Patsy was always coming home with gifts from men she knew. Vera's record collection comprised 'Because of You' and 'I Hear Music'. Patsy had loads of records and as long as Vera asked first she let her borrow them.

There was a cross on Vera's wall above the bed, and a large picture in a gilt frame of Mary holding the baby Jesus nailed opposite the bed.

Vera had stopped going to the cold Catholic church with her mother, who realised it was better to leave her daughter at home than drag her protesting down the road with all the neighbours gawping. Vera contented herself with the assembly that was held in school in the mornings and the prayers and hymns that were sung there.

Of course she believed in God and Jesus. Didn't she pray every night for God to keep her and her loved ones safe during this awful war? At any time one of Hitler's planes could send them to kingdom come.

But Vera was fed up with her mother ramming her beliefs down her throat. Quoting the bible was all right if you lived your life the way Jesus said you should. Calling Tim a drunk's spawn wasn't Godly, neither was smacking kids about, especially when it was Vera who was on the receiving end of the slaps.

Vera heard footsteps.

'Can I come in?' a voice asked. Vera went to the door and opened it and Patsy stepped inside.

She was as blonde as Vera was dark. Vera reckoned she looked just like June Haver the film star.

'I'm just off out. Going to a dance at the Co-op Hall in Queen's Road.'

Her eyes were sparkling and had Vaseline on their lids to make them glisten. Patsy got asked to loads of dances.

'I like your suit.'

Patsy had on a green silk two-piece with a peplum at the back. And not for her a pencil line up the back of her legs: Patsy wore real nylons.

'I've left you some tea on the top of the stove. If you stay up here a bit longer you'll have the house to yourself.'

'Why's that?'

'Mum's going back to the church to do the flowers as there's a christening tomorrow. I swear Father Michael sees more of her than we do.'

Vera gave a small smile. Her mother rarely entered Vera's bedroom, not even to change the bedding. Long ago, when Vera was eleven, she'd realised if she didn't wash out her own clothes they wouldn't get washed. Yet her mother took great pride in washing the delicate lace altar cloths from St John's Church where she spent most of her time when she wasn't working.

'She'll be seeing to the flowers brought to her by the congregation from their gardens and allotments. No one can arrange flowers like Mum.' Patsy giggled and Vera began to feel better.

'What'll she do when all what's growing in the allotments and gardens is vegetables? Ain't we supposed to be "Digging For Victory"?'

'Mum'll make arrangements out of cabbages an' onions, Vera. Come here an' let me see your face.'

Vera went over and stood in front of the speckled, oval mirror. Patsy gently touched the finger marks on Vera's cheek.

'She don't mean it, you know.' Ever the peacemaker was Patsy.

'What's that then, fairy dust?' Vera asked angrily. Lately the slaps occurred more often. They had become harder, too. Sometimes she bunked off school when the marks showed too much for her to explain away.

Patsy put her arms around Vera.

'She's got worse since Dad left. I reckon she knows it was her fault he went. She tries to get rid of the guilt by doin' stuff for the church. She thinks so much about that place that she forgets about us.'

Vera thought about Patsy's words and whether her life might have been different if her dad hadn't gone back to his Dublin birthplace. Would their mother have been less critical of Vera if she hadn't been her father's favourite? Daddy's little girl she might have been but he'd left her behind when he'd packed his case and sailed to Ireland.

'I need you to tell me that my hair don't look too awful.' Patsy stepped away from Vera and patted the front of her hair, which was curled in a long fringe and rolled like a sausage at the back.

'You got a slight orange tinge but what do you expect?' Patsy worked with gunpowder down the armament depot and discoloured hair and stained skin was only one of the hazards of the job.

'Is it bad?' Patsy looked worried.

'No. Bein' blonde you just got more goldy bits.'

Vera studied her own hazel eyes with their long lashes. She knew her mouth was just a little too wide for her thin face but at least she had a small nose. Her hair curled around her face, so dark brown it was almost black. She'd already decided when she was older she'd dye it black.

'Hedy Lamarr, you reckon I still look like her?' Vera asked.

Patsy, satisfied with her looks, had her hand on the door-knob.

But she came back into the room and kissed Vera on the top of her head.

'You already are a little cracker. When you're older you'll knock spots off Hedy Lamarr!'

Vera heard Patsy's high heels clatter down the stairs, then her sister called, ''Bye, Mum.'

17

Vera listened for her mother's reply but heard nothing. She went back to looking in the mirror. She tucked in her blouse, which had come adrift from her skirt, and was surprised once again how small her waist looked against the curves of her breasts and the swell of her hips. She knew she could easily pass for eighteen. She'd asked Patsy to take her when she went dancing up at Connaught Hall in town, where the servicemen went. In the end Patsy had promised to take her soon.

Sometimes she heard Patsy and her latest boyfriend giggling in the alleyway down the side of number twelve next door.

Patsy never got slapped. But then Patsy was bigger and stronger than her mother and often brought home boxes of stockings and tins of fruit that she got off the Canadian airmen at the aerodrome at Rowner or the spivs that she knew.

Much later the click clack of her mother's court shoes on the lino of the hall told Vera her mother was going out. Vera waited for the snap of the lock and the chink of the key swinging against the wood before she opened her bedroom door.

Immediately the smell of boiling washing and gas hit her. Her mother had done it again! She'd left the house with water boiling in the gas copper. How hard was it to turn off the gas? How hard was it to yell up the stairs that she'd put a wash on and Vera was to scrub the clothes before she went to bed? Suppose she'd never come out of her room but had drawn the blackout curtains and gone to sleep?

Vera ran down the stairs. One day her mother would forget something and the house would blow up or burn down. That's if a bomb didn't get it first.

The scullery stank of wet boiled washing and where the copper had been filled to the brim the water had bubbled over on to the cement floor.

Vera bent down and, with an old towel wrapped around her arm to protect her from the scalding drips, felt behind the copper for the gas tap. It didn't take her long to find the cause of the stench. The gas tap was turned on but the jets had blown out with the water dripping on them. Vera could feel the heat coming from the base of the boiler. Carefully she managed to twist the gas tap to the off position. Immediately the hissing sound stopped.

Vera extricated herself from the boiler and stood up. Knowing she would have to clear up the mess when the water had cooled, she wiped her hands, arms and knees, then she went back upstairs.

In their mother's bedroom, where Patsy's clothes were kept, Vera glanced at the bed, the two small dark-wood wardrobes and a chest of drawers with Patsy's make-up spread across the top. Her sister slept on the put-you-up in the downstairs front room because their mother didn't like being woken up when Patsy came in late, but their mother insisted that the room be kept tidy in case visitors came, so every morning the makeshift bed was folded out of sight. Yet Vera couldn't remember the last time they'd had a visitor. There was a small block of mascara with a tiny brush, a push-up tube of panstick, assorted eyebrow pencils, a jar of Pond's cold cream and several different shades of red lipstick on the chest of drawers.

Patsy had sunk nails in the wood on the back of the door to hang extra clothes. Across the back of an upright chair were cami knickers in pink and tea rose. Vera promised herself she would one day wear pretty underwear. French knickers instead of the awful passion-killers she had to wear for school. If she pulled the knicker legs down they came to her knees!

Vera pulled back the net curtain. She wanted to see if the people across the road had finished moving in.

The cart was bereft of its treasures and the horse looked fed up even though it was chewing away inside a nosebag.

The front door was open and Mrs Brady from number eighteen was standing in the middle of the road with Mrs Potter from number two. Mrs Potter had her curlers in her hair. They were staring into the open doorway.

Then a car drew up and stopped a few yards away from the horse.

A Bentley!

Vera gasped. They never had many cars drive into Alma Street, certainly nothing as posh as a Bentley. And if an owner should be foolish enough to stop, within minutes the kids swarmed over the car like ants.

Mrs Potter and Mrs Brady had stopped talking and were now staring at the spectacle before them. A man jumped out and tipped his hat to the women. Mrs Potter, clearly embarrassed, covered her mouth with a hand.

The man bent down and opened the car door nearest the house and out stepped a girl around Vera's age. She had ringlets the colour of corn. She smiled at Mrs Potter and Mrs Brady. Then she smoothed down her blue coat, which obviously wasn't a cut-down, and waited while the man handed out a woman.

Full of curiosity the girl looked about her and then upwards. She spotted Vera watching her and gave a small wave. Vera stepped away from the window. But curiosity got the better of her and within seconds she had pulled the curtain back a smidgeon to continue watching.

The woman, in a fur-collared coat that almost reached to her calves, looked about her. She too was blonde but her hair was shaped in the latest bob cut. Perched on her head was a little hat with a small veil and a large flower. Unlike the girl, the woman didn't smile. Her face was skilfully made-up but in a way that looked like it might crack if she smiled.

The woman took the girl by the hand and led her into the house. Vera turned to look at the man.

He had his back to her but Vera noted his broad shoulders. He wore a camel coat that reached past his knees. Peeping out from beneath his trilby hat was curly dark hair. But it was his moustache she liked, when he turned towards her, dark and bushy, set beneath his straight nose and above a pair of full lips that looked every bit as kissable as Rhett Butler's did when he kissed Scarlett O'Hara in *Gone with the Wind.*

'Cor! Clark Gable or what!' Vera whispered to the empty room.

As though he heard her, the man looked up. Vera's eyes locked with his and he winked.

Mrs Potter and Mrs Brady looked up and, catching sight of her, laughed. Vera dropped the curtain.

With a strange feeling in the pit of her stomach, Vera went downstairs to see if the water in the copper had cooled sufficiently for her to get on with the washing and the clearing up of the water in the scullery.

It was as she was using the tongs to transfer the steaming clothes to the butler sink that she heard her name being called. She wiped her hands on her mother's pinny and went to the back door where the huge beast of a mangle stood in the garden by the wall, waiting, its huge rollers like jaws ready to trap her fingers.

'Vera!'

She went out into the back garden with the privet hedges either side and peered through the gap towards the alley.

Two gardens separated the alley from number fourteen but standing on tip toe she could see Tim waving at her.

'Are you all right?' he asked.

'Yes,' she called back. She felt touched that he'd taken such trouble to leave his own house at the top of the street and come down to find out how she was.

'Sure?'

Vera nodded. Something moved in his arms and she saw he'd carried down the big old ginger cat, Mogs, which he loved.

'I saw your mum leave. I didn't dare knock on your door in case Patsy was home and told your mum. I know she thinks I'm rubbish.'

Vera stopped him. 'Don't you dare say another word!' And then there was silence.

Finally Tim said, 'See you at school tomorrow?'

She nodded and watched as he slowly turned away.

'Goodnight,' she called.

With a wave he and the cat disappeared into the alley. Vera felt the first spots of cold rain.

She went back into the dank stuffiness of the scullery and began rubbing at the clothes.

When at last the washing was done and the scullery was dry and clean, Vera eyed the covered plate sitting atop the saucepan of water on the stove. She made herself a drink of orange with a spoonful of orange concentrate.

Vera rinsed the glass and left it on the wooden draining board. Then she took the top plate off her meal. The Spam she wouldn't eat but she was so hungry she couldn't even be bothered to warm the potatoes up.

With every awful mouthful she longed for tomorrow.

The tapping on the window made Vera jump. She looked at the clock and saw she had been reading for only moments.

The noise on the glass continued and fearfully Vera put down *The Secret Garden*, a book she was reading for the second time, and drew back a corner of the blackout curtain.

'What are you doing here?'

Tim's face was a broad grin as he whispered, 'Let me in, I got something for you.'

'You can't come into my bedroom!'

'If I stay out here much longer one of the neighbours will see me.'

Vera drew up the sash window and Tim climbed over the sill bringing with him a newspaper-wrapped parcel, the smell of which made Vera's hunger pains more acute.

Flustered, Vera grabbed her coat and slipped it over her long flannelette nightgown and buttoned it.

Tim sat on the edge of the bed and held out the package. 'I knew you wouldn't eat the Spam, so I got you some proper supper.'

Vera stared at him in amazement. She took the parcel and began unwrapping it and as she did so the aroma of fried food filled the room.

'Thank God fish and chips aren't rationed,' Tim said. 'The chippy had a delivery of fish today.'

'I don't know what to say.' Vera was overcome.

'Don't say nothin', just eat.'

Vera looked at his face. She didn't ask where he'd got the money from to buy her the treat.

'You eat with me.'

'I've already eaten. Anyway, I have to go. Won't do for your mum or Patsy to catch me in your bedroom, will it?'

He stared at her, his eyes holding hers for a long time, then he raised his hand and brushed her cheek. Vera's heart was beating fast.

'Don't forget we're going to the fair tomorrow after school. I saw the wagons rolling down Forton Road towards the town,' he said.

Vera nodded. He looked like an excited little boy, she thought, his eyes all aglow at the proposed treat.

'It would be great if we could do more than just walk around Walpole Park,' she said wistfully. She thought how exciting it would be to go on the dodgem cars or throw balls at the coconuts. But neither of them had money to waste on frivolities. 'But it will still be exciting,' she added.

Tim moved to the window and drew aside the curtain. He looked back, smiled, almost as though he had a secret, then climbed over the sill.

In the silent house Vera felt the empty space of his leaving.

Chapter 2

'You're early,' he said. Tim was waiting for her outside the girl's entrance to the school. He sat on the steps and as she approached a big smile lit his face and he closed the paperback he'd been reading and stuck it firmly in his back pocket.

'Mrs Knight, our cookery teacher's away,' Vera said, as though it explained everything. She'd stuffed her gas mask in her satchel so there'd be less bulk to carry. The double doors slammed open behind her and a stream of girls came clattering and chattering down the steps.

Tim grabbed her hand, 'C'mon, let's get away from here before we get caught up in the after-school rush to get home.'

Vera half walked, half ran with him down Daisy Lane, the satchel bumping at her hip. Eventually Tim slowed down.

'It's nice not having to go straight back,' Vera said. She gazed at the trees, their leaves fresh and green after the rain. 'Tonight Mum's putting flowers in the church for a wedding tomorrow.' Vera sighed with happiness. 'Then her and Mrs Daniver'll give the place a special clean. What about your mum? Will she wonder where you are?'

Tim shook his head. 'She knows we're going to the fair.'

'And she doesn't mind?' Her voice was incredulous. Vera stood quite still and stared up at him.

Tim laughed. 'Of course not. We're not going into a den of

iniquity!' He suddenly put his arms around her waist, hoisting her up and swinging her around until she giggled and begged to be let go. After Tim had set her on her feet she whispered breathlessly, 'I like being with you.'

Tim ran his fingers through his hair, which immediately flopped back over his forehead. 'And I like being with you,' he said before grabbing her hand and striding purposefully down the leafy lane.

Vera heard the music heralding the rides as they walked along Stoke Road. It didn't take them long to reach the town and Walpole Park. She could smell sausages cooking, onions frying and the sweetness of candyfloss. Vera licked her lips but remembered neither of them had any money, so despite the glorious smell of the food they'd both have to go hungry. The Andrews Sisters were belting out 'Ferryboat Serenade' and the cheerful sound added to Vera's excitement.

Around the outside of the field Vera saw that the caravans were parked quite close to each other. Women chatted over stable doors and children played on the steps. Washing blew on makeshift lines.

'The dodgems first,' said Tim. They stood on the wooden boards around the bumper cars and watched as the drivers tried either not to bump into each other or to collide head on. It was noisy and exhilarating and Vera was practically jumping up and down with excitement.

'Oh, look,' she shouted. 'That bloke in the red car doesn't know what he's doing!'

She pointed at a vehicle that was getting bumped and jerked about by other cars as it manoeuvred its way slowly around the floor. A tall, good-looking young man wearing a neckerchief and a flat cap jumped on the back of the car and whilst holding on to the pole at the back bent down and turned the steering wheel, extricating the man from trouble. Then the attendant looked over and saw Tim. He swept his cap from his head and waved it to Tim with a flourish and Tim acknowledged his greeting.

'When the music stops, get into a car,' Tim said to Vera. She opened her mouth to protest but Tim said, 'Don't ask, just do it.'

Vera stared up into Tim's face but he just smiled at her.

And then the music stopped and there was a scramble as people vacated their cars and other people rushed to claim them. Snug in the driving seat of the bumper car Vera sat close to Tim. She wondered how on earth they were going to pay for the ride. But the music started up again and although the helper jumped on the back of all the other cars to extract payment from the drivers, he didn't come to them.

The ride was bumpy and exciting and Vera screamed with enjoyment while Tim laughed uproariously. Eventually the ride stopped and Tim waved towards the assistant.

'Where to now? The carousel?' Tim shouted above the noise as they scrambled off the ride.

'I don't understand' was as far as Vera got before she was propelled across the grass towards the brightly painted horses.

'Pick which one you want,' said Tim, hoisting himself on to the back of a flowing-maned horse called Teddy. He put out a hand so that Vera could climb on Dobbin and they waited a few minutes while the ride filled with customers.

A woman wearing long skirts and a headscarf came round to collect the money for the rides but once again Tim was ignored except for a smile that showed the woman's gold tooth.

Next came the swinging boats.

Travelling through the air high above Walpole Park Vera saw the town and creek from quite a different angle until the boat swung backwards and she screamed as her stomach seemed to leave her body.

Groggy with the powerful ride as they alighted, Tim held her until she regained her balance,

'That was horrible,' she cried. 'Horrible but great!'

Next came the flyer that hurtled through the air then swung backwards. Vera kept on screaming and clutching at Tim. But she loved everything the fair had to offer, the loud music and the noise of other people enjoying themselves.

Vera was screaming with fear and happiness as the rickety ghost train travelled through the creaking doors from the darkness into the light. As the passengers got off, Tim waved to the assistant and held tightly to Vera's hand.

'Hungry?' Tim's eyes were twinkling as he walked her towards the hot dog stall. 'Or do you feel too sick to eat?'

Vera's stomach was rumbling. 'I could eat a horse,' she said.

'Might have to do with a dog,' laughed Tim as they joined the food queue.

''Ow do, young sir.' The woman cooking sausages on a grill winked at him. Vera looked at them both with surprise. She couldn't work out how come everyone seemed to know Tim and be on such friendly terms with him. And then there was the question of the free rides.

'Can I have two hot dogs and two orange drinks, please?'

'An' I suppose you wants onions?' The woman picked up two bread rolls.

Vera nodded enthusiastically. She loved fried onions. On the counter were two large bottles of brown sauce and tomato ketchup.

'Help yourself to condiments,' the woman said. Vera saw her fingers were covered in gold rings and in her ears gold hoops glittered.

Vera knew the first mouthful of the hot dog was going to be as tasty as she expected.

Tim leaned up and had a quiet word with the woman, who did a great deal of head nodding and smiling before she waved them goodbye.

Vera allowed Tim to usher her towards the creek that wound its way to the Gosport Ferry. On the grass they sat side by side finishing their food.

Vera licked her fingers. 'Are you going to tell me how come we get free rides and a hot dog?' She began to sip at her orange drink.

'I'd rather not,' Tim replied. 'I wanted to give you a surprise.'

'You did that all right. But I'll be cross if I don't know how you managed it.'

He looked crestfallen. 'I don't want you to be angry with me.'

Vera persisted. 'Tell me then.' Her drink container, empty now, she put on the grass. The music from the fair was muted. Far across the creek she could see Haslar Hospital and the light breeze had turned into a sharp wind. Vera snuggled into Tim and waited for an answer.

He had picked daisies and was using his nails to make a split in the stems. Vera watched as the daisy-chain grew. When he judged it was long enough she saw him fasten the ends to make a necklace.

'Bend forward,' he commanded and slipped it over her head.

'Thank you, kind sir,' Vera said. 'But I still want to know how we were able to go on all the rides.'

Tim sat back in the long grass.

'I got up extra early before school to come down to the park

29

to ask the blokes if I could help set up the rides. I knew they wouldn't pay me with money but I only wanted free rides so I could treat you.'

Vera was silent. Tim had done all this to please her.

After a while, she said, 'I don't know what to say. No one's ever been this nice to me before.'

Vera fiddled with her necklace, a round silver St Christopher Patsy had given her. Patsy had told her he was the patron saint of travellers.

Tim put his arm around her shoulders. 'Well, they should be nice to you,' he said. 'So don't say anything.' He ran his fingers down her arm and then let them drift to her hand before holding it tightly.

'Is this why your mum knew where you would be going after school?'

He nodded. 'She let me borrow the alarm clock so I could get up at dawn.'

'My mum wouldn't have done that,' she said. She looked into his eyes. She felt warm and contented, safe with Tim. It wasn't like he was a separate person but that he was an extension of herself. Vera sighed. But she was filled with a sort of longing for him that was eating her up. Vera wanted suddenly to lay her hand against his cheek but shyness stopped her. She wanted to put her arms around him but she had never touched a boy before and although a strange tingling had started up on her skin all she could do was stare at him.

'Thank you,' she uttered at last. 'This has been a wonderful time.'

Tim's eyes were like pools of darkness. The corner of his mouth lifted to a smile.

Vera looked across at the clock on the tower of Trinity Green church. It was a quarter past six. She hadn't realised how quickly dusk had fallen. It came to her that she should be somewhere else, not out of her depth experiencing unfamiliar feelings because of Tim.

'We should go,' she said.

Tim nodded. He rose to his feet and then put out a hand and pulled her up.

In silence they walked down Spring Garden Lane. After a while Tim exchanged a joke with her and Vera felt the old companionship between them return. But she also realised something had changed between them.

Vera sat on the doorstep looking at the open door opposite.

The girl was in, because she'd seen her peeking out of the bedroom window. Vera had no idea why she wanted to talk to the girl but it just seemed rather silly to live opposite each other and not speak.

Patsy came waltzing down the passage in her petticoat. 'Shut that door, our Vera, I'm nearly naked here.'

'Well, it's not my fault if you don't get dressed, is it?'

The curlers in the front of Patsy's hair were wobbling dangerously.

'I told you before there's no point in puttin' on me best dress until the last minute. What if I spills something on it? An' I need to look ravishing tonight because there's a boatload of foreign sailors moored in Portsmouth Dockyard an' I just know they're making their way to the Connaught Hall this minute.' Patsy stood with her hands on her hips. 'Anyway, what you doin' sitting here with the door open?'

'I'm waiting for that new girl to come and talk to me.'

'Why should she?'

Vera looked at Patsy's false eyelashes. When she was older

she was going to have some and coat them in mascara so they were extra long and lush.

'Because,' said Vera, 'she don't know anyone and she could be my friend.'

Patsy began to laugh. 'It don't work like that, you silly goose!'

Vera stared at her. 'Why not?'

'Shut the door an' I'll tell you.'

Vera got up from the step, took a last look at the house opposite and closed the front door. 'Well?' she asked, sitting on one of the kitchen chairs. Patsy sat opposite her. She smelled of lily of the valley perfume.

'When someone moves into a new house it's the custom in England to take a gift round to welcome the new neighbours. In America,' Patsy's eyes went all dreamy, 'they call it a Welcome Wagon.' She suddenly frowned as she continued. 'I think it started in the nineteen thirties, in Canada.'

Vera stared at her and picked up a fork, turning it round and round in her hand.

'This ain't America or Canada. This is England and there's a war on an' I ain't got nothing to give.' Vera's mouth grew into a thin line.

Patsy took the fork away from her. 'You really want to get to know this girl?'

Vera nodded enthusiastically.

Patsy rose from the table. 'Stay there and I'll see what I've got,' she said. Vera watched Patsy's shapely figure slip from the room and then she heard her run upstairs. After a while Patsy came back and put on the table a flat box containing a medium-size pair of nylons, and two bars of Hershey's chocolate.

'Will that do?'

Vera stared at the luxuries on the table. 'Where d'you get them from?'

'Never you mind.'

'That girl don't wear nylons.'

'No, you silly goose, but her mother does. Get on the right side of the mother and the girl will be a doddle. The chocolate's for her. And a bar for you.'

Vera looked at Patsy. 'Wow,' she said. 'I haven't had chocolate for ages.' She jumped up and threw her arms around Patsy's neck. 'You'd do this for me?' she asked.

'Mind my hair.' Patsy shook Vera away. 'Sure. It's better than having you mooning about and the bleedin' front door open all day. All you got to do is put the things in a bag and go and knock on their door.'

'Oh, thank you, Patsy.' Vera slid from the chair and went to the sideboard where she foraged in a drawer until she pulled out a brown paper bag. Then she slipped the gifts inside. Her own bar of chocolate she left on the sideboard, promising herself she'd save it for after she'd done her homework and was in bed reading.

Vera heard the sound of the tap in the scullery and knew Patsy was about to have a wash.

'I'm going over there now,' Vera called.

'Good luck,' came Patsy's reply.

Vera's heart was beating fast as she crossed the street and stood outside the open door. She knocked and heard the girl running down from upstairs.

'Hello?'

Vera gulped. Up close the girl was very blonde and pretty and had the most enormous blue eyes. 'I've come to welcome you and your mother to Alma Street,' she said importantly, and thrust the open bag into the girl's hands. The bag crackled as the girl fumbled inside it.

'Oh, chocolate!'

'The nylons are for your mum. My sister got them off one of her boyfriends.'

The girl turned and called out, 'Mum!'

Wearing high-heeled shoes and a flowered dress with a sweetheart neckline the pretty woman came along the passageway. She took the bag her daughter pushed into her hands and drew out the box containing the nylons. Her gasp was long and low.

'A present for you,' the girl said, swinging her ringlets.

'That's right,' said Vera and smiled broadly.

'I can't accept these, child,' the woman breathed.

Vera frowned. 'But I'm welcoming you to our street, an' besides, Patsy gave me them specially.'

The woman looked flustered. 'I know it's rude to refuse gifts, but ...' she said, looking out into the street. 'You'd better come inside, dear. Angela's daddy has just made a cake.'

'I'm Angela,' said the girl. 'What's your name?'

'Vera,' came the reply, and Vera smiled to herself as she stepped inside the house.

Chapter 3

'C'mon, Vera, don't drag behind, we don't want to miss the start.'

Vera looked at Angela running ahead along the pavement. She decided to ask her friend the question niggling at her.

'Is your dad rich?'

Angela came to a halt outside Mason's the newsagent. The paperboys' bikes were piled against the window. 'British and Commonwealth troops capture Tobruk Airport,' said *The News*' headlines on the placard.

Angela turned, waiting for Vera to reach her side.

'Not now. He lost it all playing cards. Lost our lovely big home in the country outside Wickham as well.'

She said it so matter-of-factly Vera reckoned she'd already got used to the anguish it had caused. Vera was lost for words.

Alfred Lovell had joined the Air Raid Precautions, or ARP as everyone called it. He was a warden and Vera had seen him in the street trying to teach Angela how to spin the big wooden rattle to warn people that a gas attack had occurred. Angela had revealed that he wasn't allowed to join the services because he had an irregular heartbeat.

'But that lovely car? Must have cost a fortune?'

'Dad won that in a game of poker. It's almost new. He's trying to work a fiddle with the man in the garage at Moreland

Road as it eats petrol. He can't sell it as no one wants to buy cars now.'

Vera wasn't sure what to say. But she knew what a gambler was. She'd seen the film *Show Boat* with Patsy. Irene Dunne had played Magnolia, who was deeply in love with Gaylord Ravenal. He spent a lot of time at the gaming tables on the boat. Patsy had taken her because she didn't like going to the pictures on her own. During the film they had cried, holding on to each other for comfort.

Vera slipped her arm through Angela's as they hurried across the road. The queue at the bus stop meant they weren't too late to catch the bus to the Forum Cinema.

'Gosh, that must have been awful to lose your home?'

Vera couldn't understand why anyone who'd lived in a big house would now care to live in a two up, two down.

'Mum took it bad; she still hasn't forgiven Dad for bringing her to live in a rented house. She thinks it's so undignified. I don't really care. You see, sometimes we have money and sometimes we don't but losing the house and furniture made Mum ill.' Angela cupped her hand towards Vera's ear as though she didn't want anyone else to overhear. 'She sleeps alone.'

Vera didn't like to pry so she hoped Angela would tell her more but after a long silence it was clear she wasn't going to.

'So your dad's a real gambler?' In *Show Boat*, the men all wore smart evening clothes around the gaming tables. She could imagine Angela's dad togged up like that and sitting by a roulette wheel.

Angela sighed. 'Yes. Mum hates him going out, she says she doesn't know what he'll lose next. But since we've lost all we had I don't think it really matters, do you?'

Vera shrugged. 'He must have won sometimes; the car's

36

proof of that. An' I read somewhere that gamblers can't help themselves so they have to make bets on all sorts of things. Apparently it's an illness. Just like Tim Saunders' dad's illness, only that's not being able to stop drinking. The article stated that in the future there could be an organisation to help gamblers, like the one set up in 1935 in America, to help alcoholics.'

It was then the thought struck her.

'If you have your own bedroom and your mother sleeps alone, where does your dad sleep? Your house is like ours, it only has two bedrooms.'

'He sleeps on the sofa downstairs in the front room.'

Vera pondered that. 'Doesn't your dad get cross being kept out of your mum's comfy bed? Tim's mum and dad always share the same room and bed, so Tim says, even when they've been punching ten bales of poop out of each other.'

'If Dad's cross he never shows it to me. A couple of years ago he had a big win and he took us to Africa for Christmas.'

'Wow!' Vera wondered what it would be like to go to a different country. 'Did you stay in a hotel? Did you fly in an aeroplane? Did you see any wild animals?'

Angela laughed. 'Yes, to all your questions. The hotel had a swimming pool and the monkeys ran through the palm trees in the gardens. And nobody worried about the war.'

Vera looked at Angela in amazement. What an exciting life her friend had led. The queue was getting noisier now and longer. Thank goodness they were near the front.

Vera looked across the road to where the Crown and Anchor pub had once stood. Now it was a pile of rubble, a bombsite, and like much of the spare ground that had appeared after the bombing raids, it had become decked out with old bedsteads and stained mattresses and other rubbish.

She thought about Tim and his work-worn mum and his awful father. Then she said proudly, 'I helped Tim carry his dad upstairs to bed one morning. He'd fallen asleep, dead drunk in the garden. His mum had hurt her arm and couldn't lift him. She covered him up like he was a child. Afterwards she went through his trouser pockets and emptied them of most of the money he had left.'

Vera could see the large green Provincial bus trundling down the Crossways.

'Here it comes.' She turned to Angela. 'Tim's mum always has to do that else they don't eat.'

'Wow,' said Angela. 'How can they pay the rent?'

'They manage.' Though Vera wasn't sure they coped well.

'You talk about Tim Saunders a lot,' remarked Angela with a knowing smile.

'I do not!' protested Vera, reddening.

The bus drew up at the stop and the queue surged forward.

'Let the passengers off first!'

The conductor, his ticket machine hanging down one side of his body and his leather money bag on the other side, looked grumpy. He stood back beneath the double decker's stairs and allowed the new passengers to get on.

Vera grabbed Angela's hand and climbed up to the top deck, then she spied an empty double seat and they fell into it laughing.

'I hope we're not going to be late,' Angela said.

'It's only Pearl and Dean and the Movietone News first so we won't miss any of *Dumbo*.' Vera wasn't fussed about going to see a kid's film but Angela wanted to see it. It was a special preview as the film wasn't on general release yet.

'How come you can afford to treat me to the pictures when you haven't got the money to spare?' asked Vera.

The bus had started up again and the ticket collector was wending his way towards them.

'My dad says you're good for me,' whispered Angela. 'He gave me the money.' Vera loved the way Angela had slight trouble saying words with 's' in them. A lisp, Patsy called it. 'And he's glad you're going to look after me when I start at your school next week. He reckons it's good we'll be together if those Germans decide to make another daylight raid instead of waiting until it goes dark like usual. I was a boarder at St Clement's School just outside Petersfield. Only Dad had to take me from there when the money ran out.'

'I bet that school was fun.' Vera had read books about boarding schools and the midnight feasts, pony riding and the tennis matches that went on. But that belonged to a different world, one she'd never inhabit.

'Did your dad really say I'd be a good friend for you?' she asked.

For some reason, as she thought of Angela's dad, the warm feeling in the pit of her stomach returned. She wondered if his glossy moustache tickled when he kissed Angela's mum. He was certainly a very handsome man and didn't look anywhere near as old as the other dads in the street.

'Of course, silly.' Angela smiled at her. She paid their fares and pocketed the thin paper ticket.

Vera sat contented and happy, looking out of the window as the bus drove along Whitworth Road.

'I like standing on that railway bridge and letting the steam go all over me,' said Vera as the bus trundled over the level crossing. Opposite the Gypsy Queen pub there was a new bombsite and more rubbish was strewn everywhere. Children were playing amongst the rubble, shouting and laughing.

Another thought occurred to Vera. 'Did you ever have a

pony of your own?' In the Enid Blyton books all rich girls had ponies.

'He's called Darkie and as I can't ride him in Gosport and there's nowhere to keep him my grandad stables him for me.'

'You mean you own a pony now?' Vera was wide eyed. Nobody she knew had a pony.

They'd just passed the White Hart pub in Stoke Road when the cinema came into view.

'Come on,' Vera said. 'This is our stop.'

Squeezing around the portly conductor Vera and Angela ran down the stairs and looked both ways before they ran across the busy street.

'I hope it hasn't already started,' said Angela. She was breathing hard with the exertion of running. Patsy said Angela suffered from asthma.

'If it has we'll stay in and see it round again.' Vera didn't care what time she got home. Her mother wouldn't be in until ten o'clock as there was a prayer meeting and Patsy was going straight from work to a friend's house.

At the ticket office Angela slid the money through the opening at the bottom of the glass grille and was given two tickets in exchange.

Vera pulled her by the hand along the red-carpeted auditorium and pushed open the door into the glorious darkness.

'Come this way,' said the usherette, shining her torch to show them seats near the front where the screen loomed high and large. The blackness swallowed them. Curls of cigarette smoke drifted through the bright beams from the projector at the rear of the cinema.

As Vera settled into her seat she decided to stop thinking about Tim Saunders and Angela's dad and concentrate on the film. Just lately she'd been plagued by all kinds of thoughts she'd never experienced before. Her body seemed to be a thing apart from her. She thought it might have something to do with starting her periods a few months ago. She hated them.

'Have you started your monthlies yet?' she whispered.

Angela shook her head. 'Have you?'

Vera nodded.

'I expect it's because you've got a bust an' everything.'

'Shhh!' whispered a woman from behind.

Vera shrank down into her seat.

'You must thank your dad for giving you enough money for me to see this film,' said Vera.

'Thank him yourself,' whispered Angela. 'We're all having tea together when we get back.'

Straight away Vera panicked. She knew it was meant as a treat as Angela's parents knew she'd be on her own. But how was she supposed to behave in front of Angela's glamorous mum? What on earth could she talk to her father about? Suppose she made a mess eating her food?

After the Movietone News, Angela made Vera go and queue up for the ice-creams. She bought the two tubs that Angela had given her the money for, but she was glad to move away from the spotlight as it made her feel exposed.

'No little wooden spoons?' Angela asked.

'She didn't give me any. Make a spoon out of the lid,' said Vera and showed her how to bend the lid into a scoop.

Afterwards they waited outside the cinema and caught the bus home again.

'You're very quiet,' Angela remarked.

'It was kind of sad, *Dumbo* was, an' I think I'm fed up with seeing sad films.'

Angela laughed her tinkling laugh as they reached her house.

'Never mind, it was only a film. Now I want to see what Dad's been cooking!'

'It's great that your dad makes stuff to eat.' In Vera's experience dads didn't go anywhere near the kitchen; that was women's work.

Angela shrugged, took the key from her pocket and opened the door. 'My mum doesn't like cooking. Can't stand the flour and stuff getting under her long nails. She likes to look pretty. Cooee,' she called, and, grabbing Vera's hand, pulled her into the kitchen where a laden table groaned beneath the weight of food.

Vera gasped. She'd not seen such delicious food in ages.

Tinned peaches, tinned pineapple, Carnation milk for cream, thinly sliced bread and a plate piled high with ham. Vera's eyes must have opened extra wide at the ham because Angela's dad said, 'It came from a tin. Got it off a Canadian.'

Vera smiled at him. 'Hello,' she said shyly.

And then she found herself staring at a dish containing some kind of dessert.

'Sugarless apple dessert. Grated apples, condensed milk and orange juice. I made it this morning along with the small cakes. They're honey cakes and they speak for themselves,' Angela's dad said.

'I don't know what to say.' The smells coming from the dishes on the table were making her stomach grumble with hunger.

'Come and sit here, next to me.' Angela's mother got up from the armchair nearest the fire and pulled out a kitchen chair. Vera thought she had the longest legs she'd ever seen, and they were sheathed in nylon. Vera wondered if they were the nylons she'd given her.

'Thank you, Mrs Lovell.'

'I told you, you must call me Jennifer. Did you enjoy the film?'

'Yes,' answered Vera as she sat down at the table.

Jennifer wore a floaty green dress with long sleeves that seemed only to enhance her white skin and immaculate hands, with coral-tinted nails. It was her eyes that gave her the hard look. They were blue ice surrounded by long dark lashes. Jennifer looked at Vera as though she was looking right through her.

'Sit down, Angela.'

Angela pulled out a kitchen chair.

'The table settings are divine,' Vera whispered to Angela. Each place setting had a table mat with a hunting scene and a cloth serviette sitting inside a water glass. Water was in a glass jug. The cutlery was silver and all matching! In the middle of the table to carry along the hunting theme was a large silver tray with a horn and candle decoration.

'Mummy used to ride; we rode together.' Angela shrugged as though that part of her life was over.

'Come on, tuck in!' Alfred was fussing about. 'I suggest you try a little of my apple dessert with cream first. No standing on ceremony here.'

Vera caught the frown that Jennifer gave him but he ignored her and lifted the dish and set it in front of Vera so that she might help herself.

'Go on, Vera. It's to die for.' Angela pretended to swoon. Her mother laughed. Vera could smell Jennifer's perfume, light and flowery, competing with the smell of the apples as she spooned the concoction on to her plate.

'Can I pass you the dessert?' Vera couldn't bring herself to call Angela's mother by her Christian name as she handed across the dish.

'I daren't. It will go to my hips immediately. Besides, this tea is in your honour.'

That was a funny thing to say, thought Vera. After all, *they* had to eat, didn't they?

'I'll make tea, shall I?' Alfred didn't wait for anyone to reply but got up and disappeared into the scullery where Vera could hear him clattering about. Vera thought she'd never met such a nice man as Alfred Lovell.

'What do you think?' pestered Angela.

Vera scraped her plate clean and sighed. 'I've not tasted anything so nice for ages.'

'It's one of Alfred's specialities,' Jennifer said. 'Of course when we had the means and food was more readily available, my dear husband would try out all sorts of recipes.' She gave a thin smile.

Alfred came back in, china clinking as he poured the tea.

The layout of the house was similar to Vera's home. But there the resemblance ended. The moquette three-piece must be in the front room, she thought, for the small kitchen was filled with a Welsh dresser and matching table and chairs. Hunting scenes adorned the walls. A slate clock stood on the mantelpiece. But what impressed Vera the most was the atmosphere, the warmth, the obvious affection Angela's parents had for their child.

Vera felt very uneasy sat there with them, conscious of Alfred's watchful gaze. Every time Vera looked towards him, he seemed to be staring at her, looking her over as though she were for sale in a shop window. She looked about her. No one else seemed to be noticing.

Eventually Vera knew she had to leave. She thanked everyone profusely.

'Come over any time you want,' Alfred said.

'Any time,' stressed Jennifer.

Outside in the night air, Vera said to Angela, 'Your mum and dad are really pally considering they don't sleep together. I thought you said your mum was angry with him?'

'She is.' Angela put her arm around Vera's shoulder. 'But she also loves him so much she'd follow him to the ends of the earth. And he knows it.'

Chapter 4

'Why ain't you got a dad, Vera?' Tim propped himself up on one elbow and looked down at her. Angela was lying next to Vera, her face towards the wintry sun.

Vera stared up at him then back towards the ground again. The new grass growth showed itself in tiny spears of green. They were sitting in Forton Recreation Ground and there was hardly a soul about.

'I was a tiny girl so I don't remember much about him except he smelled of fresh tobacco and had a moustache that tickled. He used to throw me up in the air and catch me and we'd laugh a lot. Patsy says one night him and Mum had a row to end all rows and he walked out. We ain't never seen him since.'

Angela nudged her. 'Don't you remember what he looked like?'

'If I met 'im in the street I wouldn't know him. Mum destroyed all the photos so she wouldn't be reminded.'

'That's a cruel thing to do,' Tim said.

'That's when Mum started goin' to church every five minutes. She didn't start gettin' funny and forgettin' stuff until a couple of years ago.'

Vera thought back to the scullery incident and the overheated boiler. She'd complained to her mother but she'd had

46

no explanation except, 'I told you I'd turned the copper on.' Vera preferred to think her mother had *thought* she'd told her. That was better than thinking her mother had lied to her.

'I wish my dad would go,' Tim said with a sigh.

'Don't talk like that! You don't mean it.'

'I do, Vera.' He'd stopped smiling at her and his expression became serious. Vera always felt like she wanted to hug him when he looked like this. She hated it when Tim was sad.

'It's 'orrible being in a house where your dad is drunk all the time. Him and Mum are always arguing about money and every time she tries to make the place look nice he comes home and falls about smashing stuff. As soon as I get old enough to leave school, I'm going to make some money, get a place and take my mum with me so she don't 'ave to put up with it any more.'

Angela was staring at Tim in horror.

'Sometimes he wets himself and doesn't even know it. He stinks.'

Angela put her hand over her mouth in disgust. You could tell she wasn't used to revelations of this sort, thought Vera.

'What if your mum loves him so much she won't leave him?' Angela said.

Vera frowned at Angela's words. She knew all about love. Patsy bought *Photoplay* every month and Vera read all the true love stories about the stars like Franchot Tone and Joan Crawford, who was one of her favourites. Joan had two children, Christina and Christopher. She'd seen the pictures of them all looking so happy together in Joan's lovely new house. It was obvious by their big smiles that Joan and Franchot were deeply in love.

'My dad loves my mum but she ignores him all the time. She hasn't forgiven him for losing her money,' Angela confided.

'Her money?' Vera and Tim chorused.

'Yes. My dad worked for my mum's dad and when my mum's gran died she left my mum the big house near Wickham. That had to be sold to pay off the people dad owed money to. Dad hated working for my grandad. Grandad made my mum choose between staying with "that blackguard", as he called Dad, or going to live in the family home in Sussex. Of course, my mum stayed with Dad.'

'What did your dad do when he worked for your grandad?'

Angela shrugged. 'He sat in an office and answered a phone.'

'I wouldn't mind gettin' paid to do that,' Tim said.

'Your dad's lovely,' said Vera. 'He's always smiling.'

'Mum don't think he's lovely; she nags him.' Angela shook back her golden ringlets, which shimmered in the sunlight. 'He says she ought to go to Germany and nag Hitler, then the war would soon be over.'

Tim laughed loudly.

'It's not funny,' warned Angela. Tim mumbled something to her and it put the sparkle back into her eyes. 'Anyway, my dad had a mistress,' said Angela importantly.

Vera wasn't sure what a mistress was. She knew a married woman was a Mrs and that she was a Miss.

'So he's been unfaithful to your mum?' Tim probed.

Vera could see Angela liked being the centre of attraction.

Angela nodded. 'It was a couple of years ago. We'd been shopping in London and we came home early and my mum went upstairs and they were in Mum's bedroom. The girl used to walk the estate dogs and she was only seventeen. I really liked her; she used to let me walk with her. She had curly dark hair.' Angela pointed to Vera's head. 'A bit like yours, Vera. Mum was furious,' she added.

48

Tim was silent, but Vera was curious. 'What happened then?'

'The girl got the sack. Dad said she'd thrown herself at him. Grandad said he was a bloody fool.'

'Your poor mother,' said Tim quietly.

'We went on holiday to Athens. That's where the Parthenon is,' Angela said.

'Wow,' said Vera. She knew that Athens was in Greece. How lucky Angela was to have travelled so much.

Tim gazed at Angela in envy and then decided to change the subject. 'That church in Stoke Road got bombed last night along with some shops in the town. For once we was in the shelter. Why don't you ever come to the shelter, Vera?'

'Mum makes me sleep under the table in the Morrison shelter when the siren goes off. Last night our Patsy was out with her mate. Her friend lives in Avenue Road. That's just up the street from that church. She says it was all rubble and a couple who was out late walking their dog got it.'

A moment of silence followed. 'We've got our own shelter.' Angela looked pleased with herself. 'It's an Anderson, bigger than your Morrison.'

'Only because the people what lived in your 'ouse 'ad it dug in the garden,' said Vera.

Angela looked crestfallen.

'My Mogs was out in that lot. I was worried sick about him.'

Vera could read Tim like a book. He didn't want bad feeling between the girls.

'You an' that daft orange cat,' said Vera. 'I bet he was fine.'

'Yeah.' Tim laughed. 'Got nine lives, ain't they, cats?'

Vera looked at the darkening sky. 'We ought to be getting 'ome.'

'Okay, we'll walk through the alley.' Tim got up and then put out a hand first to Vera and then to Angela, pulling them up.

'I like Saturdays,' said Angela to no one in particular.

Vera brushed grass from Angela then turned to Tim. 'Turn around,' she said, 'and I'll get it off your jumper.'

He stood in front of her. Already his shoulders were showing the breadth he would gain later in life. Vera had to reach up on tiptoe to pull grass strands from his hair.

Her heart began its strange fluttering sensation as her hands touched him. She suddenly remembered the dream that had woken her that morning. She was being kissed by Tim but he'd changed into a man and his ragged clothes became an expensive suit. Vera shook her head to settle her thoughts.

'That's you finished,' she said. 'How about me? Have I got stuff clinging to me?'

Angela brushed the grass from her back.

With Vera leading the way, they walked towards the alley that would cut short their journey home. Tim and Angela were close on her heels as she entered the narrow passageway that divided back gardens from a factory wall.

'Mind the dogshit,' she called.

She could see a dark form lounging against the wall at the end of the alley. It was a man and he seemed to be doing something that made his arm shake. Even from this distance she could hear the man making noises to himself as he faced the wall, his hands hidden beneath his long coat.

'Stay back, you two.'

Tim pushed past her and Angela and strode ahead. The pair of them halted. Vera wondered what was going on. Then she heard him say to the man, 'Put it away, mate. I got two young girls here.'

The man paused and for one dreadful moment Vera thought he was going to lash out at Tim. But Tim stood almost a head taller than him. The man didn't speak.

Vera, who'd been about to give Tim a mouthful for shoving her out of the way, closed her mouth and listened.

The man eyed Tim then, pulling his coat about himself, swung away and stumbled out of the alley into Inverness Road.

'What was he doing?' asked Angela.

'You don't want to know,' said Tim firmly.

'Having a wee?' Angela asked.

'More than that,' said Tim.

Vera was mystified. 'What then?'

Angela wasn't going to let Tim keep her in the dark. 'Tell us!'

'He was rubbing his thingy until it squirted,' said Tim, his face reddening in embarrassment.

'Will you shut up now?' Vera said to Angela. 'C'mon, let's get back to Alma Street.'

'No I won't,' said Angela, her voice rising to a shriek. 'You think just because I'm the youngest that I don't know about men and their thingies.' She shook her ringlets. 'That's not how men do things with their willies. I know *exactly* what happens.'

Vera stopped and turned to her.

Angela had got their attention. Vera could see she wanted to impart her knowledge. She looked at Tim for reassurance but he shook his head as though he was bored with the whole subject.

'A man lays on top of a woman then moves around a bit then he gets off her and has to pay her some money. Sometimes the woman has a baby. That's what married people do.'

Vera was still looking at Tim but his face was shut tight.

'It's what my mum and dad do,' insisted Angela. 'I watched them from behind the door. My mum said, "If you can waste your money you can afford to give it to me. So in future you can pay for it." It's called doing people.'

The silence was palpable.

Vera didn't know why but she suddenly felt sorry for nice Mr Lovell. Still no one spoke until Vera suddenly blurted out, 'Well, my mum doesn't do anyone because she sleeps alone.'

'I bet your Patsy does it!' Angela was breathing heavily. She looked puffed up as though she'd just said something of great importance. Vera was angry. She didn't think for one moment her Patsy did anything with men.

Vera felt Tim squeeze her hand.

'I'm sorry, I didn't mean to say that,' said Angela. 'I just got carried away. My mum's got some funny ideas about things. She doesn't even like Dad having a drink of whisky. "Drink is a tool of the devil," she says.'

'So it is,' said Tim.

'Oh, Tim, I didn't mean it. I didn't. I'm sorry. I'm getting all mixed up about stuff,' Angela said.

'That's all right. I wish my dad thought it was the tool of the devil; he might not spend his wages on it then.'

Angela stood in front of them. Vera could see she didn't know what to say that might change the cool atmosphere between them.

'I'm not waiting for you two slowcoaches. My dad's making a suet pudding an' it's my favourite. See you tomorrow.'

And then she ran towards the chip shop, turned into Alma Street and out of sight.

'I'll walk to the end of the road with you,' Vera said. 'My mum will be down the church sorting flowers for tomorrow morning's Sunday service an' Patsy won't be in. She's very pretty.'

'Patsy?'

'No, Angela, silly.' She wanted to see what effect her words had on Tim.

'*You* look like a proper woman.' Tim's voice faltered and Vera knew he wasn't used to giving out compliments. The pit of her stomach started feeling like it was full of butterflies.

'Thank you,' she said. 'When I get older I'm going to dye my hair black.' She stared into his eyes.

'You'll look even more lovely, then,' he said softly. Vera suddenly thought of how Tim had got up at dawn and gone down to the fairground to help erect rides so he could take her to the fair. She couldn't imagine how she would feel if he wasn't her friend.

'Thank you,' Vera said again, accepting Tim's compliment.

They walked close together up Alma Street and then turned into the small alley that led to Tim's back door.

'Are you invited to Angela's party?' She suddenly remembered the birthday party planned for next week.

'Yes. She's going to be fourteen, isn't she?'

Vera nodded. 'You and me are just that bit older, aren't we?'

Tim stopped and pulled Vera around to face him.

'Will you let me kiss you? I've never kissed a girl before and I'd really like to kiss you.'

'I don't think you ought to practise on me then,' Vera said, unsure of what to say.

His face darkened and she could see she'd hurt his feelings.

Her mother's voice was talking inside her head: 'You're a woman now you've started your monthlies and you've got to keep yourself pure. Men are only after one thing and once they've got it, they don't want you any more.'

What that one thing was her mother hadn't actually told her.

The thing was she actually wanted to kiss Tim. But she didn't intend to lay down and let him wriggle all over her. She wondered if it would be all right if she kissed him standing up. Only she'd never kissed anyone before either. And she really liked him.

He put his arms around her and she smelled the sweetness of his breath. It was nice being held by Tim. It felt exciting but right. His face was nearing hers. And again she heard her mother's warning voice: *'Men are only after one thing.'* She twisted away from him. Until she knew what this one thing was, she'd better not let him kiss her.

'No.'

He stepped away, eyes downcast.

Without any explanation she turned and ran swiftly back into the street.

Chapter 5

'Can I wear some of your red lipstick? *Please?*'

She picked up the tube of ruby red that was practically empty and then stared into the mirror admiring the fake rose pinned in her hair.

'Okay, but you'll have to use your fingernail to get some out. I wish we could buy lipsticks like we used to.' Patsy stood back and appraised Vera. 'My green two-piece looks better on you than it does on me. You fill it out more at the bust.'

'Do you really think so?' Vera twirled round and then faced her sister. 'I'm so excited. I've never been to a proper dance before.'

Patsy frowned. 'Yes, well, if Mum hadn't decided to go to the night prayer vigil you wouldn't be going. But I'm damned if I'm going to waste a night staying in with you.' She shook a finger at Vera. 'If one word of this gets back to Mum, I'll kill you.'

Vera started laughing. 'If one word of this gets back to Mum, she'll kill you!'

Patsy, in her knee-length flowered dress with the sweetheart neckline and small puffed sleeves, was now putting the final touches to the rolled curls at the front of her hair. The back of her fair hair hung in waves almost to her shoulders. Vera sniffed appreciatively at the Evening in Paris perfume being sprayed on Patsy's pulse spots. The blue glass bottle had a rubber spray attachment, another present from some man.

'I suppose you want some?' Vera nodded as clouds of perfume mist settled on her neck. 'You going to be all right in my shoes?'

Vera looked down at the lace-up court shoes. She'd never worn heels before but she'd practised walking up and down stairs in them and they seemed fine. 'I couldn't very well wear me school sandals, could I?'

'Draw a line up the back of your legs with this black eyebrow pencil.' Vera looked at Patsy's legs covered in sheer nylon. 'If you think I'm wasting a pair of my stockings on you, you got another think coming. And hurry up. I need to paint your face. I don't want people to see I'm out with a kid!'

It was on the tip of her tongue to answer back but Vera held back, worried Patsy might change her mind and leave her at home.

Ten minutes later, Vera opened her eyes and stared at herself in the mirror.

'Oh!'

'Do you like the transformation or not?'

'I ... I look like a woman,' answered Vera as she studied her reflection from different angles.

'Well, I wouldn't be seen dead at a dance with a sister who's only fourteen, would I? So remember, if anyone asks, you're my mate.'

Vera nodded. 'When are we leaving?' She glanced again at the stranger in the mirror. She actually looked pretty as well as grown up. 'How are we getting there?'

'One question at a time. We're going now and we walk.'

Vera couldn't wait. She ran down the stairs, opened the front door and stood impatiently on the step. Across the road,

Albert Lovell was polishing his car in the last of the evening light. He looked up, stopped what he was doing and stared at her. And then he smiled. One of those dazzling smiles of his that seemed to light up his face.

'Hello, Vera,' he called. His eyes on her made her feel funny.

Just then Patsy pushed her off the step and slammed the front door and shoved Vera's coat and gas mask at her.

''Lo, Mr Lovell,' she called. Then she practically dragged Vera down the street. 'We got to hope he doesn't tell Mum you was dressed up to the nines. And you won't be allowed in the Connaught if the management thinks you're underage.'

'I'm so excited!'

'There's a couple of rules though.' Patsy stopped by the secondhand shop and turned to her. 'Don't get too pally with the blokes. Don't tell anyone your real age or address. And the most important rule, don't go out of the hall and round the back with anyone. Promise?'

'Whew! It's like being in the secret service!'

Patsy's fingers were digging into her arm. 'Promise me.'

'All right, there's no need to draw blood.'

It wasn't far to the town and Vera certainly didn't mind the approving looks and wolf whistles they got. She wondered if men always acted like this when they saw pretty girls. Patsy was a knockout. She had a way of swinging her hips that made her bum waggle.

The nearer they got to the Connaught Hall the more apprehensive Vera became. She'd kept on at Patsy to take her to a dance but now she was really going she suddenly felt very nervous.

At the entrance there were a few men and women standing about. Some were smoking and one bloke was tipping a small bottle to his lips.

'No alcohol inside,' said Patsy. 'Only cups of tea and orange. Do not go outside if anyone asks you if you want a drink!'

'I'm beginning to wish I'd stayed at home,' grumbled Vera. But then she heard the music and her spirits lifted as Patsy propelled her into the crowded, dimly lit hall. 'Is that a real band?' She nodded at the men playing instruments on the stage.

'Of course, stupid. Later on they'll have a break then some-one will play records to dance to.'

A blonde woman in a slinky dress was singing 'We'll Meet Again'. She was holding the microphone like it was a toffee apple, thought Vera. She badly wanted to rub her eyes as the smoke was making them smart but she remembered the mas-cara and eyeshadow that Patsy had painstakingly put on her so didn't dare. Couples were dancing to the slow tune. Not just men and women but here and there girls were dancing together.

Vera heard Patsy's name being called and found her elbow grabbed once more.

'Over there, Jeannie's saved us chairs.'

As Vera's eyes grew accustomed to the gloom she saw many of the men were in uniform. Before she got to the empty chairs a man pushed in front of her.

'Care to dance?'

Vera looked to Patsy for help but Patsy was nodding her head and laughing. Apprehensively Vera allowed herself to be swept into the sea of bodies.

The woman on the stage was now singing 'Taking a Chance on Love' and the dancers were doing a slow jive to it. Vera had practised jiving with Angela. The man was talking to her, trying to make himself heard above the noise and the crush of people. He was shorter than her and had lank greasy hair and suddenly she found herself in the middle of the crowded floor trying to keep up with his steps.

She was just getting used to dancing with him when a young man in a sailor's uniform cut in. Now she had a different partner but she soon found the rhythm and after a while, despite the change of partners, she was enjoying herself immensely.

'What's your name?'

'Vera,' she said.

'That's a nice name.'

'What's yours?' Vera asked. Now she could see he wasn't as old as she'd first thought. He clutched her tightly to him. 'Kenneth.'

Then a very strange thing happened. The young man began to cry, very softly like he didn't want anyone to see. Vera pulled away from him, frightened he might make wet marks on Patsy's dress.

'What's the matter?' she asked.

He stopped dancing and wiped his hand across his eyes. 'Can we sit down?' He steered her towards a couple of empty seats at the back of the hall. He wasn't crying now but he was looking very sheepish.

'You won't think I'm being silly if I tell you, will you?'

'Depends,' said Vera. He had silver-blue eyes and fair hair and he looked barely older than her. His bell-bottoms were clean and well pressed and his collar very white.

Kenneth sighed. 'I'm going to join the *Royal Oak*.'

'But that's a great ship, aren't you excited?'

He shook his head and tears filled his eyes again. 'I'm scared, Vera.'

She took his hand and squeezed it. 'I don't suppose you're the only sailor who's scared.'

'But they aren't me. I didn't want to join the services. I wanted to stay on at college.'

'But don't you want to fight to save England?'

'Yes.' He suddenly looked defiant. 'I'm no coward.'

'Of course not, you wouldn't be in the services if you was,' said Vera. She saw he had relaxed again. Then he shook his head and said sadly, 'But my mum's brother got killed at the Battle of Jutland in the last war. She's never got over it. I joined up to show her that men will come back from the war.' He stared at her. Vera saw the fear in his eyes and the sheen of sweat on his top lip. 'I won't die, will I?'

'No,' Vera said. She felt a fraud. How could she give advice about something she knew nothing about? Her fingers twisted automatically in the silver chain at her neck and an idea took over. 'Look, I've got this St Christopher. It's supposed to keep travellers safe. Well, you're a traveller, aren't you?'

She saw her words were being digested.

'I can't let you.' His voice tailed off.

'You can't stop me,' she said. ''Ere, undo the clasp for me.' Vera bent her neck forward and felt his fingers fumbling at the clasp. When the silver necklace was in the palm of her hand she said, 'Bend your head down.' Then she slipped the chain around his neck and did it up. He lifted his head.

'Does it look silly?'

'Lots of men wear them.' Vera tucked the chain out of sight behind his white vest.

He gave her a watery smile. 'Thank you,' he said and sniffed. At least he'd stopped crying, she thought. 'How old are you, Vera?'

She looked at him in surprise. Then, crossing her fingers behind her back, she lied, 'Eighteen.'

Kenneth put his arms around her and gave her a quick squeeze.

'No wonder you're so wise, you're two years older than me,' he whispered.

'That means you're not old enough to be in the navy,' she began.

'I forged my birth certificate,' he said. 'Plenty of other men have done the same to enlist.'

Vera stared at him. He was only a boy. He had every right to feel frightened.

He put his hand up and felt the imprint of the St Christopher beneath his vest. 'Thank you,' he said. 'I feel loads better, now. Do you want to dance again?' 'In the Mood' was fast and many of the dancers were already jiving to it.

Vera nodded and jumped up.

'I could write to you while I'm away,' Kenneth said.

Vera froze. 'No, oh. No. My mother's very strict, she wouldn't like me getting letters from a serviceman.'

His face fell. Vera had a moment of sadness but she knew it wasn't only her mother who would be upset if she wrote to Kenneth. Tim wouldn't like it either. And if there was one person in the whole world she didn't want to be hurt by her actions, it was Tim.

'Excuse me.'

Vera looked back at Kenneth as a tall serviceman in army khaki whirled her away. Kenneth was standing on the floor and he looked more miserable now than ever. And then he was gone from her sight as her new partner guided her to the middle of the dance floor.

'Where have you been all my life, darlin',' said the man. He had a red face.

'Just dancing,' said Vera above the noise. The music had

changed once again. 'I Don't Want to Set the World on Fire', was a slow song and the girl up on the stage had changed into a different long glittery dress and was singing her heart out. The soldier had taken the opportunity to hug Vera against his itchy uniform and she didn't like being held so close.

At first the man's hand was on her waist but inch by inch it was slipping until it had cupped her bottom and he was pressing himself into her. She wriggled away.

'Oops, I'm sorry, my hand slipped,' he said. But Vera knew it wasn't an accident that his hand had strayed.

Vera tried to pull away from him and his breath that smelled of bad meat. But he would insist on holding her too tight, lowering his head and nuzzling into her neck. He was a disgusting man, she thought, and couldn't wait for the woman on the stage to finish her song so that perhaps a faster tune would be played and she could dance with someone else.

Nothing like this had ever happened to her before. All she really wanted to do was walk away from him. But what if he shouted after her and she made a fool of herself in the dance hall? Patsy would never bring her again and Vera had so enjoyed the dancing, until now.

'Do you fancy a little drink?' he whispered in her ear. 'A mate of mine 'as got some of the hard stuff outside.' His hand had once again landed on her bottom.

'No, thank you,' Vera said. She remembered Patsy's words. *"Don't go outside with anyone."* 'I don't go outside,' Vera said. The woman on the stage had ended her song. Now was Vera's chance to get away but another man had caught her arm and she found herself doing the quickstep.

Vera breathed a sigh of relief that she was no longer dancing with the man who had hands like an octopus. She wondered how Patsy coped with all the different men. But then, Patsy was older and she knew how to treat them.

'Sorry,' said the man. He'd trodden on her toes. She didn't mind, as he was at least holding her properly and not trying to take advantage of her.

When the quickstep ended she looked towards Jeannie. Patsy had vanished. Vera walked swiftly across the floor and gratefully sat down on a chair.

'Where's Patsy gone?'

Jeannie looked uncomfortable. 'Oh, she's gone to get a bit of fresh air. She'll soon be back. You're a natural dancer,' she added, changing the subject. 'You'll never be a wallflower.'

'What's a wallflower?'

'A girl who comes to a dance and never gets asked to dance so has to sit on her chair near the wall. Don't worry, that'll never happen to you.'

Vera nodded, she loved the band. There was an accordionist, trombone player, piano, drums and a saxophonist. The musicians were led by a conductor, who was a small man wearing evening clothes and white gloves and waving a baton.

Even dances like 'The Dashing White Sergeant', Vera thought were wonderful. And 'Knees Up Mother Brown' and 'The Lambeth Walk' didn't faze her.

More men asked Vera to dance.

All too soon Patsy tapped her on the shoulder saying, 'We've got to go. Mum'll be home by eleven.'

Vera didn't argue. It had been the most wonderful night but she was tired and knew her mother would kill her if she got in first to find both her daughters out of the house.

It didn't seem so cold walking back. They were singing along to 'The Last Time I saw Paris'. Patsy had a square package in her hand. She slid her arm through Vera's and asked, 'How was your first dance?'

'Bloomin' lovely,' said Vera. 'I had a wonderful time, except for the blokes who reckoned because they'd asked me to dance they could put their hands in all the wrong places.'

She didn't tell Patsy about the young sailor. Perhaps Patsy wouldn't notice she was no longer wearing the necklace. Vera prayed the St Christopher would keep Kenneth safe.

'Anything else you want to tell me?' Patsy asked.

'Only that my feet hurt from being trod on by army boots. Anyway, what you got in that package?'

Patsy tapped the side of her nose. 'That's for me to know and you to wonder about.'

'Go on, tell me.'

'Okay, nylons.'

'Who gave you those?'

Patsy didn't answer.

'Oh, I know, you must have got them when I came looking for you. Jeannie said you'd just popped out for a minute, to get some fresh air. Can I have a pair?'

A blush suddenly covered Patsy's face.

'No,' she said. 'You're too young for nylons. But you did all right tonight. But if we go again, just make sure you don't accept any alcohol. Sometimes the blokes bring it into the hall in little bottles in their pockets.'

'Oh, Patsy, we're going home an' you're still moaning at me.'

'Sorry, but you're my little sister an' I got to take care of you. C'mon, let's sing again.' And Patsy started them off with 'Rose, Rose I Love You'.

The house was still in darkness when they arrived.

'Go and wash yourself, quick, and get all that make-up off.'

While Vera scrubbed at herself in the scullery Patsy laid the table for the morning then put hot water bottles in the beds.

The blackout curtains had been checked, so when Vera had her nightdress on she went and kissed Patsy goodnight.

'You didn't want to come home with a bloke tonight?' Vera asked.

Patsy stared at her with a funny look on her face.

'Too busy looking after you, wasn't I? I can 'ave loads of blokes but I only got one sister.'

Chapter 6

'They're obviously a well-bred family, even if Jennifer does wear too much make-up. And, since Angela's father came over especially to ask if you can go to her birthday party, I said yes.' The ash on her mother's cigarette was dangerously long. Vera watched, mesmerised.

'Thanks, Mum, but you're only letting me go because they're the poshest people in the street.'

Seeing her mother's furious expression, Vera quickly rose from her chair and made a dash for the scullery. She waited a moment, staring at but not really seeing the shelf of saucepans and the tin bath hanging on a big nail on the wall.

They used to keep the bath outside but once Vera had accidentally brought it in with the biggest and hairiest spider she'd ever seen. Now the bath stayed in the scullery to be hauled in front of the kitchen range once a week when the regulation five inches of water would provide a soak for the three of them. Vera got the last bath. She hated the scum on the water.

She could hear the steady click clack of her mother's knitting needles so ventured back and sat down at the table once more. The last thing she needed was a swift slap round the ear. The cigarette ash had disappeared but the cigarette was in exactly the same position, clamped between Vera's mum's lips as she knitted what was to be a cardigan for Vera.

The wool had come from a jumper bought from a second-hand shop and unravelled. Vera watched the crinkled wool she'd helped wind into balls. Her mother had called the colour Heather Mixture. To Vera it looked a yucky brown with bits mixed in it. She vowed when she grew up she'd wear silk and frills and jumpers that weren't made from secondhand wool.

Her mother set down her knitting and got up to poke the fire. Next to the fire was an oven that also helped to heat the room. Vera had blackleaded the range only that morning. They mostly used the gas stove in the scullery to cook on. The range held a small fire just enough to take the chill off the room and Vera's mum poked at it vigorously. Sparks and yellow flames spurted on to the fender.

'I don't know what you'll get to eat at the party, there's precious little food about for luxuries.'

'Angela's dad is going to make sausage pancakes and carrot fudge.'

Vera might just as have well spoken to herself for her mother replied, 'I'll take over a tin of Spam.'

Vera ignored her. 'I expect there'll be tinned fruit salad and jelly and evaporated milk for cream, an' I'm looking forward to playing pass the parcel and hide and seek and sardines. I know they're kids games but we'll have a good laugh at all the antics everyone will get up to.'

Tim had been invited. Whether his mum would let him go was another question.

Would Tim ask her to kiss him again?

Vera closed her algebra book. She picked up the copy of *Black Beauty* she was reading.

'I'm goin' to bed, Mum.' She didn't kiss her mother good-night as her mother didn't like displays of affection. Vera stuffed her exercise books in her satchel ready for Monday and left it hanging by its strap over the back of the chair.

'Don't put the light on; you don't need it. And check the blackout curtain in your room. Just leave it open a smidgeon so you can read by the moonlight. And I don't want Patsy coming in and switching on the passage light and the place looking like Blackpool Illuminations.'

Vera was sure because of the war Blackpool had stopped lighting up the sky with its Illuminations but she wasn't about to risk her mother's wrath by saying so.

Upstairs, she undressed and slipped into her flannelette nightdress.

Vera's bed was near the window for maximum light. She knelt on it and peered out of the curtains. The stars were bright in a velvet sky.

And then the silence was pierced by the screaming of the air-raid warning telling everyone that Portsmouth and Gosport were once more under attack.

The first thing she thought of was Alfred Lovell up a ladder this morning putting tape over his windows so the glass wouldn't blow into the rooms. Many of the people in Alma Street had given up mending the damage the bombing caused, so there were boarded-up windows and broken fences everywhere.

Vera's heart was beating fast as she left the bed, slipped her school shoes on and grabbed her coat in case she had to go out in the street. She hoped the raid wouldn't last long.

The Morrison shelter was small and with the big kitchen table on top of it was twice as effective, or so her mother said. But there wasn't a great deal of room inside and the wire covering it made her feel like she was a rabbit in a cage.

'Mum!' Vera ran downstairs to find her mother already

inside the shelter. She was lying on her side with one of the pillows over her head. It was on the tip of Vera's tongue to say something sharp about her mother looking out for her own skin first but she thought otherwise. Vera ran back down the hall and turned the electric off at the mains then back into the scullery to switch off the gas and the water. Bedding was already in the shelter.

'I've got candles,' her mother said, looking out from the safety of the pillow. 'Can you hear anything?'

'Just bombing far off,' Vera said. If they got through the night or however long the bombing lasted, Vera knew when she opened the front door she'd smell cordite, brick dust and something that smelled like meat frying. Dust would cover everything.

She always wondered how much protection the table and shelter would be if their house took a direct hit.

Last week Vera and Patsy had been at home when the siren went. Their mother had been at a church meeting. They'd taken all the right precautions and settled themselves in the shelter with a pack of cards. After a while Vera got fed up listening to the noise outside and persuaded Patsy to watch what was going on out of the bedroom window.

There were searchlights in the skies and a dogfight was in progress. Vera knew the spitfires would beat the German planes into submission. They were small planes flown by men barely older than boys. The aircraft were almost dancing in the sky, sometimes whirling, sometimes ducking, leaving white trails and orange lights that burst like fireworks. They watched until the all-clear siren sounded and as Vera crept into her own bed that night she had to stuff the corner of the quilt in her mouth to muffle her sobbing. She knew not all those brave men were going safely home.

'I don't know why we don't go to the proper air-raid shelter at the top of the street.'

Her mother raised herself up, lit a Woodbine, drew on it deeply then blew the smoke towards Vera. It seemed to fill the small space. Vera coughed.

'That shelter might be underground and made of corrugated steel but I've heard if a bomb falls nearby all the people will suffer from damage to their eardrums. We're fine here.'

The shelter was used by most of the street's families. Her mother didn't like mixing with the heathens.

'If God intends our name should be on one of Hitler's bombs, then there's nothing we can do about it. It's His will.'

'I wonder where Patsy is?'

'She'll be safe. We have to trust in the Lord.'

There were muted bangs and sound of stuff falling about. Strange colours and smells came seeping in from outside through the blackout curtains.

'How long d'you reckon we'll have to stay here?'

Her mother was furiously knitting, the needles clacking away almost as quickly as the strange sounds invading the room. It was as though finishing that cardigan was the most important thing in the world.

Vera was scared. When would she be able to go to bed knowing that she could sleep the whole night through without being wakened by the sirens? She pressed her face into a cushion. Then she heard a whistling sound and it was coming closer.

'Jesus,' said her mother, 'save us.'

The droning became louder and louder.

And then the silence was painful to Vera's ears as she groped for her mother's hand, but the knitting needles were in the way. Vera threw herself down on the mattress and covered her ears with her hands.

The crash caused the whole house to shake.

The big dresser with the best crockery fell across the table and dust swirled.

'Mum!' screamed Vera. Her mother had both hands in front of her face. At first Vera thought she was crying then she realised she was praying.

Vera again reached for her mother's hand but was shaken off. The praying grew faster.

More plates smashed and the smell of dust was everywhere. Her mother was coughing now. Vera pulled back the chenille cloth in time to see plaster falling. The room was filled with a grey mist.

Vera realised the worst was over, for now. She hoped with all her heart that wherever she was, Patsy was safe.

'Are you all right, Mum?' Her mother nodded and picked up her knitting, examining the row to make sure she'd not lost any stitches.

There was a stillness. Vera peeked out again and saw there was room for them to crawl beneath the heavy dresser and into the shattered room. Her mother tried to tuck a stray lock of hair back into her bun.

'Where's my fags?' Her mother had a vague look in her eyes.

Vera found the green packet and handed it to her.

Then there was noise. Shouting, calling, torches showing up strange patterns on the walls made by furniture that had shifted. Her mother lit her cigarette, blew out a stream of smoke, and then went back to her praying, her eyes tightly closed.

Vera crawled out and managed to stand upright. She stared at the dresser that lay drunkenly across the Morrison shelter.

The windows had blown in and she could smell burning.

'I won't be a moment, Mum, I'm going to see how much damage has been done to the house.' There was no reply.

Her heart beating a tattoo inside her chest, Vera began a tour of their home. The stairs looked secure so she slowly ascended.

Her mother's room seemed untouched, except the sash window was broken and the curtains were hanging through it. Broken glass crunched beneath her feet.

Her own bedroom was untouched.

Downstairs the scullery was whole although all the pots and pans had been blown from the shelf. Vera opened the back door.

The sky was alive with colour. Everywhere, fires seemed to be burning, filling the air with acrid smoke that began to sting her eyes and hurt the back of her throat.

The noise was coming from the top of the street.

Suddenly, fear gripped her.

'The place is fine, Mum,' she shouted. 'Nothing we can't sort.'

She opened the front door and ran out straight into the arms of a man.

'Careful,' he said. It was Angela's dad in his official uniform as ARP warden. 'You'd do better to stay where you are. I've just contacted the fire and ambulance. If we're lucky they might get here.'

Vera didn't answer but ran with him, stepping over rubble to get to the top of the street.

'Not the air-raid shelter?'

'No.'

Miraculously a fire engine passed them, crunching over gravel. People were trying to douse the flames enveloping the last two houses in the street. They were using buckets of water passed from neighbour to neighbour.

Vera tried to push her way through but strong arms held her back.

'You can't do anything. It was a direct hit,' Alfred said gently.

Vera looked upwards to see part of a bedroom floor with a dressing table precariously perched on the edge. The wall had blown out.

And then Vera heard screaming. Loud wailing that eclipsed the other noises around her. It was only then she realised it was her.

Then Alfred's arms like bands of steel went around her. 'Shhhh!' he said.

Tim's house was a smoking pile of rubble.

'You can't do anything. Best let the fire fighters do their job.' Alfred tried to lead her away.

'But Tim's in there.'

'I don't think anyone's left in there.'

And then Vera saw him. Sitting on a kitchen chair nursing a cup of tea, a blanket around his shoulders.

'There's Tim's dad!'

It took Vera a while to push through the helpers. When she reached him she knelt at his feet. Despite the strong smell of the smoke and sweat, Vera caught a whiff of beer. She looked into his unshaven face.

'Are you all right? Not hurt?'

He shook his head.

'Where's Tim?' Vera looked about her then back at him.

His eyes focused on her face. 'Tim's with his mum.'

Vera felt light-headed with relief.

She felt a furry softness against her knees. It was Mogs. Dust was falling from the cat's orange coat.

'Oh, your poor thing,' she said, hoisting herself upright then picking up the cat. 'We'd better get you to Tim. He'll be glad you're safe.'

Tim's dad was staring at her.

'Tell me where they are. I'll take the cat to them.'

He looked at her as though she was daft.

'In there.' He pointed to the ruins of his house. 'They wouldn't go to the air-raid shelter without me. I was down the Alma, see?'

Vera stared at the charred remains of the house. 'No!' she whispered.

Her Tim, her funny Tim, always with a book in his back pocket, gone for ever. He would never travel round the world, never get to write about it. He would never again ask her to kiss him.

Vera gathered Mogs to her and wept into his purring body.

Chapter 7

Vera turned her head to see Angela snuggled down in the quilt. Pushing herself up on to her elbow she could see the orange ball that was Mogs, asleep at the foot of the bed. He lifted his head and stared at her as though his yellow eyes held all the questions and answers of the universe.

Tim was dead. Tears filled her eyes as memories came rushing back. She remembered pushing through the crush of people, screaming, with the cat in her arms, not caring where she was going only that she had to get away from the awful man who was Tim's father.

And then she was hauled to a sudden stop, twisted around so that both she and a struggling cat were pressed into a rough uniform. Alfred Lovell held her until her screams had faded.

'I think that cat belongs to you now,' he said. 'C'mon, let's get you back home where you belong.'

At number fourteen, the front door was wide open. He didn't wait for an invitation but with his arm across her shoulder he walked her down the passage.

It was as if she had never left the house. Her mother was still beneath the table. 'God help us,' she was saying over and over again. A cigarette was clenched between her nicotine-stained fingers.

'Fucking hell,' escaped Alfred's lips.

He let go of Vera and said, 'Stand back.'

With an almighty heave, the dresser was back in its place. He walked along its length, testing that it wouldn't tumble back down of its own volition.

Vera, still holding the now struggling cat, felt as though she was in the depths of a dream. She watched as Alfred knelt down and whispered to her mother, who shook her head but continued her mumblings.

He looked up. 'I need to explain to your mum how you're feeling but it seems she's in a worse state.'

Her mother's voice droned on and on. Every so often she paused, raised the cigarette to her lips and pulled in the nicotine, then carried on praying.

Just then footsteps fell in the hall and Patsy's cheery voice called, 'Jesus Christ, it'll take more than a tin of polish to sort this.' Her expression turned to one of horror as she took one look at her mother beneath the table. 'Oh, God, not again.' To Vera she asked, 'You all right, love?' Without waiting for an answer she turned to Alfred. 'What's wrong with our Vera?'

Vera's tears began again. 'I thought you was dead an' all, Patsy.'

'Take more than that ol' bleeding Hitler to get rid of me.' Patsy scooped Vera and Mogs into her arms.

Alfred chimed in, 'I can't let Vera stay here. Why don't I take her over the road and she can spend the night with Angela?'

He whispered to Patsy that Tim Saunders' house had taken a direct hit.

'He was my best friend,' whispered Vera.

'Oh, my love.' Patsy looked at Vera with tears in her eyes. 'With Mum like this,' she shook her head, 'and the place in this state, I reckon it's best you take her, Mr Lovell. I can cope 'ere.' Her eyes fell to the cat, who'd given up struggling. 'Take that thing with you over the road, then. I don't want you blamin' me if the animal runs off. I've got to get this house,' she paused and looked at her mother, 'and Mum, in some semblance of order. Mum gets herself in a state like this at times, Mr Lovell. Usually she comes out of it by herself.'

'I've seen men back from the front break down like this,' he said kindly.

'Started after Dad left.'

Patsy planted a kiss on Vera's cheek and said, 'Go. Get out of this shithole. Hopefully tomorrow things will look better.' And then to Alfred, 'I don't suppose we could find a doctor?'

Alfred shook his head. 'You'll never get a doctor to come for this. Too many people elsewhere are injured. I gather Gosport and Portsmouth took a fair battering tonight. The ship builders caught it and the hospital. I was lucky to get in the shelter near the recreation ground before running back here to find this little lot. My neighbour had sounded the alarm.'

Vera saw Patsy was listening intently as Alfred stroked the cat's head. 'You don't mind taking the pair of them, do you?' she asked. 'What about your wife, will she mind?'

'Leave her to me.' To Vera he added, 'Come on, love.'

As though in a dream, Vera had allowed herself to be taken across the road. She clutched Mogs' soft body. It's all I got left of Tim, she thought desperately.

In Angela's house the smell of polish was strong.

'We've done upstairs, nothing damaged except a broken window, thank God,' Jennifer said, appearing in the hall as if by magic. Looking at Vera, she asked, 'What have we here?'

'A crisis, my dear.'

Alfred led Vera to the sofa and sat her down.

77

To Angela he said, 'Go and make some cocoa. And see if there's a drop of milk for the animal.'

Angela went out into the scullery and soon Vera heard the gas pop. She put the cat down and it scurried behind an armchair.

She could feel the tension between Alfred and his wife as they spoke in hushed tones. Vera knew part of the conversation was about her as every so often Jennifer narrowed her eyes at her. The last words she heard before her head began to droop was Alfred saying firmly, 'The cat as well.'

Alfred's voice shook her awake and she stared at Angela peeking round the scullery door. Alfred gently touched Vera's shoulder and said, 'Go through and wash, you won't be disturbed.' Vera got up and went into the scullery. She was too tired to think for herself as Angela poured warm water into a bowl and then handed her an oval of Pears' soap. 'That's clean,' she said, pointing towards the back of the door where a nail held a white towel.

Vera remembered drinking the cocoa, which was sweet and strong. Angela led her upstairs to the back bedroom and tucked her beneath the feather quilt on the double bed. She sat on the bed beside her and smoothed her hair, softly humming a song Vera knew but couldn't place.

She remembered the feeling of sinking down into something she had no control over.

And now she carefully crawled out of the bed, trying hard not to wake Angela. She slipped down the carpeted stairs towards the scullery.

'Good morning, Vera. I trust you're feeling better?'

'Oh!' The voice startled her. She whirled round towards the armchair to find Alfred, dressed in twill trousers and a collarless shirt, sitting holding a cup of steaming tea. Folded on the sofa were blankets and an eiderdown topped by a pillow.

'I usually rise early,' he said.

'I … I need the lavatory,' she stuttered. He gave her an understanding smile. She went through to the scullery and slipped the latch on the back door.

The toilet was whitewashed inside and out and on a holder was a roll of Izal toilet paper. Vera perched on the scrubbed wooden toilet seat.

Memories of Tim swam in her head. She remembered the night he'd thought she'd gone hungry so he'd brought her fish and chips. Her bottom lip quivered. She thought of the way his hair flopped over his forehead no matter how many times he pushed it back. He was the kindest person she had ever known and she'd been able to confide in him all her fears, hopes and aspirations. He was her Tim. Vera blinked her tears away.

Two minutes later she was back in the scullery to find Alfred had poured her a cup of tea. She grasped it, muttered her thanks and followed him into the living room to sit carefully on a chair. Aware that Angela's long white flannel nightdress was stretched tight across her breasts, she tried to shield them with her arms.

Alfred, an amused smile on his lips, was watching her. Damn, she thought, why was she always so tongue-tied when he was around? Finally, after sipping the hot tea, she plucked up enough courage to say, 'Thank you for being so kind to me.'

He brushed away her words with, 'Don't worry about it. You're going to miss the boy. Angela said Tim cared deeply for you.'

Vera said nothing, but his words struck at her heart. She

had cared for Tim more than anyone had ever guessed. She sighed. Alfred was still staring at her.

Vera didn't know how to answer him and she wished he'd stop talking about Tim and intimate feelings. She sipped her tea and stared at the floor.

'You remind me of Clark Gable,' she blurted, knowing she was talking simply to fill the awkward silence.

'I wish I had his money,' he replied, setting his mug on the floor and rising to his feet. He came towards the sofa and sat down next to her. Vera's heart started thumping wildly.

'So you like Clark Gable?'

Vera nodded and took another swallow of tea. It went down the wrong way and she began to cough. Her eyes were watering as he took the cup from her and placed it on the floor. Then he began to rub her back in a gentle circular motion. The cough subsided and Vera wished more than anything that Angela was in the room with her.

'There, there,' he said, as though whispering to a very young child.

She wriggled away asking, 'Can I have my tea back now?'

He abandoned his stroking and passed her cup to her. Vera took another mouthful thankfully. Now the liquid had cooled she realised he'd used saccharine to sweeten it. Trying to think of something else to say, and remembering Angela had told her he'd lost a great deal of money through gambling, she asked, 'Don't you have any money at all?'

'Very little at present,' he said. 'But next week I may have plenty, who knows? Tea all right?'

She nodded. Vera felt safer with the cup in her hand. She breathed a sigh of relief as he shifted away to the far end of the sofa.

'I suppose Angela has explained that my wife has a legacy

she won't allow me to touch and her father owns property. Both she and Angela will always be looked after. Me? I'm waiting on a reply for an Australian business venture I'm involved in, a sheep farm. We don't plan on staying in Gosport long.'

'Gosh,' cried Vera, 'I can't see Mrs Lovell being happy on a sheep farm.' As the words left her mouth she realised once again she'd spoken without thinking.

He threw back his head and laughed. Vera saw his teeth were large, even and very white. 'Oh, we won't be living together. Not at first. There's a huge house in Alice Springs for Jennifer to pretty up.'

Vera was unsure how to keep the conversation going. While Alfred was talking he wasn't trying to sit closer to her. Yet she was afraid to simply get up and move away. After all, he was Angela's dad and she knew he didn't mean any harm. He was happy to have her being Angela's friend and she liked being in their nice house with its abundance of food.

'I've put some board in the window you lost last night. Seemed silly not to fix your window while I was mending ours.'

Her mother, God, she'd almost forgotten her! When these fits occurred, her mother usually emerged with little recollection of what had taken place. Her heart beating fast she asked, 'My mum?'

'Your mum's a lot better. I was over there at first light. Your sister's embarking on a massive clear-up as she's not going into work today.'

'Was Mum cross about me being over here?'

'She wasn't in a state to refuse last night, was she? And this morning she never mentioned it.'

'Did she say anything about Tim and his mum?' At the

mention of his name Vera's eyes began to prickle with more tears.

'Yes.' A frown crossed his forehead. 'You've got to remember your mother's a sick woman.' His voice was a whisper: '"The Lord giveth and the Lord taketh."'

'That sounds like me mum's back to normal.' Another wave of sadness overtook her that Tim was dead and no one seemed to care.

'She's going to clean the church today. Says it will be filthy after last night.' He looked at the mantelpiece clock. 'She'll be gone by now.'

Vera sighed. It wasn't hard to see where her mother's priorities lay.

Just then Mogs slid into the room and made a beeline for her.

She picked him up but Alfred said, 'I'll let him out. Jennifer's not fond of animals at the best of times. She'll be getting up soon and I don't want to upset her.' He must have seen the desolate look on Vera's face. 'Don't worry, he'll find his way back to you if he wants.'

He took the cat from her and went through to the scullery. Vera heard the latch lift on the back door.

'I'd better get dressed and go home,' she called. She was glad he'd left the room. Now she could think more clearly. When he stood close to her it made her feel almost as strange as it did when Tim had asked her to kiss him. 'I can't leave everything to Patsy, it's not fair,' she said, trying to appear as normal as possible.

Alfred put his head round the scullery door and said, 'Come over any time. We'll always be here for you.' He gave her a smile that made the butterflies return to her stomach.

Chapter 8

'I don't know why Alfred and Jennifer have decided to go ahead with Angela's birthday party. It's not right with young Tim fresh in his grave.'

Vera was at the sink in the scullery washing her school blouse. Her mother was running a shoe brush over her court shoes. She always liked to look smart when she went out on a cleaning job.

Vera, amazed that her mother was thinking about Tim, said, 'I think it's precisely the reason why the party's still on. Tim wouldn't have wanted it any other way.' Vera scrubbed at the collar with a nail brush, wishing the brush wasn't so decrepit.

'Everyone has to take what enjoyment they can in this war, Mum,' said Patsy. She had her foot perched on the seat of a chair and was painting a black line down the back of her leg. 'Bugger, I've smudged it.' She sighed. 'I wish I had some proper nylons.'

'You never wore out that big box you 'ad?' Vera couldn't believe her sister had laddered all the precious packs.

Patsy looked up and grinned. 'I swapped some for a lipstick, and some for a dinky red hat that's all froth and red flowers. I'll soon get hold of some more nylons, don't you worry.' She winked at Vera. 'It's all about supply and demand, our Vera.

You'll soon find that out.' One leg painted to her satisfaction, she started on the other.

'We're all going to say a prayer for him and his mum,' Vera said.

'I suppose that makes it all right then, does it?' Her mother stared at her. 'Good thing I let the hem down on your flowered dress, isn't it?'

Vera had her back to her mother. She closed her eyes tightly and gritted her teeth. She didn't want to wear the flowered dress because it was too tight across her bust. Her only other dress was a cast-off of Patsy's cut down to fit, but it had a ruched top that only emphasised her bosom. Vera wiped her hands on the tea cloth, picked up the blouse and opened the scullery door.

As she pegged the blouse on the line she thought about the party and Angela dressed in her pretty clothes. Vera had planned on wearing the dirndl skirt she'd made in sewing class at school and a white blouse with the sleeves turned up. Now she'd have to go in the flowered dress or her mum would get upset. She jammed the last peg on and went back inside and upstairs to her bedroom.

On the back of the doornail was her flowered dress. There was a white line about two inches from the bottom where the hem had been let down. Everyone would know it had been altered. But why was she worrying about a stupid dress when the one person she'd cared about wouldn't be there to see it?

Angela had a red moustache from the colouring in the jelly. She scrubbed at it with a red crêpe-paper tissue but it made it worse.

'Come into the scullery and I'll use your flannel to get rid of it for you,' Vera said. She pushed her chair away from the table and waited while Angela followed.

The noise in the living room was tremendous, thought Vera, with a dozen children shouting and laughing at once. She'd be glad to get out into the scullery for a bit of peace and quiet. At least there she could think about Tim and how much she missed him being with her. Vera knew she couldn't give way to tears but she wanted to. It was only now she realised that Tim had been more than a friend. He'd been her confidant, her rock when things went wrong, and whenever she was upset about anything it wasn't long before he made her laugh again. Angela was a good friend but she was a child compared to Tim. And now Tim was gone. Vera sniffed. Stop being so melodramatic, she told herself. 'Look at all the washing-up to be done!'

'It won't take Dad and us long to plough through that,' Angela said.

Vera wasn't so sure; she'd never seen so many dirty plates in her life. She picked up the white cotton flannel and rubbed soap on it then started wiping Angela's top lip.

'Hurry up.' Angela was wriggling like a worm on a hook. 'I don't want to miss playing musical chairs.

'Well, they'll all laugh at you if you start parading about with red on your face like a clown. So stand still.'

For about five seconds Angela was still, then she started talking again. 'My dad likes parties.'

'So I can see,' said Vera. 'All the girls loved him when he was dancing about playing pass the parcel with everyone.'

'He's always full of fun,' said Angela.

Vera surveyed her handiwork and saw the red moustache had disappeared. 'You're done,' she said.

*

'It was a good party wasn't it?' Her lisp had become more pronounced because she was so excited.

'Yes,' replied Vera. Arm in arm, they walked the length of Angela's garden.

'I'm sorry my mum wasn't around, she said she needed to go shopping. Though what on earth she could buy when there isn't anything in the shops, I don't know. I heard her tell my dad that she didn't want to be a nursemaid to a pack of kids. But she said she'd bring me back something nice.'

Secretly Vera was pleased by Jennifer's absence; she had a way of looking at Vera like she was something the cat had dragged in.

Angela began to prattle on about her presents and the party. Vera liked to listen to her talking happily about her family life. Angela was an undemanding friend but Vera had spent a few sleepless nights wondering how to buy a present for her. Vera had no money and asking her mother for some was out of the question. Angela had been thrilled when she'd torn away the tissue paper to find the coral necklace.

Earlier Patsy had urged, 'Go on, take it, Vera. Joe gave it to me and I'll never wear it.' Patsy had tied a green ribbon around the tissue and sent Vera on her way.

'I liked the way your dad made serviettes out of that red crêpe paper and decorated the table with all those paper flowers. And the food was scrumptious, but fancy inviting fourteen kids to trample all over the house,' Vera said. She couldn't imagine her mother allowing such liberties.

Angela said, 'Dad said one child was invited for every year of my birth.'

Vera wondered who had been invited to take Tim's place.

'I was glad that Father John said Tim would want us to

celebrate. I don't think even my mum could dare to argue with Father John,' Vera said.

Angela smoothed down her new blue flowered dress that with her ringlets made her look like a doll. Vera thought how nice it was in the garden with all the flowers beginning to bloom and the leaves green on the trees. It was good to be away from Angela's dad, who kept watching her with that strange look in his eyes. Then, as if on cue, Alfred's voice cut into her thoughts.

'Angela, I want you to take Mrs Wilkins' plate back to her.'

Alfred was hanging out the back door with a tea towel tucked in his trousers as a makeshift apron.

Vera extracted her arm from her friend. 'And I must go home. Mogs'll need feeding,' she said hastily.

They went into the scullery, which still smelled of baking. Alfred handed Angela the blue and white plate.

'Don't drop it and come straight back,' he said.

'I'll come out with you,' said Vera.

'Wait, what about the cat's meat? I saved a chicken carcass. I just need to pick the meat off then you can have what's left for him.'

With food at a premium she could hardly say no. 'Thank you,' she replied quietly.

'See you later,' said Angela, slamming the front door as she left.

Mrs Wilkins lived near the Criterion Cinema so Angela would be a while. Vera watched as Alfred went to the meat safe and took out a newspaper-wrapped parcel which he put on top of the stove.

'There,' he said. 'Dinner for Mogs.'

Vera was confused. He hadn't needed to strip the chicken after all.

'I could have gone with Angela,' she said. He was standing so close she could smell cigarette smoke on him. He was looking at her and breathing heavily. She said, 'Why did you tell us you had to cut off bits of chicken when you'd already done it?'

His voice was husky. 'Because it would give me a few moments alone with you.'

His glossy moustache was inches away from her face. That fluttery feeling had invaded her stomach again. She put out her hand to lift the parcel of meat but he pulled her round to face him. 'You're a very beautiful girl, Vera. But I suppose you know that. I expect Tim told you that all the time.'

Vera tried to move away but she was trapped between the gas stove and Alfred. She was suddenly reminded of the panic she'd felt when the serviceman had groped her at the dance hall. This time there was nowhere to run.

'I saw you when you went dancing with your sister. Made up to look much older. Tell me, did you dance with many men?'

She was scared. This is no business of yours, she wanted to say, but no sound came from her mouth. She was leaning so far back on to the stove that the gas taps were digging in her back.

'I bet you're a right little goer when you get warmed up.'

His lips suddenly covered her mouth and his tongue forced its way between her teeth. Alfred pulled her shoulders towards him and began lowering her towards the coarse coconut matting. One of his knees pushed her legs apart while his hand raised the hem of her dress. Vera tried to push him away but she was powerless against his strength, and so frightened her whole body was trembling as he pulled away her white cotton knickers. Something hard was pressing against her, entering her. He was moving fiercely, not kissing her now, and she was crying.

'Get off me. Please get off me!'

With a thrust he cried out and then lay still. She felt a sliding sensation as he rolled off her.

Then he sat up, fixed his clothing and leaned his head on to his arms.

'If Jen finds out about this it'll be the end of my marriage.' Vera scrabbled for her knickers. 'Don't you dare tell a soul!' he stressed.

Vera saw she was bleeding. 'I'm hurt, Mr Lovell. And it's not my period.'

Alfred looked up at her. 'You're just a kid,' he said. 'I ... I never realised. You'll be all right. It's your first time, that's all.'

Vera didn't know what he was saying but he rose and pulled her up with him.

He handed her a pile of red crêpe serviettes and Vera scrubbed at herself, the paper staining her skin. She started crying as she pulled on her knickers.

'I felt so sure you and Tim—'

And then the front door opened with a clatter. Alfred whipped the dirty papers away and thrust them into the rubbish bin beneath the sink. Vera smoothed her clothes into place.

Angela bounced into the room. 'You still here?' She grinned at Vera.

'She's just on her way,' Alfred said.

Vera couldn't meet Angela's eyes.

'That's my dad all over,' said Angela, tucking her arm through her father's. 'He can talk the hind leg off a donkey.'

Vera pushed past her and ran down the passage. There was still grit and bricks on the street from the last bomb blast. She put her hand through the letterbox and felt for the key on its string. She opened the door, practically falling into the safety of the hallway. The house was quiet. Mogs was curled on an armchair. Vera bent down and put her face in his warm fur. She realised she'd forgotten the meat for his tea.

Chapter 9

'Vera, why won't you talk to me?'

Vera lay on her bed. She had slipped the bolt across and knew Angela wouldn't dare force the bedroom door. She was cross with Patsy for allowing Angela into the house, but if she refused to answer her Angela would eventually get fed up and leave.

'Vera, what have I done?'

Vera stayed silent.

Finally, Angela clattered downstairs, the front door banging behind her. Ever since Angela's birthday party Vera had carefully avoided her at school and, though it meant leaving earlier, she'd evaded walking to school with her. She simply couldn't face her and she certainly wouldn't set one foot in Angela's house again.

This morning Vera had overslept and she didn't care. She lay staring at the dirty plaster cracks in the ceiling. Then she heard voices.

She rolled off the bed and put her ear to the door. It sounded as though her mother was home.

'She'll come out when she's a mind to. If she doesn't feel well enough to go to school, one day off won't hurt. Now, if you don't mind, I've got another job to go to. I only popped back because I'd forgotten me purse.' Her mother was cleaning for Mrs Patterson at the big house near St Vincent Barracks.

'But what's the matter with her? She's been treating Angela badly for weeks now. Any other girl would have taken the hint ages ago that Vera doesn't want to talk to her.' Vera could hear the concern in Patsy's voice.

'I don't know, do I? Vera's highly strung. Perhaps she's pining for that Tim, waste of space that he was.'

'Don't speak ill of the dead,' said Patsy.

Once again the front door closed and Vera guessed her mother had gone.

All kinds of things were happening to her body since Alfred Lovell had kissed her. Her breasts were swollen and tender. Her periods had stopped, but it was the sickness that upset her most of all.

She wanted to ask her mother to take her to the doctor. But now her mother was over her bad episode after the bomb had hit the street she didn't want to worry her.

She could ask Patsy to take her. Patsy had a day off work today. Vera slipped into her school clothes and brushed her hair. If only Tim was still here. He would have listened to her. Vera had always been able to trust Tim.

She drew back the bolt then crept downstairs to the scullery where Patsy was curling her hair with a pair of tongs propped over the gas flame. The scullery smelled of singed hair and Vera put her hand over her mouth to stop herself from throwing up. She flew down to the lavatory at the bottom of the garden where she heaved until she thought her insides would end up in the lavatory bowl.

When Vera returned to the scullery, Patsy looked up from the *Photoplay* she was leafing through and smiled at Vera.

'Tea's in the pot,' she said, waving towards the brown earthenware teapot. Vera got down a cup and saucer and took off the tea cosy. Patsy's head was now covered with small sausage-like curls ready for the dance that evening. In that moment Vera knew she couldn't ask her sister anything because Patsy would ask questions that Vera wouldn't want to answer.

'Now you're finally downstairs you'd better look slippy, else you'll be late for school. Mum's not very happy with you.'

After drinking the tea, Vera scrubbed her teeth then un-hooked her satchel from the back of the chair and trudged down the passage.

As she opened the door she noticed Alfred standing on his doorstep. He was staring down the street. Then he glanced across at her, and, with a dark look on his face, went inside, closing the door. Vera's heart plummeted. How could Alfred like her enough to kiss her and then ignore her? What had *she* done?

All morning she barely heard or cared what was going on in the classroom.

'Pay attention, Vera!' Mr Brown bellowed.

Vera turned her gaze from the window and looked at the blackboard. Algebra and Mr Brown: Vera didn't know which of the two she hated most. Would she really need algebra when she left school? And the sooner she got away from Mr Brown and his creepy eyes and his way of knowing she'd always give the wrong answers, the better. She tried to make herself as small as possible so he wouldn't pick on her.

She ignored the questioning looks from Angela sitting in the next aisle.

Her mind began to wander again. She thought about *Jane Eyre*, the novel they were reading for English. Why if she loved reading the book was she unable to concentrate on the words?

Sometimes she read the same sentences over and over again and yet they still made no sense. All she could think about was Alfred Lovell and what had happened after Angela's party.

At last the bell rang to end the session and she gathered up her books.

It was break time and Vera hurried to the far side of the playing field. She sat on the damp grass and again felt her skirt waistband cutting into her even though she'd already moved the button back twice. Whatever was the matter with her?

And then she saw Angela with Sue Barnes over by the art room. They were talking earnestly, their heads close together, and every so often Angela would look towards her and laugh.

The bell went and Vera trudged unhappily back. Angela, arm in arm with Sue, walked in front of her. What could they be giggling about? It must have something to do with her because Angela kept turning around. As the class filed into the geography room, Vera kept on walking. She strode into the cloakroom, picked up her coat and then ran out, running breathlessly until she reached Alma Street.

Her mother was sitting at the kitchen table smoking a Woodbine. The room reeked of stale smoke.

'You've not had a period lately,' she said accusingly before Vera had a chance to hang her satchel on the back of the chair. 'I've not seen your rags washed and drying on the line. And why are you home early?'

Vera shrugged.

'Don't you shrug your shoulders at me, young lady. I'd have to be blind not to see you're behaving strangely and putting on weight.'

'Will you take me to the doctor?'

'He won't tell you any different from what my own eyes see. Who's the father?'

Vera looked at her as though she'd gone mad. 'I don't know what you mean,' she said.

Her mother's hand connected with the side of her face. Another slap caught her mouth and the ring on her mother's hand cut into her lip. Vera crawled to the corner of the room but her mother was in her stride now, lashing out at her. Vera curled up, her hands coming up to protect her head.

After a while her mother's frantic thrashing paused and Vera cried, 'Mum, what are you doing? I didn't do anything.' She looked at her mother's face, red from her exertions.

'You're going to have a baby, you silly cow. Fornicating is sin and you well know it. You're a prostitute like Mary Magdalene. You've brought shame to me and my house!'

Vera took in the words. Baby? She managed to crawl to her feet and stagger towards the door. Making her way slowly up the stairs and into her bedroom, she pushed the bolt across.

Sitting heavily down on the bed, Vera numbly gazed out of the window, not even noticing as the room grew slowly dark about her.

'We must pray for the sin you have allowed to descend on our family. God will show us the answer.' Her mother's whispered voice cut through the silence in a lull during the mass. Vera adjusted the scarf that covered her head and looked across at the stained-glass window that so far had escaped the bombing.

Vera found the gazes of the saints and the outstretched arms of Christ nailed to the crucifix an awesome sight. The smoky smell of the burning candles made her feel ill and the gloom seemed to crowd in on her. She had committed a sin. If only she could do something that would appease her mother. She glanced at the shining brass goblets and altar rails, testament to her mother's vigorous polishing, and then her gaze shifted to her mother who, eyes closed, knelt and prayed. The church was sparsely filled.

Vera turned her head and looked at Patsy. There were tears in her sister's eyes.

The two of them had gone to church with their mother, knowing she was very near the edge again. For the past couple of weeks she'd spent most of her time either talking to Father Michael or Father John or being sullen and forgetful while at home.

The priest was now droning on in a monotone voice that was sending Vera to sleep, despite the bitter cold in the church. Patsy poked her in the ribs with her elbow. Father Michael echoed the words of the news reporters and the wireless reports, then said, 'We must pray for the sailors missing from the *Ark Royal*, sunk by the Italian U-boat. We must pray.'

When the service finally ended Vera's mother said, 'I'm going to collect the hymn books and put them away. Father Michael wants to talk to me so you two go on home.'

There was ice on the pavement and Vera clung to Patsy's arm.

'You should have confided in me, Vera. About the baby, I mean.' Patsy tucked her long knitted scarf inside her coat for extra warmth.

'I didn't know, did I? Anyway, what difference would it have made?'

'We could have tried some methods to get rid of it that have worked for some of the girls at the factory.'

'Like what?' Vera was chilled to the bone and longed for a cup of tea and her bed.

'Drinking gin and sitting in a bath of scalding hot water, that's what Millie did.'

Vera looked at her sister and made a face.

'I don't like gin.'

'Pennyroyal pills then. Or, as a last resort, an abortion.'

'What's that?'

'A sure way of doing away with an unwanted pregnancy. One of my mates knows this woman who lives round in Old Road who'll get rid of it. She got rid of Pearl's "little trouble".'

'How?'

'She sticks a knitting needle up there.'

Vera shivered. 'Well, she ain't gettin' the chance to do that to me.' Vera knew Patsy was only trying to think of ways to help her but Vera didn't want help.

Last night, she'd felt strange movements. She'd clasped her stomach in amazement. There really was a baby growing inside her! She thought she'd be scared but instead she felt strangely happy. She would at last have someone to love of her very own.

Chapter 10

'I don't want to go anywhere!' Vera put her hands on her hips and stared defiantly at her mother. 'You can't make me!'

'Don't you shout at me; I'll knock some sense into you!'

The poker was in her mother's hand and she raised it.

'Mum, Mum don't hit her, she's 'avin' a baby!' Patsy's voice filled the kitchen. Vera saw the poker halt above her head. Her mother's knuckles were white where they gripped the fire-iron's handle and then the blood slowly returned to her hands as she relaxed and the poker was lowered and thrown to the grate, where it clattered noisily.

Patsy let out a long breath, walking across to her mother and leading her to a chair.

'I need a fag,' her mother murmured. Patsy took a Woodbine from the packet on the table and put it between her mother's thin lips. Then with a shaking hand she struck a Swan Vesta and her mother inhaled.

Vera lowered her lids over tear-swollen eyes. 'I don't want to go to no 'ome for unmarried mothers.'

Her mother sighed heavily and blew out a stream of smoke in her direction. 'Father Michael is only thinking about what's best for you.'

For someone who only moments ago was ready to kill her, Vera thought her mother seemed remarkably calm. Perhaps now was the time to try to make her understand how frightened Vera was of leaving Alma Street and all she'd ever known.

'I want to stay 'ere.' Vera sat down.

Her mother lifted her head and glared at her with blank, dark eyes. 'Can't you see what you're doing to me?' Vera couldn't stand the whiney voice. 'I can't 'ardly hold my head up to the neighbours for the shame I feel. I go to church and imagine the congregation pointing their fingers at me. Me, a mother with a harlot for a daughter.'

'Mum, no one knows about the baby,' Patsy soothed. 'Vera hasn't left this house in weeks. And now the grammar school's closed because of the bombing it's hardly likely to become common knowledge, is it?'

Vera knew however much Patsy tried, her mother wouldn't change her mind. If the fifty pounds needed for expenses had been in her mother's possession, Vera knew she wouldn't be sitting in the kitchen now, begging to be allowed to stay at home. She'd have been carted off already.

'They'll all know about the child when it's screaming its head off, won't they? The shame of the birth will kill me, I know it will.' Her mother flicked the ash into a saucer then took another deep drag of her cigarette.

A spark crackled in the grate and Vera turned towards the flames, watching the blaze, until Patsy's voice broke into her thoughts.

'Vera, just listen to me. If you go to this place, after the baby's born I could come and get you. Right, Mum?' She didn't wait for a reply but carried on speaking, her face turned towards her mother. 'Vera could bring the baby home and we could say we'd taken the kiddie in as it was an orphan of the bombing. A baby belonging to a friend of mine.'

'An' me? Where am I supposed to 'ave gone while I'm wait-ing for the birth?' Vera cried.

'Been evacuated, haven't you?' Patsy looked pleased with herself. She pushed her fingers through her blond curls. 'The neighbours will understand. Lots of youngsters are still being taken to the country to escape ol' Adolf.'

Vera looked at her sister then narrowed her eyes. 'Got it all worked out, ain't you? But you've forgotten somethin'.'

'What's that?' Patsy looked worried.

'I ain't goin' nowhere!'

Vera's retort was drowned out by a loud knock on the front door. Their mother rose from her seat, saying, 'Vera, get up them stairs. We don't want no one to see you in that condition.'

Vera shuffled towards the stairway and began the climb. Alfred's voice reached her in the darkness and she paused. What was going on? Vera pressed herself against the shadows.

Her eyes adjusted to the darkness and she saw the tall figure enter the kitchen closely followed by her mother. Vera could smell his aftershave wafting up. She waited, listening to Patsy announcing she'd put the kettle on for tea, followed by the movement of scraping chairs on the lino as the three of them finally sat down.

Alfred's voice was a low rumble. 'I can understand why you've asked me to lend you some money; after all, it's com-mon knowledge about my good fortune.'

Even Vera cooped up in the house had heard how Alfred had had a large win on the Epsom Derby with Owen Tudor. 'Changing the racing venue to Newmarket because of this war was a lucky break for me,' he said. 'It means I can take the family out to Australia sooner than I expected. It doesn't mean I can say yes to all the hardship cases that have come knocking at my door, though.'

Her mother's voice was calm and clear. 'Fifty pounds. That's what I need. I'll pay you back. I don't want to be beholden to anyone.'

Vera silently fumed. Here was her mother, begging Alfred Lovell for money to send her away to give birth to his child!

'I'd have to know what you want it for,' she heard him say.

'It's Vera. She's having a baby. She's too young to bring up a child, and with my nerves and the shame of it, I just can't cope. The church has suggested a special home in the country where she can have the baby. She'll also be safer in Warwickshire than down here near Portsmouth. They don't get the bombing we do, not now the blasted Germans have flattened Coventry.'

'Has she said who the father is?' Vera could detect a note of panic in his tone.

'She won't say who the father is but we reckon it belongs to young Tim Saunders, the lad who died in the bomb blast.'

There was a pause then Vera heard a long intake of breath from Alfred, who said, 'She did think a lot of him.'

'You're not shocked?' Vera noted the strike of a match that meant her mother had yet another cigarette on the go.

'No, why should I be? They were always together.'

Vera felt her anger rising. How could he sit there and insinuate that Tim, gentle Tim, had taken advantage of her when it was he who had pushed her to the scullery floor and, and . . .

Vera couldn't contain herself any longer. She burst into the room with such force that the door slammed against the wall. Her voice high with indignation, she shouted, 'You awful man! You know whose baby it is!'

Against her weight, the table shifted and cups of tea over-turned, streams of liquid running across the oilcloth then dripping to the floor. Alfred looked horrified and his mouth had dropped open at the sight of her swollen belly.

'Don't start Mum off again,' Patsy implored Vera. 'I don't think I can take much more of this.' Patsy moved forward to restrain Vera, but Vera struggled free and turned once more to Alfred.

'Liar,' she whispered hoarsely, fighting back her tears.

'Now you can see why we want the money.' Her mother's face was emotionless, as she pointedly ignored Vera's sobs. 'I have to get her away.'

Vera looked at Alfred once more. His face was grey and his mouth hung slightly open in disbelief.

'If it wasn't for you . . .' she began before turning back to her mother. 'And you, you ask him for money to send me away?'

Her mother raised her hand and struck Vera across the side of the face. So forceful and unexpected was the blow that Vera stumbled and fell to the floor.

'I'm sorry, Mr Lovell.' Vera's mother reached for her cigarettes, lying in a pool of tea. 'You see what I have to put up with?'

And those were the last words Vera heard before she passed out.

'Caught you at last!' Vera tried to slam the front door on Angela but she forced her way into the hall. 'My dad says I'm not to call on you any more. He reckons you're a bad influence and a liar.'

Vera was glad she had her coat on so Angela couldn't see the swell of her stomach. She pushed the door to and stared at Angela.

'Did he say anything else?'

Angela pushed her face close to Vera's. 'Yes, you've done

things with a boy, most likely Tim Saunders, and tried to put the blame on him because Tim's dead.'

'That's not true! Your dad forced himself on me.'

Angela shoved her hard. 'No! My dad said you was always rubbing yourself up against him and giving him the eye. My mum said you only came to our house so you could see him. Because you don't have a dad, you wanted my dad! That's why you put the blame on him.'

Angela was breathing fast and her face was red.

Vera took a deep breath. 'That's not true. You were my best friend. Do you really think I would do a dreadful thing like that?'

'Yes. Mum says you're jealous of me, of our nice house, of the things I've done before we came to Alma Street.'

Vera shook her head. 'That's not true,' she repeated.

'Why did you let me go on knocking at your door and begging to see you? Why didn't you talk to me then?'

Vera saw the tears in Angela's eyes. Never had she seen her so upset and angry.

'How could I talk to you? Your dad had—'

'There you go again with your lies.' Vera could hear the anguish in Angela's voice. Angela turned and pulled the door open. As she ran across the street, Vera heard her say, 'I never want to talk to you again.'

Vera's mother stood beneath the huge painting of *The Last Supper* and continued listening to the Reverend Mother's speech. 'Until the child is born, Vera will work light duties. As you're aware, the only way we can keep the home running is by the work the inmates do. We believe by servitude and the greater glory of God, Vera will find salvation in heaven for the sin she has committed.' There was no hint of a smile to soften her severe features. 'Of course, donations too help finance our burden.'

Her mother opened her handbag and withdrew the roll of notes that she had borrowed from Alfred Lovell. He had left for Australia only days before. Vera had watched the furniture van being piled high with their belongings. She'd hidden behind the curtain in her mother's room and seen the family get into their car. Alfred was the last to leave, closing the door with a bang that smacked of finality. He never once looked towards Vera's house.

Her mother held out the money, which was immediately taken and deposited within the folds of the voluminous black robes worn by the nun. 'There's no need to stay. Vera will be well taken care of. It's a long journey from Wellesbourne back to Gosport.' The nun waited for Vera's mother to make her swift goodbyes.

'I'll come and see her—' her mother began.

'Oh, no, we don't advise that. If we allow parents to turn up at any time, our girls become unsettled. We don't want that, do we?'

The Reverend Mother took her mother by the elbow and guided her towards the door. Vera went to follow but was met with a sharp, 'Wait here.' But she ran forward anyway, throwing her arms about her mother.

'Don't leave me, Mum!' Despite everything that had happened between them, she needed to be held, to be comforted. Her mother's body was stiff and unyielding. The Reverend Mother clutched at Vera, pulling her back into the cold room. Then the door closed and she was left alone.

Vera's eyes stared at each piece of the heavy polished furniture that cast shadows in the dull light. She was alone in a strange place. Abandoned by her mother. Abandoned by her best friend, Angela. And Tim was gone for ever. Then Vera felt the baby move and she placed her hand over her stomach, glad that she wasn't totally alone. She waited for what seemed like hours before the nun returned, sweeping into the room.

'Rule one, child: I told you to stay here but you deliberately ignored me.' The Reverend Mother fixed Vera with a steely glare. 'You will never ignore my wishes again.' A bony finger poked at Vera's chest. 'Do you understand?'

Vera nodded. 'Yes.'

'Yes, Mother. From now on I am Mother to you.'

'Yes, Mother.'

'Right. You now belong to the Magdalene Home For Girls. It is a house of correction. You will rise at five in the morning, go to mass, labour in the morning in the washhouse and in the afternoons you will work in the garden and grounds. Bed is at half past seven.'

Vera looked at the floor, too scared to ask questions.

'You will wash clothes. By hard work you will wash away your sins. You are a Magdalene now and your work will help put a roof over your head and feed you. You are unclean. You have known a man's body before marriage. Hard work and prayer is the only way to atone for your sins. You are no longer Vera. You will be called Sheelagh: a new name for a new life.'

Vera almost opened her mouth to speak but was interrupted by a timid knock on the heavy oak door.

'Come.'

The door creaked open and a girl came into the room. The girl's arms and legs looked all the more stick-like because of her huge belly. Her hair was cut close to her head and her eyes were downcast.

'This is Aileen. She will take you to the bathroom. And no talking.' Aileen hesitated. 'The bathroom, Aileen!'

'Yes, Mother.' Aileen turned to go. Not once had she raised her eyes to Vera, who quickly bent to pick up her cardboard suitcase.

'Leave that!'

'My clothes are in—'

'To wear clothes other than those we provide is vanity. You will scrub your body and wash your hair. Sister Selia will watch over you. Go!'

'Yes, Mother.' Aileen and Vera spoke together. Aileen held open the door and Vera walked out into the hall, waiting until the girl had closed it behind her, then she said, 'Is she usually so grumpy?'

Aileen turned her head and spoke softly. 'We're not allowed to talk. I don't want to get into trouble.'

Vera, in silence, followed Aileen down the wooden floored hallway. At a scratched blue door, a nun stood guard.

'So this is Sheelagh? You may go, Aileen. And you, child, will call me Sister Selia.' The nun was tall and thin and her nose was like a squashed potato on her dough-like face. Over her arm was a large towel. 'Inside on a chair you will find clothes to put on after you have bathed.' She held out the towel to Vera, who took it, and before she could say a word the nun pushed open the door and clouds of warm vapour escaped. 'Don't take all day. I'll be outside waiting for you. And leave your own clothes on the stool.'

Vera began tugging at the belt of her coat. She'd long ago given up trying to button it. When she was naked and her clothes in a heap on the floor, she climbed into the white cast-iron bath and slid into the steaming water. There was no lock on the bathroom door. The smell of disinfectant hung in the air, sickly and strong.

A wire mesh soap dish hanging over the edge of the claw-foot bath contained a bar of strong-smelling lye soap similar to the kind her mother used to scrub whitewood tables. Vera picked it up and began to scrub her swollen body.

'Don't take all day!' The door had swung open and Sister Selia marched in. 'You were told to wash your hair. You've not begun yet. Bend forward!'

Vera leaned over the bulge of her belly and the sister rolled up her sleeves and began attacking Vera's hair. Tears sprang to Vera's eyes. The nun's fingernails raked Vera's scalp. Vera had become proud of her long dark waves and a ring the nun wore kept catching in her tresses. Vera closed her eyes tightly, too frightened to ask the nun to take more care.

'I'm not wasting warm rinsing water on an ungrateful wretch who refuses to wash her hair. Turn around and put your head beneath the cold tap.'

The ice-cold water froze Vera's scalp and washed over her shoulders as her head was held beneath the tap. Just when Vera thought she would surely drown beneath the freezing torrent, the nun turned the tap off.

'Dry yourself and get dressed,' she commanded, wiping her hands on the towel before passing it to Vera. 'And fold those up.' She kicked at the clothes on the floor. The door slid closed behind Sister Selia as tears started running down Vera's face.

As Vera rubbed at her hair, trying to dry it and bring back some warmth into her chilled body, she tried hard not to think about the reality of her mother abandoning her here in this frightening place. Leaving her in the charge of nuns who cared nothing for her or her baby. She longed to be back at home. If only her mother had listened to Patsy begging her not to send Vera away. Vera wiped her eyes and slid into the clean, scratchy clothes that didn't belong to her.

Vera pressed her hands over her belly. 'No one's ever going to treat you this way,' she whispered.

Chapter 11

'Don't cry.'

The touch was light on Vera's shoulder. She recognised Aileen's voice and twisted round beneath her cold sheet to look at her. Aileen was wearing an identical flannelette nightdress. The room was dark, the blackout curtains in place, though Vera doubted many of Hitler's planes dropped bombs here in the middle of the countryside.

'Can't you sleep?'

'No,' Vera said, wiping her eyes. 'I'm cold and hungry.'

She thought of the greasy stew that had been her supper in the enormous dining hall, served in silence by the two girls at the top of each table. So many girls and so little noise, other than the scraping of cutlery on plates and the rattle of tin mugs on the wooden tables. Most of the women and girls were in various stages of pregnancy. And after came the long prayers on her knees in the vast chapel, conducted by a priest with a red face and large pudding-like hands.

The girls had lined themselves in the pews and then almost as one had sunk to their knees. Nearer the altar, priests and nuns sat, heads bowed. Vera had felt chilled to the bone and longed to be in bed for warmth. But in the long dormitory that Vera shared with eighteen other girls in separate wooden beds, she was still cold.

'You'll get used to it,' Aileen whispered.

'Never,' sniffed Vera. 'Anyway, I thought you weren't supposed to talk to me?'

'To get caught means a hiding from Sister Selia.'

'What kind of a hiding?'

'A strap about the backs of the legs or a ruler on the knuckles.'

'Jesus.' Vera was appalled. 'Has she done this to you?'

The girl nodded. 'But I've been here a long time so my punishments have been many. And now I have a further misdeed to atone for, for the baby I'm carrying.'

Vera frowned. 'How long have you been in the care of the nuns?'

The girl shivered. Vera pulled back the thin bedcovers. 'At least be warm while you're chatting to me.'

Aileen crawled in beside her. 'The nuns are eating their supper now, else I'd dare not come to you.'

'Go on,' Vera whispered.

'I was born here. My mother died giving birth to me. I was always scrawny, so when the couples came to choose babies for adoption I was always overlooked.'

'But you're having a baby. You must have got out of this place sometime.'

'No. Never.'

'Who's the father, then?'

Vera felt Aileen stiffen. 'I can't tell you.'

Vera put her arms around the thin girl. 'Someone's done it to you same as it was done to me, haven't they?' She couldn't blame Aileen for not wanting to talk about it. Vera didn't even want to think about Alfred Lovell.

Aileen sighed. 'I'd better go back to my own bed. If one of the nuns comes in and finds my bed empty, I'll get into trouble and so will you.' Without waiting for a reply she climbed from the bed and Vera realised she was at last warm.

'Goodnight, Aileen,' she whispered.

'Goodnight, Sheelagh,' came the soft reply.

A bell woke Vera.

After cold showers and mass came breakfast. Vera sat at the table and poked at the meal in front of her with a spoon. It could have been porridge, she thought, except for the green-grey glutinous mass in the middle. A giggle caused her to look across at one of the servers watching her. The server was about her own age with long ginger hair tied in pigtails. All the girls were slyly watching her now. Vera knew immediately that the server had spat in her porridge. The girls hung their heads towards the table.

Vera sighed. To eat was unthinkable. So too was to complain to one of the nuns wandering alongside the tables. She wasn't a snitch and never would be. She climbed with difficulty from her place on the bench, picked up her porridge and walked calmly to the head of the table.

'You did this an' I reckon you can have it back again.' Without another word she grabbed the girl at the back of her head and forced her face into the sticky mess.

Vera walked back to her place. She sat down, picked up her mug of weak tea and gulped it down. The silence was broken by a loud wail from the girl.

The girl sitting on Vera's left whispered, 'She needed taking down a peg or two. My name's Maeve.'

And then a hand clamped Vera's shoulder and a voice said, 'Come with me. Settle down the rest of you. Go and wash yourself, Bridget.'

Vera was half pulled from the bench and marched by the

nun along highly polished corridors until she stood outside the room she recognised as the Mother Superior's.

After a short sharp knock she heard Mother's 'Come'.

'Stay here,' the nun said and disappeared into the room only to reappear moments later to haul Vera in front of the Mother Superior. The door closed.

'It wasn't my fault—' Vera began.

'Did you or did you not cause a scene in the dining room?'

Vera couldn't lie. 'Yes. But it was because—'

'Because, Sheelagh, you are a disruptive influence.'

Vera wanted to shout that her name wasn't Sheelagh but Vera.

'Sheelagh, you will learn how fortunate you are to be here with us in this safe environment. According to the news this morning, the Japanese have devastated Pearl Harbour and many American lives have been lost. It's possible now with the Americans entering the war that the British Isles could be even more at risk. Thus your home in Gosport, because of its forces connections, might be razed to the ground at any time.' Mother had been walking around the room while speaking, her steps measured and slow. 'To be here is a God-given honour for you, a Magdalene. Do you understand?'

Vera looked towards the ground. 'Yes, Mother,' she replied.

'And do you know why you are called a Magdalene?'

'No, Mother.' Vera wanted to sit down. She hadn't minded the sickness her pregnancy had brought, but now she was growing larger her ankles had puffed up, making it difficult for her to squeeze her swollen feet into her shoes. She moved from one foot to the other, trying to ease the pain.

'You are a penitent, a sorry excuse for a human being. A Magdalene in remembrance of Mary Magdalene who scrubbed away her sins and became one of our Lord's closest friends.'

'Thank you, Mother,' Vera said.

'Humility is a lesson for you to learn.' Mother opened a drawer in the desk and took from it a large pair of scissors. 'Pride is a sin. I think you need to understand we will not tolerate pride here. Sister Selia tells me you were unhappy about her washing your hair?'

Vera knew what was coming. And she knew there was nothing she could do to stop it.

'Yes, Mother,' Vera said. She was ushered to a chair and sat down. And then the first curl of her long, glossy locks fell to the wooden floor.

Afterwards, Vera was led by Sister Selia to a large brick building. When the door opened the noise of machinery assaulted her ears. The smell of bleach made her eyes water as she was marched through the machines to wooden tubs where girls were bent over, scrubbing clothes.

'The dirty laundry arrives first thing in the morning,' Sister Selia said. 'We have contracts with nursing homes and hospitals.' Billows of damp steam filled the air. 'It is washed and dried and ironed and collected by van each evening. We do not abuse our employers with sloppy work or late supply.'

Then Vera was led to a thin padded table that was set up as an enormously long ironing board. From light fittings in the ceiling swung electric cords and each cord was attached to a heavy-looking iron.

'This is where you'll work. You're to be pressing personal clothing and gowns belonging to the nuns and priests. You do know how to use an iron?'

'Yes, Sister Selia,' said Vera.

'Individual garments are to be ironed and set in piles according to their owners.'

Vera realised she must have looked perplexed.

'Staff nametags are sewn into their personal clothing. Inmates, garments are sorted by size.'

Vera nodded. She knew it was going to be hard standing all morning ironing but it was much better than scrubbing washing. She looked about her. Maeve stood at another ironing board. Behind Sister Selia's back she winked at Vera.

'Aileen.' The girl seemed to appear from nowhere. 'Watch Sheelagh, will you?'

'Yes, Sister Selia,' said Aileen. Aileen and Vera neither greeted nor smiled at each other. Vera looked along the line of girls, all busily working. She saw no one else she recognised and no one was speaking. But there was the sound of women coughing, and as she had walked past huge vats containing bleached water and the women scrubbing at the soiled clothes, Vera had seen their hands were rubbed red raw. On a table behind the ironing board was a rush basket full of clothes. Her heart fell as she looked at the mountain of linen she had to conquer.

'So you're the trusted one, are you, Aileen?' Vera whispered as soon as the nun had left. Vera saw one of the brothers sitting in the corner. She realised he was supposed to be watching them but he had his eyes closed and was obviously asleep.

'Only because I've been here the longest.' Aileen spoke so softly that Vera had to listen hard above the noise in the room. 'I'm sorry about your lovely hair.'

'So am I,' sighed Vera. She looked at Aileen's short locks. 'Did it happen to you, too?' Aileen nodded. 'I'm going to get out of here,' said Vera. 'No one is going to treat me like, like,' she cupped her hand and leaned into Aileen's ear, 'shit.'

Aileen didn't look shocked by Vera's language. 'There's no way out. The doors are locked, the walls are too high and topped with glass. And supposing you have your baby outside in the countryside? How will you manage?'

'So I'll have to wait until my baby's born then I'll go as planned,' Vera replied.

Aileen frowned. 'I don't know what you mean by a plan but you'd better try and escape very quickly after you've given birth.'

Vera looked puzzled. 'Why?'

'The babies are taken away for adoption.'

Vera laughed uneasily. 'I don't believe you.' But her heart was beating fast.

'The Mother Superior has a ledger in her desk with all the children's names and their adoptive parents, from as far away as America and Canada. And the prices they were sold for, too.'

For a moment Vera was dumb. Then she spoke. 'No, that's not true of my baby. I'm only in this place because my mother's nerves are bad and she couldn't stand the shame of me being with child. She's telling all the neighbours that I've been evacuated. When I go back with my baby, the story will be that the little one is the sole survivor of a bombed-out family and we're going to bring it up.'

Vera suddenly realised Aileen was looking at her in a strange way. Then tears sprang into the thin girl's blue eyes. She reached across and held one of Vera's hands.

'Is that what they told you?'

'Yes. Why?'

'Because it's not possible. It's rare for any of the girls or women to leave here. Except in a casket.'

Vera just stared at her.

'You've been told a lie. The truth is that when your baby comes, you will feed it for a week or so in the sanatorium then it will be taken from you and put in a special nursery, not on these premises. Wet nurses will take care of it and you will return to your duties here. Have you not wondered why there's no sound of infants crying?'

'That's not true! My mum and my sister will come for us. I know they will.'

Aileen was silent.

Maeve looked over towards Vera. 'She's telling the truth. I thought my man was telling the truth when he said he loved me. He got what he wanted from me and then ran when I told him I was carrying his child. Mam turned me out, so here I am.'

Vera stared at her flat stomach.

'I had twin boys three months back. They've been sent to Australia with a couple who emigrated.' Tears welled up in her eyes. 'I'll never see them again.'

Vera put her hands over her stomach and felt her child moving. *Her child.*

No one was going to take her baby. *No one.*

Chapter 12

Vera's fingers were frozen and the thin woollen cape she had on didn't do much to keep out the wind. It had rained during the night, enough to make it easier to pull weeds from the rose garden. The rose bushes were Vera's favourites. Hanging heavily from the thorny branches were the glorious orange rose-hips.

Christmas had come and gone. As Christmas hadn't been a celebration except for the extra long masses, Vera wasn't surprised when the day of her own birth was ignored.

She stood up and looked around the walled garden that gave the bushes and climbers protection. She knew the leaves would soon appear and then the buds, followed by the weighty heads of the roses. But it was the wild dog roses she loved and they grew in abundance, their fruit still clustered despite the cold weather.

The house of correction was celebrated for its rose-hip syrup, which was sold countywide. Fruit during the war, especially oranges, was difficult to come by but it was acknowledged that the syrup of the rose was especially rich in vitamin C. Some said it could keep colds away all winter and babies thrived on it.

The only thing Vera didn't like was picking the fruit and breaking the skin. If that happened, the fibres inside made her hands itch like mad and she had to be careful not to touch any other parts of her skin.

This afternoon she was alone in the garden. As her baby's birth was imminent, she had been excused the chore of clearing out the big shed backing on to the gravel road near the vegetable garden. Some of the wood had rotted and the women were restoring the roof and building. But first the contents had to be taken out and laid upon a canvas sheet and then, in case of more rain, be covered by a tarpaulin. She took a moment to ease the pain in her back and watched as lawnmowers, steps, ladders, rakes, spades and other garden equipment were carried out.

Usually there were other women, girls and the guardian nuns about her. She enjoyed being alone, able to think and daydream a little. The cast-iron bucket was almost full of fruit.

She wondered how Aileen was today.

For the past week, she'd been depressed and more nervy than usual. Yesterday she'd seen Aileen coming from Brother Andrew's room. She looked as though she'd been crying. Yet when she'd mentioned it to Aileen, Aileen had glared at her and said she must have been mistaken. There was something about Brother Andrew that made Vera fearful. During mass she had caught him staring at her with those odd bulbous eyes.

Vera could feel her child low inside her. It gave her great pleasure to experience the baby moving about. Although she knew she'd lost all sense of time, she guessed it couldn't be much longer until the birth. Her legs were like tree trunks and she walked like an old woman. Surely, she thought, her time must be very near now.

And what then? Somehow she would escape from this awful place, taking her baby with her. Of that she was determined.

She stretched, bent down carefully, picked up the pail and slowly walked towards the kitchens.

Bridget was sitting on a stool peeling potatoes. Amazingly, she was quite alone. Vera didn't speak to her but went to the draining board and heaved up the bucket of rose-hips. As she let go of the handle someone pushed the bucket, spilling the hips in the sink and down on to the floor.

'What!' exclaimed Vera, twisting around to face Bridget, who still had the potato knife in her hand.

'I'm so sorry,' the red-haired girl sneered. 'My hand slipped.'

Vera moved towards her but the girl waved the knife. 'Don't try to be clever; this knife is sharp.'

Just then the door opened. Bridget, fear on her face, turned her eyes towards the sound and Vera grabbed hold of the knife, wresting it from the bigger girl's hand.

'What's going on here?' Maeve ran towards them and the door slammed shut.

'My friend Bridget is offering to pick up every single rose-hip. Isn't that so?' Vera pointed the small black-handled knife at Bridget. Prickles of fear had risen on the back of Vera's neck. She knew if she ever let Bridget get the better of her, her life in this awful place wouldn't be worth living. 'If she doesn't, Bridget might accidentally get hurt. Isn't that correct?'

Bridget's face was stormy and Maeve looked scared.

'Nothing to worry about, Maeve,' said Vera as calmly as she could.

Bridget had scooped up the hips on the floor and had started picking the ones out of the sink.

When the chore was almost complete, Vera said, 'I reckon you ought to rinse them off, I don't want to get into trouble for bringing in dirty rose-hips.'

Maeve was smiling as she watched Bridget rinse the red fruit.

'What did you come in here for?' Vera asked Maeve.

'Sister Selia wanted the kitchen scissors.' She opened the cutlery drawer and took them out. Vera handed her the potato knife.

'Might as well put this away. I've finished with it.' To Bridget, Vera said, 'I'm off now, but keep away from me. I might not be so nice next time.'

Having left the rose-hips there, Vera walked down the great hallway. She was shaking with fear at what had happened in the kitchen. Amazed that she'd stood up to Bridget.

She just had time to wash her hands before afternoon mass. In the bathroom that was used by her dormitory, she heard crying coming from the toilet cubicle. Trying to ignore it, Vera washed her hands with the lye soap and dried them. But when the crying still hadn't ceased, Vera decided to knock on the door.

'Hello?' she tried tentatively.

'Go away!'

'Aileen, is that you?'

There was no answer. She tried again. 'You do realise that if Sister Selia had asked that question and got the answer you gave me, you could be in bad trouble?'

The door swung open.

From the waist down, Aileen's clothing was covered in blood.

'Jesus, we have to tell someone.'

'No.' Aileen pulled her inside the cubicle and shut the lockless door.

'You have to tell me what's happened.'

'And if I tell you and you tell Mother, I'll get into more trouble and be branded a liar.'

'Aileen, you're bleeding. Think of the baby. You need help.'

'Like Brother Andrew helps me?'

Vera looked into her eyes. 'What do you mean?'

'He said it wouldn't hurt, to do it that way might even bring the baby along.'

Vera was quiet. 'How long has he been doing this to you?'

'I can't remember a time when he didn't fondle me, but I don't always bleed, not like this.'

Vera felt sick. Sick that someone who should be looking after children could do something like this. 'You have to confide in someone. Someone who'll make it stop.'

Aileen was shaking her head. 'They wouldn't believe me and my punishment will be to be treated worse than I already am. I'd have to be made an example of, wouldn't I?'

Vera threw her arms around Aileen. She understood only too well. Who would believe two young girls that the nuns and brothers of such a holy establishment were abusing the very children it was supposed to protect? And there was nothing Aileen and she could do to protect themselves and other inmates from the abuse.

Aileen lowered her head, looking at her bloodstained clothes. 'Will you help me, Sheelagh?'

Vera sniffed. 'I'll try but only if you stop calling me Sheelagh when the nun's ain't around. My name is Vera. What's your name, your proper one?

'Aileen, just Aileen.'

'Right, just Aileen, take them bloody clothes off.'

Aileen looked ashamed. 'I don't have any other clothes to put on. It's four days until our regular clothes change.'

The girls were allowed fresh clothing once a week.

'Doesn't matter. I happen to know where Sister Selia has left today's ironing. Our ironing didn't get locked away because the van collecting sheets and bedding had to wait while the stuff from the shed was moved.' Vera looked at Aileen, who had pulled her chemise over her head. Vera saw dried blood between her legs. Her heart churned with pity for her friend. 'While I'm gone, get yourself bathed. If we ain't discovered missing from mass, we got time to sort you out.'

With her eyes and ears alert, Vera hobbled down the corridor. At the bottom of the stairs, near the Mother Superior's room, was the large wicker hamper containing clothes she'd ironed earlier. As quickly as she could, she fumbled for an outfit for Aileen. Once she had a set, she turned back towards the bathroom. Footsteps made her freeze. They were coming nearer. She looked for somewhere to hide. The hamper was too small for her large body.

She tried the glass handle on Mother's door and it opened. She darted in, closing the door behind her, praying that Mother was at mass. The room was empty. Vera knelt behind the desk and listened to the footsteps growing closer.

Her heart was beating like a drum. She held her breath. The footsteps passed by. Vera let out a sigh of relief. Using the chair as support, she rose. That's when she saw the heavy set of keys on the table.

Without a further thought, she scooped them up and slipped them in her pocket. Then she opened the door and scooted as fast as she was able back to the bathroom, where Aileen, standing amidst bloody clothes, was drying herself.

'Are you still bleeding?'

Aileen shook her head and grasped the clean clothes, shrugging herself into them as fast as her swollen body would let her.

'How are we going to get rid of these?' Her toe poked at the soiled clothing.

'Don't worry, I'll sort that.' Vera knew she couldn't take them to the wash-house. The eagle-eyed brothers and nuns on duty would soon spot her washing them when she should be ironing. She would bundle the clothes up as small as possible and bury them in the rose garden. 'Just pray it rains tonight, Aileen. A heavy frost could spoil everything.'

'You're going to bury them in the garden?'

Vera nodded. 'I'll stuff the bundle down me knickers to get it out of the house and with the others busy re-building the shed, Bob's your uncle.'

Aileen threw her arms around Vera. 'You're a true friend.'

The keys jangled in Vera's pocket. 'What have you got there?'

Vera drew out the keys.

'You stole them!'

'I'd like to think I borrowed them.'

'When Mother finds her keys are missing, there'll be hell to pay.'

'But unless we're discovered missing from mass, she won't be able to blame us.'

Aileen clutched at her stomach and moaned.

'Are you all right?'

'Just a twinge.' Aileen gave Vera a watery smile and Vera pushed open the cubicle door. She'd already stuffed the soiled clothes inside her large white knickers.

'A quick clean up in here,' she said. 'You go and hide some-where so you can mingle with the others when they leave the chapel.'

Again Aileen put her arms around Vera, their bumps press-ing against each other.

After Aileen had left, Vera marvelled how long it had been

since someone last hugged her. She mentally shook herself to stop feeling maudlin, wiped around the sink, took a last look to see that all was tidy, then peered around the door before leaving.

In the dormitory, Vera looked about her. To hide the keys beneath her thin mattress was unthinkable. The nuns often searched the room looking for personal mementos. To have in one's possession any item without the house of correction's consent was considered vanity. Painful repercussion was the outcome.

Vera's eyes scanned the beamed ceiling. Behind a beam would make a good hiding place. She dragged out a chair and stood up on it. She looked carefully at the keys. None was marked but surely the large one had to be for the oak front door that was locked after mass each evening. The other keys were small. Desks, interior doors, cupboards, she reckoned. But where was the key for the main entrance that was set in the wall? She'd worry about that later. Tucking the keys out of sight over the dormitory's entrance, she put back the chair and then, with difficulty, she slid beneath her bed, knowing the girls would come first to the dormitory to shed their coats before going for the evening meal. Vera hoped she might be able to slip from the bed and join the others going down to the dining room without anyone noticing.

She lay on the dusty floor. Vowing once again that she would escape this place and take Aileen with her.

Chapter 13

The pain began at her back then squeezed its way around to the front. Vera clung to the banister at the bottom of the stairs.

'Sorry,' she gasped as the women and girls had to make a detour around her to get to the hall.

'Come on, don't cause an obstruction,' bellowed Sister Selia, coming to see what was causing the hold-up and the extra noise.

The pain was excruciating and Vera could hardly stand. She felt the wetness covering her legs and shoes and her belly was as hard as iron.

'I think your waters have just broke,' Aileen said.

'I think me baby's coming.' Vera was terrified. She had no idea what she had to do. Would they cut the baby out of her?

'What's the matter with you?' Sister Selia's face was full of anger.

'Jesus,' groaned Vera as another wave of pain enveloped her. She was suddenly bathed in sweat and everything seemed unreal except for the agony pouring through her body. All she could do was hold on to the banister; without its support, she'd slump to the wooden floor. She *knew* the baby was coming.

'Help me, Sister. I feel like I'm being split in two.'

Women and girls had gathered about, their faces full of expectation, their voices hushed.

'The rest of you carry on to the chapel and be quiet. Aileen, hold her up.' The sister peered at her. 'The baby shouldn't be coming this quickly.'

Was she going to have her baby here on the stairs? Was she going to die? She had no control nor understanding of what was happening to her. All she wanted to do was push.

'Don't leave me, Aileen.'

Aileen put her arms tightly around Vera.

'We'll get her to the sanatorium. The midwife can take over then.' Sister Selia's voice was entirely without emotion.

Terrified, Vera allowed herself to be half dragged, half pushed along the hallway. She was hardly aware of walking outside and across the gravel path that led to the sanatorium.

'I want to lay down.'

'Oh, God, try to hold on until we get you inside.'

'Do not take the Lord's name in vain, Aileen. Try to remember you are a Magdalene,' barked Sister Selia.

Vera saw the open door of the sanatorium. Filling it was a rounded figure dressed in nun's clothing and a white apron. She came down the steps towards Vera.

Tears and sweat stung Vera's cheeks but the sight of the woman's kind face filled her with hope.

'We need to get you in bed, don't we?' Vera could smell alcohol on the woman's breath. Then to Sister Selia and Aileen, 'Get her to the labour ward. You can leave then.'

Vera felt as though she was in a play. Someone undressed her. Things were happening but she had lost all sense of order and time. The only thing that was real was the pain coming in ever increasing waves, tightening her stomach and making her grunt and scream.

'We're nearly there,' said the nun, then to another nun, 'Get Doctor Parker.'

To Vera she said, 'Breathe out and in and when I tell you to push, push.'

She tried to concentrate on breathing but her mind didn't want to focus on anything except making the pain go away.

'One big push!'

A thin wail started up like a far-away cry.

'You've a boy!' The cry was stronger now and, pain forgotten, Vera used her elbows to push herself up to see the nun holding a mucus- and blood-covered baby who Vera thought was the most beautiful child she'd ever seen. A repulsive-looking cord hung from the baby.

'Give him to me,' Vera demanded. The child was placed over Vera's body. A fuzz of dark hair covered his head and he was yelling, his pink mouth a small cavern, his tiny fists clenched tight. Feeling a rush of love, Vera vowed to herself this child was *never* going to be taken from her.

'We have to cut his cord where he's attached to you, weigh him and clean him.'

The midwife started attending to Vera and the baby then called another nun who carefully lifted the child and wrapped him in a piece of sheeting. And Vera realised that sheet was his first garment and she, his mother, was unable to provide him with any clothes at all.

'Can he come back to me?'

The nun wiped her bloody hands on her apron. 'Doctor Parker needs to sort you out first.' The nun pressed her hands on Vera's flabby belly and Vera felt something slide from her.

'Good girl, that's the afterbirth.'

Vera lay back on the bed.

She had a son. Her son. Her little boy.

She heard, as though in a dream, the doctor saying, 'Just a little prick and then you won't feel a thing.'

James had the bluest eyes she had ever seen and they gazed at her with rapt attention while she held him close and he suckled from her breast. Vera was overwhelmed with love for him.

'You've been in the infirmary for two days now.' Sister Selia stood over her, a look of disdain on her pinched face. 'Tomorrow you'll be sent back to work in the laundry and gardens.'

'What about my baby?' Vera didn't call him by name; already she'd been told by another nun that naming the child wasn't her job. But in her head and heart he was James, named after James Stewart, the movie star, one of her favourites.

'He'll stay here for another few days and you will return at four hourly intervals to breastfeed him.'

Now Vera had got used to having him in her life, she couldn't imagine being without him. She thought of all the bad stories Aileen had told her and every day another truth emerged. She had been lied to by her mother: she wasn't being sent home with James. If she allowed it to happen, James would be taken from her and she'd never see him again.

Vera had made up her mind to escape but first she had to return to the gardens and laundry and there were scores to settle and plans to make and only days to resolve them.

'My next baby won't be treated like an object,' said Vera.

Sister Selia smiled as she replied. 'There will be no punishment this time for speaking to me in such a discourteous manner. They have obviously not told you that you have been sterilised. Spawn of the devil, Magdalene girl, there will be no more babies for you.'

For a moment Vera was silent. Whatever did the sister mean? Then she found her voice. 'I don't understand.'

'No more babies means exactly that. Your fallopian tubes have been severed. It's not reversible. You will never carry a child again.'

The hot iron skated along the sleeves of Brother Andrew's tunic; the rest of his freshly ironed garments were piled neatly beside the wicker basket. Vera's eyes scanned the wash-house. Everything was as usual: women working without speaking, the noise of chesty coughing the only sound apart from the clatter of the machinery breaking the silence.

Vera tried to push away the grief she felt at having her body treated as though it didn't belong to her. She loved James to distraction but surely the sisters had no right to prevent her ever having more children? And Brother Andrew? Wasn't he supposed to look after the girls? She thought of Aileen and the way she was being treated. The pair of them needed to get away.

Vera pulled out the orange-coloured hips from her pocket and used her nails to set free the hairs and seeds. Along wrists, collars and neckbands of Brother Andrew's clothing, she rubbed the bright insides of the fruit. None of his clothing escaped her attention and his long johns received the most consideration. Smiling to herself, she refolded the clothing and swept the remains of the seeds into her pocket to dispose of later.

As she continued with the never-ending ironing, her back aching and her insides feeling as though they were about to drop on the floor at any moment, Aileen swayed past carrying a box of soap. She looked as though she was about to give birth any day.

'Tonight,' Aileen whispered.

It wasn't a question but a statement. They planned on

escaping tonight. Too bad, Vera thought, she'd never see Brother Andrew scratching away at his inflamed skin.

'Tonight,' mouthed Vera.

Clouds hid the moon and even Hitler's bombers appeared to be silenced for once. Vera held tightly to Aileen's arm. She was still weak after the birth and the work she had done had tired her more than usual.

Aileen was strangely quiet. Vera pulled her cape about her and the keys jangled in her pocket. Mother had never queried the missing keys, which surprised Vera.

Vera had been correct in thinking the very large one was the key to the front door. But it seemed there was no key to unlock the wrought-iron gate in the wall. Vera had crept out late one night to check. Which meant they'd have to use a ladder. But first they had to get into the sanatorium and bring her baby out.

'Time's against us,' puffed Aileen. 'If that last feed you gave James didn't send him to sleep, we could have a crying child on our hands and he could wake the whole place up.'

'I know,' whispered Vera. The gritted path crackled beneath her feet and she moved to the grass to suppress the sound. 'But if we don't take this chance to escape now, James may be moved from the sanatorium and lost to me for ever.'

The building came into sight, wreathed in darkness. Vera turned the brass knob on the door. She knew that only one nun guarded the small hospice at night and that one nun was very fond of the bottle. With a bit of luck she would be out for the count, but Vera couldn't take chances. She knew that the nun's bedroom was the other side of the nursery. When she'd fed James earlier, she'd noted that just four babies were in residence and no Magdalenes sleeping there.

'Stay here.' Vera put her fingers to her lips and then entered the sanatorium as quietly as she could.

In the nursery, four small cots lined one side of the room. James lay on his side, breathing deeply. Vera lifted him gently and scooped up his bedding. Terrified he would whimper, she clutched him to her and returned to Aileen. Even in the darkness, Vera could see Aileen looked frightened.

Away from the sanatorium, Vera and Aileen walked quickly towards the garden area.

'We need to prop the long ladder against the wall,' whispered Vera. 'With both of us hauling at it, it should work.'

'Where is it?'

'Beneath the tarpaulin. If you pull the top sheet away, I can make a sort of nest for James on the ground. I can't do much with him in my arms.'

Vera suddenly froze. She could hear humming.

'Shh! Get under the tarp!'

Aileen clumsily fell to her knees and slid beneath the wet tarpaulin and Vera followed her, the baby held to her breast. Vera pulled the sheet above their heads. The baby sniffled. Tighter she pulled her child into her and willed James not to start crying.

Footsteps were loud now and so was the humming. The person passed within feet of them, and as the footsteps receded Vera let her breath go as she lifted the corner of the sheet.

'That was Mother,' she said incredulously.

'Taking a night-time walk,' said Aileen. 'Is she gone?'

Vera looked towards the front door, and after a couple of minutes saw the sliver of light as the door was opened then quickly closed again.

'She's gone.' James wriggled. In the darkness his eyes glittered like tiny stars and the sight of her baby tugged at her heartstrings. His tiny mouth puckered and she bent forward and kissed him, tasting the milky sweetness of his skin. Then Vera wrapped him as best she could in the bedding she'd brought from the nursery and set him upon a dry bit of the tarpaulin away from the ladders.

'You don't know how much I love you,' Vera whispered, tucking James in safely.

It didn't take as long as she thought it would to prop the longest ladder against the wall. Aileen was holding on to the bottom of it. Vera thought how tired she looked as she began piling heavy rockery stones against the bottom of the ladder.

'We don't want it to slide,' she said to Aileen, then, 'You know what to do?' Her friend nodded. Vera collected a few empty sacks and stuffed them inside her cape. Then she picked up James and started to climb, going very slowly and looking around to make sure Aileen was close behind her.

Vera's heart was beating rapidly and it was difficult climbing with James in one arm. 'Don't you wriggle or cry, my sweetness,' Vera said softly. She didn't look down until she reached the broken-glass ridge.

'I'm putting the sacks down now.' Balancing carefully, Vera, still clutching James, made a rough padded seat on the top of the wall. She hoisted herself off the ladder to sit on it and waited until Aileen climbed level with her.

Sitting on top of the wall they smiled at each other. Vera felt her adrenalin pumping.

'Now we have to get down the other side. Pulling the ladder up and swinging it over isn't going to be easy, especially not with you in your condition. Hold James and I'll draw it up. It's a pity this wall is so high, otherwise we could have jumped down.'

Aileen looked terrified.

Inch by inch the ladder rose until it was lying across the wall. Vera felt she'd never worked so hard in all her life. And then she swung it round and finally it was propped on the outside of the wall.

Vera took a breather. Her arms felt as though they were practically pulled from their sockets. She faced the wall and gingerly put one foot on a rung to test the steadiness of the ladder. 'Hand me James,' she said.

Vera could see the fear on Aileen's face as she held out the precious bundle that Vera clutched thankfully to her.

'I'm not coming.'

'What?'

'I'm staying here.'

'But we're almost free!'

'I've never been outside the gates before. I don't think I could cope.'

'You'll be with me. I'll look after you.'

'Vera, you're the first person ever to show me kindness but I'm not sure you're going to be able to look after yourself, let alone me. I don't want to hold you back. And ... and, I'm aware it's only a matter of days now before my baby comes. How will we cope if something goes wrong? I'm staying here.'

Vera, standing on the rungs near the top of the ladder, pleaded. 'But you know what Brother Andrew's like. He'll not stop because you've had your baby.'

'I know he won't. But I'll try to keep out of his way. Nothing you can say will make me change my mind. I'm helping you get away then I'm going to drag this ladder back. No one will ever know I had anything to do with your escape and this is the way I want it to be. You'll be better on your own, you know you will.'

'If you stay here they'll take your baby and cut your insides the way they cut me. Please come?' Vera whispered tearfully.

Aileen shook her head. 'I'd always be thinking about Brother Andrew and how he got me pregnant. I couldn't love the baby, Vera. It's best if I stay and let them take my baby away.' Aileen looked about her, then said, 'All right. You'd better get going. James'll start screaming then you'll not be able to leave because we'll get caught.'

With tears in her eyes, Vera climbed down the ladder. At the bottom she laid James on some dry leaves and pushed the ladder towards the top of the wall. Aileen gave her a sad smile and then she was gone, leaving Vera to wonder if that would be the last time she'd ever see her friend.

Vera picked up James and started walking. It was cold and she hugged James tighter to her body underneath the cape. She thought about Brother Andrew and how his skin would itch like mad and she began to laugh. But her laugh quickly turned to sobs as she thought of Aileen left without a friend there.

A tiny cry came from her precious bundle. Vera knew James was hungry. When she was far enough away she would feed him. She pulled her garments aside and peeked at him and his blue eyes stared unblinking back at her.

'I love you,' she whispered.

The road seemed to be widening now and ahead Vera could see another road with vehicles crossing it. If only she knew where she was. South, that's where she must head. Her mother could hardly refuse to take her and the baby in if she turned up on the doorstep, could she? And Vera knew her sister would do everything in her power to help, once she'd shown them she wouldn't be parted from James. With hope in her heart, she trudged on.

Vera wished she had some money. Sooner or later she would

reach a village. She had nothing to eat or drink. Her mouth watered at the thought of food. But first she had the night to get through.

She began to get used to the small scuffles in the undergrowth, realising they were only tiny night creatures foraging. Vera reached a bigger tarmac-covered road. There was no pavement but every so often a charabanc or a lorry passed. When she heard the trundling, Vera would try to hide, just in case the home had sent someone to look for her.

Occasionally the silence would be broken by the far-away sounds of planes and the discharging of their bombs. Then lights would fill the sky and just as suddenly disappear.

Woods loomed large and dark. Vera crept towards the trees and discovered beech leaves and pine needles soft beneath her feet.

'C'mon, my pretty,' she cooed. 'I'm laying you here, nice and warm, and I'm going to make us a bed. Then I'll clean your bottom and feed you and we'll sleep together like peas in a pod.'

Vera collected as much dry stuff as she could and fashioned a makeshift mattress. After attending to James, she rolled him in his blankets and cuddled him next to her warm body. Her whole body ached with the exertions of climbing and lifting and a dull ache had started up in her groin but she was too tired to care. She was free! Free of that awful place. Her last thought was that if Mother sent anyone to look for her, they'd never find her here. Matching her breathing to her son's, she slept.

Chapter 14

A tickling sensation on her face woke Vera. Snowflakes had forced their way through the leafless trees and were drifting on to her face. She moved her arm from around James, clutched close to her body for warmth, and stretched it to relieve the numbness. He awoke and began to cry, his tiny face puckered with frustration, so she immediately latched him on to her breast and sat back with her body propped against a pine tree. Inside her cape she could feel dampness where her son had urinated. After he'd suckled she cleaned him and then herself as best she could. Her body was stiff and hunger pains gnawed at her. She knew without money for food and shelter, being exposed to the elements would be the end of them.

The main road would be her best option. If only she knew where she was she'd know the correct direction to Hampshire.

Luckily the snow must have just begun for only a light fall covered the verge at the roadside. With James bound tightly against her body for warmth, she began walking. The walk warmed her and she sang softly to James. Not knowing any lullabies, she sang her sister's favourite song, 'The Last Time I Saw Paris'. If only Patsy was with her now.

A few cars passed going in the opposite direction and Vera kept walking. One of her shoes was letting in water and her feet were cold but she knew she couldn't afford to slow down.

A lorry drove past her, soaking her with snow and slush. And then it stopped. As she drew nearer, a curly-haired man leaned out and stared.

'Bit cold for walking today, girly. Want a lift?'

Vera swallowed back tears of gratitude as she answered her thanks.

He put out a hand and pulled her into the cab. Immediately Vera was settled on the seat, she searched in the layers of her clothing for James, who silently stared at her with his luminous blue eyes. Vera leaned back on the bench seat, savouring the warmth inside the cab.

'Why, you got a babby in there,' the man exclaimed as he pulled away, turning to her with a smile. Vera looked at him tearfully while he glanced at her muddy cape and her battered shoes. 'You're from the Catholic place, aren't you?'

Vera gazed fearfully at him. 'Please don't take me back! I ran away because they were going to take my baby from me.'

'Lordy, I ain't goin' to take you back. I've heard bad things about that place that would fill a book.'

Vera relaxed. Already the heat in the cab had sent James to sleep and Vera's fingers and toes tingled. 'Thank you,' she said quietly.

'When did you escape?' His voice was deep and musical. Vera decided he must be Irish.

'Yesterday.'

'You've never slept rough?' His brow furrowed.

'I had no choice.'

'No money?'

Vera hung her head.

'I don't suppose you've eaten then?'

Vera shook her head.

'I've no food but I've a flask of tea. Help yourself to that, girly.' He pulled a large plastic flask from the door well and gave it to her. 'I been drinking from it; there's only the one cup.'

'I don't care.' Vera smiled at him and unscrewed the flask top, pouring a little of the warm liquid into the cup. She drank her fill, feeling it warm her insides as it went down.

There was a newspaper folded on the seat and Vera picked it up. She saw the headlines. '*Royal Oak* torpedoed in Scapa Flow. 833 men lost.'

'Oh!'

'What's the matter?' he asked.

'I ... I once knew someone on The *Royal Oak*,' she said, remembering the young man who'd cried at the Connaught dance hall.

'Nasty business that,' said the driver. 'Apparently, the ship was sunk by a series of explosions from an enemy submarine. Crying shame; some of them men were no more than boys.' Vera could see herself, back in the hall, fastening her St Christopher necklace around his neck. He was a nice boy. But she knew believing in a silver chain wouldn't bring *her* luck, she had to make her own.

'What's your name?' Vera asked.

'Me mates call me Paddy but the missus calls me Patrick. I won't tell you what she calls me when she's cross with me.'

Vera smiled.

'How long you been married?'

'Thirty years, an' I got a girly about your age and my boy is seven and a right little bugger! But I wouldn't have him any other way.' He pulled down the sun visor and Vera saw a family photo pinned there.

'They look nice,' she said, looking at the woman in a

sun-dress with her arms about two children, both of whom looked like him. 'Where are you heading?'

'Waterlooville. I got packing cases of china to deliver to a store. I've just loaded up at Stratford-upon-Avon.'

Vera could hardly believe her luck. Waterlooville was near Portsmouth and Portsmouth was just across on the ferry from Gosport. 'Could I stay on until then?'

'Sure you could. Tell me where you're heading an' I'll see if I can drop you a bit nearer.

'Gosport. But anywhere near there will do.'

'Well, I have to look in on my wife's mother, who lives at Hambledon.'

'Oh, yes, please.' Hambledon was a village about twenty miles from Portsmouth. Vera's heart lifted. She sat looking out of the window at the passing fields and cottages before sliding into a deep sleep.

'C'mon, Sleeping Beauty!' Vera's shoulder was being shaken. 'We're at a transport caff. Don't tell me you aren't hungry.'

Paddy's door slammed shut and she heard the crunch of footsteps before her door was opened and she was helped down to the gravel.

'I don't have money for a meal,' Vera mumbled.

'No, but I do, so get your arse into gear, girly, I'm starving!'

Vera looked towards the steamed-up windows. She could hear laughter and smell bacon and fried bread and her mouth began to water. Cigarette smoke surrounded her as she stepped inside the door.

'Full fried breakfast?' Paddy put his hand on her shoulder.

'Oh, yes, please,' Vera said.

'Righty-o!' But instead of yelling it across the Formica counter at the curvy woman frying bacon at the gas stove, he went round the counter and began whispering something in the woman's ear. She looked back at Vera, then continued talking as she turned over the delicious bacon rashers. Paddy came back and said, 'That's Ida. She's a good sort. I told her about you and the baby and she says you can use the facilities in her rooms at the back. I figured you'd like to bathe yourself and the babby and you'll feel better feeding the little one in private, won't you?'

Moved by his kindness, Vera nodded as she felt tears slide down her cheeks.

Paddy foraged inside his coat pocket and brought out a white handkerchief.

'Keep it,' he said, when she offered it back.

Vera settled into a booth, only half listening as the men talked loudly about the war and the two hundred aircraft from RAF Bomber Command that had carried out a heavy and successful raid on Germany's Ruhr valley. For the first time in a long while Vera felt safe.

It wasn't long before a huge plate of eggs, bacon, liver, fried bread, tomatoes and crusty bread was set in front of her.

Ida put her hands on her hips and said, 'We have our own hens and pigs, so enjoy your food. Ol' Hitler ain't starvin' us. When you've finished, come over to the counter. Can I see the little one?'

Vera drew back her cape, revealing a sleeping James. 'God love the little mite,' Ida said.

Later, Ida showed Vera into her living quarters and began running a bath. 'Can't fill it to the top, I'm afraid. But I reckon we can go a little better than the regulation five inches. After all, you are sharing it, aren't you?'

Vera had lain James on the bed.

'I've always wanted a little one,' Ida said wistfully. 'Had

one, too. Only he didn't live to be a year old. Can I hold him?'

Vera nodded. She was sure James gave Ida a toothless grin.

'I don't know how to thank you ...' began Vera.

'You don't have to. If Paddy's taken a shine to you, then you're okay.' She began rifling through drawers, finally pulling out a skirt, jumper and underwear and a red belted coat. 'I reckon these clothes'll fit you. All the time you're wearing that Catholic uniform, it's a dead giveaway where you're from. These should keep you warm an' all.' Then she pulled a cardboard box from beneath the bed. 'There's plenty of towelling for you to use as nappies and I'd be honoured if you'd kit out the little one in these baby clothes.' She showed Vera a pile of cardigans, bootees and romper suits. 'Ain't fair he should be dressed in them damn Catholic bed rags.'

'I couldn't possibly—'

'You'd be doin' me a favour. Stop me gettin' them out an' lookin' at them an' thinkin' what might 'ave been.'

'I don't know what to say.' Vera felt close to tears again, unable to believe the kindness of a complete stranger. She touched a shawl that had obviously been hand-knitted.

'Say nothing then,' said Ida briskly.

Ida shut the door behind her and Vera undressed and slipped into the hot water. She gave a great sigh as she found a fresh bar of Pears' soap in the dish.

Once out of the bath, she towelled her hair and then she caught sight of herself in the mirror. There were no mirrors at the home, for vanity is a sin, she'd been told time and again by the nuns. Gazing at her reflection, she saw that her hair had grown to a curly shiny cap of darkness and that she looked much older. Why, she could easily pass for eighteen now, she thought. Vera the girl had gone and Vera the woman stood in her place.

Safe in the centre of the bed, James was kicking his legs, dribbling and making noises. Vera lay full length beside him. She moved her face close to his so that his eyes, like dark blue shiny currants, became distorted and he gurgled as though he was quite aware she was playing a game with him. She couldn't resist putting her arms around him and hugging him tightly to herself.

A while later, with James fed and clean, Vera returned to the caff.

Paddy was reading a newspaper but when he looked at her, he whistled.

'You look a treat,' said Ida.

'We got to go,' said Paddy.

Vera went and hugged Ida. 'Thank you,' she said.

'You just keep that boy safe. Come back and see me sometime.' There were tears in Ida's eyes.

Back in the lorry, Vera put her hand on Paddy's. 'Thank you,' she said. 'There are some truly kind people in this world.'

Paddy, embarrassed, gave a curt nod and then started the engine. As Vera stared out of the window, all she could think about was going back home, back to Gosport, with her beloved son safely by her side. Oh, how she looked forward to seeing her mother and Patsy and settling James into a proper home. That was all she wanted for him: a home where she could look after and love him. But her excitement was outweighed by overwhelming tiredness and, unable to resist its pull any longer, Vera's eyes began to close.

Vera could see the village of Hambledon spread before her. The small cottages were ivy covered, a church was set back down a lane and the soft drinks factory faced the road. Paddy's mother-in-law's house was behind the factory, he told her.

'Are you sure you can find your way home from here?' Paddy looked concerned. Vera gathered up James and tucked him inside her coat.

'Yes,' she said. She waved her arm. 'Over there is Fareham and the next town is Gosport.'

'If you're sure?' Paddy asked.

Vera climbed down from the cab and smiled up at Paddy. 'Your wife is a lucky lady,' she said. Then she walked swiftly towards the pub on the corner of the lane. She waved back to Paddy as she turned into the lane and saw that he was still watching her with that same concerned look on his face.

Vera walked steadily on down the lane, passing a duck pond and a cluster of cottages. Gradually the houses disappeared, leaving only fields either side of the lane, sometimes punctuated by trees, but mostly hemmed by high hedges.

She was trying to ignore the low pain throbbing in her groin. Without disturbing James, she put her hand to her breast. It was hot and tender. Her first thought was that James had suckled a little too long, and made her sore. She pulled back her coat and the shawl to make sure James was sleeping and saw, tucked inside James' blanket, a ten-shilling note. She clutched it, silently thanking Paddy.

It was growing dark now. Vera hoped there would be another pub ahead. Perhaps she could stay the night there now she had money to pay for a bed. She was so tired she could hardly keep her eyes open. But it wasn't the tiredness that worried her, it was the feverish hot and cold flushes and the awful dragging sensation down in the base of her stomach.

Vera made a bargain with herself that if a pub wasn't on the next bend she would sit down inside the next field she came across. Just a small rest until she felt able to carry on.

Around the next bend of the lane was a ribbon of grit as far as her eyes could see. She sighed and at the next five-barred gate she came upon she untied the rope and with great difficulty pushed it open. It was a fallow field with long grass and weeds. Vera made herself a nest of dry ferns, every movement becoming more laboured.

A drink, if only she had a drink. She was so hot. She tucked James down against her skin and closed her eyes. She knew there was something wrong with her. And it was then that Vera gave into the darkness.

Chapter 15

Vera woke to the smell of broth and a wood fire. It took an effort to prop herself on one elbow and look about. Her head felt heavy, as though it didn't belong to her. She was in a wooden bed that was built at the end of a sort of oval wooden room. There was a lit stove near the door and from this came the heady smell of pine logs. The broth was in a tin dish on a small table next to the bed. A warm patchwork quilt covered her. She was alone. Her hair and body were wet with sweat.

James? Where was James?

The door opened and in stepped an elderly woman dressed in black clothes. Atop her plaited black hair, woven in coils about her ears, was a man's trilby hat.

'You're awake then?' The woman's voice crackled with age.

'Where's my baby?'

'Safe, dearie, he's in good hands. But if my grandson, Luca, hadn't heard the lad crying, neither of you would be alive.'

Vera's arms felt lifeless as she tried to push back the quilt.

'You lay still until the strength comes back, and it will return all the quicker if you eat and drink.' The woman pushed Vera back on to the bed and replaced the covers. Then she picked up the bowl and spoon and said, 'Let me get this inside you and then I'll bring you your little one.'

Vera opened her mouth and took each spoonful offered. A

mug of cool water was produced from a tin jug and the woman held it to her lips. When Vera had finished the woman took a large tin bowl from a wall cupboard, shook some powder from a glass vial into it and then poured in water from a blackened kettle standing on the stove.

'Now, dearie, I'm going to wash you down below. I've put in some herbs that'll help with the soreness. No need for you to feel embarrassed about this, you got nothin' to see that I ain't got meself, and 'sides, I been washing you all the time the fever was a hold of you. You've got what we call childbed fever. In other words, you've given birth in dirty surroundings and you could have perished,' she said. 'Your little one too, if my grandson hadn't found you.'

Vera heard the words and tried to make sense of them in her head. She thought about the sanatorium, the drunken nun and the doctor who had made it impossible for her to ever carry another child. She lay back exhausted on the bed while the old woman struggled to slip a towel beneath her. Then she felt the heat from the warm water soothing the rawness.

Vera felt clean and refreshed after she'd been washed and dried. The woman removed the towel and went over to a basket on the table.

'I've a potion here that will help. You've already shown me you can fight against the fever.' Three small bottles were opened and their drops collected on a spoon. 'Open wide.'

'What is it?' Vera asked wanly.

'You don't have to worry your head about that, but there's pennyroyal, aconite and belladonna amongst other herbs here, and together they'll sweat the rest of the fever out of you. You'll feel tired and you'll sleep.'

Vera drank from the spoon, then asked, 'But James? Where is he?'

'I told you not to fret about him. Nellie has more than enough milk for her own little one and your boy. What you need is sleep.'

Vera smelled the clay pipe. The old woman sat swamped in a blanket on an armchair next to the bed. Immediately her button-black eyes opened and she took the pipe from her mouth and put it on the hearth by the stove.

'Good, you're awake. I'll bring in your child, but he can stay only for a wee while as you need to sleep some more.' She put her wrinkled hand on Vera's forehead. 'You're doing fine.' She moved with the grace of a young girl towards the door and closed it behind her.

Vera looked about her. Small windows were covered by sparkling white lace, and fringed oil lamps and brightly coloured cushions filled the caravan. *A gypsy's caravan.* But how had she got here? The grandson of the old woman had found her, she'd been told. Vera remembered sitting down in a field because she felt unwell, after Paddy had dropped her off. But that was all. She'd obviously been more ill than she thought and this kind gypsy woman had taken her in and cared for her.

Vera heard footsteps and the door opened to reveal James well wrapped up in the woman's arms. Vera put out her hands and her heart leaped with happiness as she felt the weight of her boy in her arms.

'Oh, my love,' Vera whispered. His eyes were open, his skin clear and she swore to herself he felt heavier. Then her nose wrinkled at a greasy smell coming from the blankets surrounding him.

'I've slathered his little chest in goose fat. He's over the worst of a chest infection.'

'That's my fault!' Vera was angry with herself. 'I ran away from the home because the nuns were going to take him away from me. I should have realised he was too small to be out in the bad weather.' Vera put her face against James and held him tight. 'I'm so sorry.'

'What's done is done. You mustn't look back. No! Stop that!'

Vera was unbuttoning the flannelette nightdress in an attempt to feed James.

'The medicine I'm giving you will be passed on through what remains of your milk. It's not fit for him to suckle. You could harm him!'

Vera looked tearfully at the woman. 'I can't feed my baby?'

'No, and I've dosed you with Epsom salts to help discontinue your milk. Otherwise your breasts are going to be in a terrible state. It's not wise for you to feed James, but Nellie can, and you can see by the look of him she's done a grand job these past two weeks.'

'Weeks? I've been ill for two weeks?'

The woman nodded. 'When you're better you can leave the camp, if you want. We're only a small gathering and I've made sure you're welcome to stay. But I won't be answerable for the boy's health if you take to the road again with him. My advice is to stay with us until your child can eat solid foods. Stay until you are well.'

Vera nodded gratefully. It was only then it dawned on her that she had been sleeping in the woman's bed.

'But it's me who should sleep in that chair, not you.'

'Don't you worry, girl, as soon as you're properly on the road to recovery you'll be on the floor,' she said with a throaty laugh.

'How can I ever repay you?' Vera said quietly.

'You don't need to thank me, it was Luca who carried the both of you back to the camp.'

Vera had imagined Luca to be a child. But how could he have carried the both of them?

James started to cry. Vera laid him on his belly and rubbed his back. He was having none of it. He was hungry. The woman pulled out a basket from beneath the bed and from the pieces of cloth stored there picked out a creature made entirely of patchwork. It resembled a rabbit.

'I bin passin' me time makin' him a toy. I hope he likes it.' The woman pushed the toy into Vera's hands.

'Thank you,' Vera said, unable to find words to express her gratitude.

The old woman picked up James and rewrapped the shawl around him, making sure his toy was with him.

'Rags,' said Vera. 'We'll call the bunny Rags.'

'That's as maybe,' she replied gruffly, as she turned to leave, 'but for now Nellie can sort James out. I'll bring him back tomorrow.'

As the woman disappeared out of the door with James still crying, Vera felt angry with herself that she was so useless she couldn't comfort her own child. After a while she lay down and then drew back the net curtain beside her. Outside she could hear music and laughter.

Children ran, shrieking and laughing. A man sat on an upturned crate with a fiddle providing melodic music for two couples dancing. Ashes of a fire burned low. One young woman had dark hair pulled back from her face by a ribbon and she was as tall as the man she was dancing with. The second couple danced close together. He had his arms tightly about the girl and he leaned his dark curly head against her glossy black hair which floated unrestrained in the light breeze. Almost as though sensing someone was watching him, the man looked towards the caravan and, catching sight of Vera, smiled, showing white teeth set in a strikingly handsome face. Vera felt her breath tighten in her chest. She suddenly felt alone and vulnerable. She let the curtain drop.

The dancing made Vera think of the time Patsy had taken her to the Connaught Hall and she'd danced the night away, held in the arms of servicemen fighting for their country. A lump rose in her throat. Where was Patsy now? Where was her mother?

'What, not asleep yet?'

The woman had come back.

'Where are we?' Vera remembered Paddy had dropped her at Hambledon but where she was now she had no idea.

'Oakfield, not far from Hambledon. We're waiting on relations who'll bring back the horses they borrowed to tow roundabouts to Titchfield. Always a fair there this time of the year; cheers people up, it does. Our group's been working for a farmer and it's his land we're on now. But the work has come to an end and it's time to move on again. There'll be hop-picking later. Now you're in the mood for asking questions, perhaps you'll tell me who you are?'

Vera watched as she set the blackened kettle on the wood stove.

'Vera.'

'Well, Vera, me name's Rosa and I'm the oldest in this camp. Coming from the most respected and highly regarded family, the Smiths of Hampshire, I gets the last word on decisions. When you're up and about, I'll show you a thing or two to make some money. Can't afford to keep you for nothin' and you ain't leavin' me until you can care for your babby properly, understand?' Vera looked at her animated face and the thousand wrinkles that told of a life outdoors. She nodded.

Rosa spooned tea from a caddy into a red teapot and stirred it, leaving it to draw upon the hearth. 'A cup of tea will do you good.' Her eyes took on a far-away look. 'Maybe when you're well, I can get you to do a bit of hawkin'. That's goin' out with a basket. I reckon you'd make a good caller, selling door to door. Everyone in the camp works, even the little ones with their small hands, weaving the rushes or twisting the crêpe for paper flowers. Luca was out looking for budding flowers when he spied you. Aye, he found a flower all right, two of you. The lad's been back three times asking about you. Esme, his betrothed, is not too happy about that, I can tell you.'

'Well, I thank the man for saving my life but if he walked in here now I wouldn't recognise him. I must have been totally out for the count.' She thought for a moment then asked, 'Flowers? Why was he looking for flowers?'

'We picks 'em then bunches 'em then sells 'em door to door.'

Vera thought how nice it would be to be out in the open air knocking on people's doors asking if they'd like to buy her flowers. She could even take James with her. It would be easy compared to the hard work she'd been made to do in the home. She started to tell Rosa about it.

'I was scrubbing sheets, ironing and gardening in that home. Some women's hands were cut and bloody with sores.' It seemed a long time ago that she'd said goodbye to Aileen. She wondered if her friend had had her baby. And if Aileen had been subjected to the same brutal procedure that she had.

Chapter 16

Vera spooned the porridge into James' mouth. He swallowed, leaving a big dribble on his chin, then grinned at her, his two small teeth gleaming. He'd made short work of the sweet gooey mess so she set him down on the grass with Rags so he could crawl back towards the other children. They were giggling and chattering as they sat on the ground sorting through the rags and woollens Uncle Billy and Luca had brought back from the town. The children's grubby hands scrabbled in pockets of trousers and coats. Sometimes people left money in clothes, brooches too were often found pinned to jumpers and ladies' coats.

Rosa said they never bought clothes because 'ragging' turned up good warm pieces. Uncle Billy, Luca and a couple of cousins had taken the horse and cart and gone into Southwold, buying anything they could make a profit on from the house-dwellers: iron, lead, brass, old bedsteads, furniture and, of course, rags and woollens.

Vera leaned back against the high wheels of the caravan as she watched over the children. She studied her brown legs and arms. She was the colour of a cob nut and thanked God she'd put weight on again after being so scrawny and poorly for so long.

Vera now slept on the floor of the van so Rosa could have

her bed to herself again. James slept on a small palliasse next to Vera but inevitably he clambered up into bed with his Nana, as he called Rosa.

The summer had passed in a blur of Hampshire villages and country lanes and fields where the gypsies settled. Vera loved the way every new place became a challenge to earn a living. It was a traditional way of life, catching rabbits and pheasants, poaching, and sometimes, with a bit of luck, a farmer would offer work to the men. Luca was especially proud of his fencing and hedging. Vera liked to watch him at work, his strong brown arms and hands bending the hedge branches to his will.

Luca would sense her watching him and turn and stare arrogantly until Vera felt shy and turned away. She loved the shape of Luca's lips, sensuous and full, always ready to laugh. It was always with a jolt that she remembered. Luca belonged to Esme.

Vera put her face up to the sun, closing her eyes and savouring the blissful heat.

Tomorrow they would be on the move again.

'You ever been to Ditchford afore?'

Nellie walked over to her, momentarily blocking out the sun before sitting down.

Vera shook her head. 'I don't even know where it is.'

'Kent, silly. We allus goes 'op-pickin' in Kent.'

'So there'll be no calling round the doors then, it'll just be field work?' Vera had never even thought about picking hops, yet here she was getting excited about living in a wooden shed with a tin roof for a few weeks.

'Course. An' in the evening when the babbies are abed an' the meal's gone down, we'll dance.'

Vera liked the sound of that. 'Will I like picking hops?'

'Don't be a boro dinellos. Nobody likes 'op-pickin' but we

do like the money.' Nellie began to laugh, her plump body jiggling. She was pregnant again.

'What did you call me?' Vera asked.

'A boro dinellos; it means big fool!'

'You cheeky madam!' Vera loved Nellie. She was a couple of years older than Vera but she'd been married for some time, after a true gypsy wedding, and had three small children. Vera watched James rolling on the grass with Tom, Nellie's youngest. James saw her and crawled over. When he reached her Vera made a noise like a cat meowing and James bent down to look beneath the caravan steps. Nellie started to laugh and James hid his face in Vera's skirts, only peeking up to say, 'More.'

Vera began tickling him and James rolled away, back to his friend.

'Did you have to get married?' The words were out before Vera could stop herself.

Nellie picked at a bit of grass and put it between her teeth. 'No, me an' George was promised together as babbies.'

Vera thought about the big man who looked like an ox but had the temperament of a teddy bear. He'd provided Nellie with a caravan the size of a house that he'd mostly built himself and he had two Shire horses to move it. He cared about his horses almost as much as he loved his family.

'Didn't you mind having a husband picked out for you?'

'Not really. But marriage ain't always like that. If we ain't promised we can choose who to love, but when our parents makes an alliance it's usually better to trust their judgement. It worked for me.'

Vera flicked away an ant that was crawling on her knee. 'What about non-gypsies?'

'You mean a gorgio.'

'That's what I am, aren't I?'

'Of course. Only with your dark hair and skin tanned by bein' out in all weathers, no one would guess.'

'So no one would want to marry me?'

'If you're thinking of Luca, stop it right now. He's promised to Esme, and he's a Smith; they keep the faith.'

'I wasn't—'

'Yes, you was. A blind man can see how you look at him. And don't think I haven't seen his sly glances at you.'

Vera felt herself blushing. She remembered Alma Street and the shy glances Tim used to give her. Now she was older she realised that in his own way Tim had loved her. Sometimes she lay awake at night wishing she'd kissed him. Wishing she'd followed her heart instead of her head. What would her life have been like if Tim was still alive?

'Anyway, our sort, girls that is, don't have intimate relations before marriage.' Nellie nudged Vera's arm and winked at her. 'You know what I mean. When the girl weds, she must be a virgin for her man.'

'What about the man?'

Nellie shrugged. 'Oh, they be's a different kettle of fish. But they mustn't bring shame to their families by sleeping with a gypsy girl. Definitely not.'

'Vera!'

Vera looked towards Rosa, who was standing on the top step of her caravan.

'I'm coming,' she called back, then to Nellie, 'Could you watch James and the rest of the children for me while I see what Rosa wants?'

'I'd be glad to. Be as long as you like; I'll take him back with my brood and give him some tea later. The others'll be having their food soon.'

'You're a true friend,' said Vera.

Rosa was in the doorway, her black ankle-length skirt fluttering in the breeze. A shawl, as usual, covered her shirt which was belted at her waist.

Vera too now wore ankle-length skirts, aware always that the gypsies frowned on women who showed their flesh. A green silk frilled blouse with her long sleeves rolled up complimented the green of her skirt. She'd topped the outfit with a man's waistcoat. She was mindful, as usual, that her large breasts emphasised her tiny waist.

'I've got a surprise for you,' said Rosa. 'Come you 'ere, close your eyes and hold out your hand.' Rosa was smiling.

Vera ran up the steps. 'Why?'

'Don't ask daft questions, just do it.'

Vera closed her eyes and held out a hand to feel something cool and light slide on to her palm.

'Can I open me eyes now?'

'Of course.'

In her palm were two earrings. Vera scooped one up, letting the gold and jet dangle against her fingers.

'These are real, aren't they?'

'Nine carat and Whitby jet. I wouldn't give you rubbish, pet.'

'I've never seen such beautiful earrings in all my life,' said Vera. Her mother had frowned on trinkets and Patsy wore what was called costume jewellery, pretending the glass jewels were diamonds.

'They're a present to you for making me feel young again. All that looking after you and running about after James was good exercise and has given me a new lease of life.'

'Oh, Rosa.' Vera put her arms around the small woman and held her tight. 'You're like a mother to me,' she said, and thought, no, you're better than my mother ever was to me.

'Pshsst.' Rosa pushed her down on a small stool next to the stove.

Vera turned the earrings in her hand. 'I'm goin' to keep these for ever.' She studied them intently. 'They're for pierced ears an' I don't have holes in me ears.'

Rosa twisted Vera's head towards her and looked deep into her eyes. 'You soon will 'ave, my girl.'

Vera watched as Rosa assembled two corks, a needle and a pair of pliers.

'Don't you dare move off that stool, and when I ask for an earring give it to me.' Then she reached up to the shelf and dumped a large jar of Vaseline in Vera's lap. 'Just you do everything I asks.'

'Are you goin' to hurt me?'

'Put it like this, dearie, "Pride's painful", whichever way you looks at it. But I promises you you'll be happy later that you can put such delicate jewels in your ears.' Rosa flicked her own dangling earrings. Then she opened the door in the side of the woodstove.

'OK then, get it over with. I'll be like all the other women then, won't I?' Vera thought of Esme and her gold hoops.

Rosa used the pliers to hold the needle in the glowing furnace. When the pointed end glowed she said, 'Have an earring open ready. Don't fidget.'

She deftly brought the needle up and then suddenly Vera smelled burning flesh. She saw the cork lifted by Rosa and the needle pushed into the cork. The earring was whisked from Vera's hand. Rosa's touch was light as the wire of the earring passed through Vera's lobe.

And then the pain started.

'Jesus Christ!'

'Don't blaspheme! Give me the Vaseline.'

Vera saw a dollop being scooped from the jar then felt her ear being slathered.

'Am I bleeding?'

'A bleedin' nuisance. Sit still!'

'I don't think I want this.'

'Well, you got it now an' you'll look pretty stupid with only one earring. Turn around. I told you not to look.'

This time Vera turned away and let Rosa get on with it.

'All over now.'

Vera felt as though someone had cut off her ears.

'They look beautiful.' Rosa went and picked up her hand mirror and gave it to Vera. All Vera could see were two gobs of Vaseline coating her lobes. She went to touch her ears. Rosa slapped her hand away. 'You 'ave to touch, don't you? Take my word for it, I've done a good job. In future, wash your 'ands before touching your ears an' keep them slathered in grease for a while until you can turn them without the gold wires sticking. Ain't one woman in this camp that I ain't pierced the ears of,' Rosa continued. 'The babby girls now, I does 'em young.' She looked at Vera. 'You *can* move, you know.'

Vera got up from the stool, keeping her head quite still.

'Oh, for God's sake, anyone'd think I cut yer bleedin' throat! Get out of here and give me some peace.'

Chapter 17

Vera couldn't believe a place could be in the middle of no-where, yet Ditchford was. The caravans followed a track that led past the small railway station. There were crowds of people and children waiting, sitting on crates or suitcases.

''Tis an 'oliday for the townies,' said Rosa, taking a suck on her clay pipe. 'They're waiting for the farmer to send carts for his 'oppers.'

'Good job it ain't rainin' then,' Vera said. 'I wouldn't fancy bein' crowded on a cart like that lot.'

Vera held the reins and let Gordy the horse pick his way over the stony lane. Rosa was holding James, who was still for once. Vera smiled at her. James was a proper boy now he could move about.

'If I wasn't allowed me own accommodation, you would be crowded in with somebody,' said Rosa. 'Having me own hut is me payment for the fifty years I been picking 'ops for Crawford.'

'Fifty years?'

Rosa nodded. 'That man knows he can trust us lot. That's why we can park our wagons next to the 'op fields.'

'I can't wait to see the hut.'

'Well, now's your chance as we're comin' up to the farm. Give me the reins and git down an' open the farm gate.'

Vera jumped down and lifted the iron hoop that kept the gate closed. A stocky man was coming towards her, with mole-skin trousers and strips of leather tied around the legs.

'Well, bless my soul, if it ain't my Rosa,' he said. He tossed a smile at Vera but went and stood near Gordy and smoothed his muzzle. Gordy snorted. 'See you got another addition to the Smith clan?'

''Tis me granddaughter an' her babby,' Rosa answered.

''Nother few years an' the kiddie'll be pickin' then.' He swung the wooden gate wide and added, 'You got no fears about the war 'ere, gel. We gets a few planes comin' over but there ain't nothin' out here old Hitler wants. Not when we got RAF planes dropping a hundred thousand bombs on Dusseldorf in under an hour.'

'Is that so?' Rosa asked. Her eyes were wide. Vera thought about the German town that would surely be flattened by the English planes and their bombs.

'It is, Rosa,' he said. Then, 'Where's Luca?'

Rosa tossed her head. 'He's in a van at the back, still staying with Dec and Mari. I can't 'ave the great clodhoppin' lump in my van.'

'I warned all the village women to keep their daughters locked up against your Luca,' he said with a laugh. 'Come on, Gordy, take your missus where she needs to go.' He slapped the horse's rump and Gordy began his slow amble to the sheds.

Vera walked alongside the horse. She could see a line of huts opposite a huge field of high climbing plants.

'Them's the gardens,' said Rosa. 'And that's the bines. Smell that air.'

Vera took a deep breath of air that smelled of sulphur and as she touched one of the acorn-shaped flowers, a shower of yellow pollen tumbled down. Rosa laughed. 'That'll teach you to respect the bines. Your hut is the third one in. I'm behind you in the wagon. Luca sleeps with Dec and Mari but he picks with us.'

Vera's heart leaped in nervous anticipation.

'Your kiddie's gone to sleep, tucked in with his rabbit. Take my advice and sort out the hut while he's quiet. The key should be on the top of the door frame.'

Vera watched the wagon pull to the back of the huts then she searched for number three. Her hand felt for and found the key and she inserted it in the lock. But no matter how she tried, she couldn't open the door.

Nellie and George were next door at number two.

'No good asking George, his big hands'll break the key in the lock. It's Luca you want. He can open anything.' Nellie squinted along at the horses pulling vans. 'There he is. Luca! Come over here.'

Vera saw him put his hand to his eyes, shielding them from the sun, to see who had called him. Then he jumped down from the wagon and came towards them.

'Key's stuck,' Nellie said. 'I told Vera you'd look at it.'

Luca didn't speak but squatted down on the hard earth and gently jiggled the key. He pulled it out then peered into the keyhole, then at the key, and then looked up at Vera.

'Sit down and I'll show you what's happened.'

Vera sat beside him. She could feel his closeness and he smiled at her before fingering the lock's surface.

'In the lock are pins. These pins need to be raised at the same time. This is what a key does and why it's the shape it is. Sometimes the pins won't move.' He turned to face her and Vera was aware of the deep brown of his eyes and the lashes that curled. 'If you squint into this lock, luckily it's a large one, you'll see what's stopping the key from lifting the pin.'

He moved out of the way and Vera looked inside the lock. 'There's something in the way.'

Luca nodded. 'These huts been empty all winter; all kinds of creepy crawlies gets inside. Give me that hairgrip pinning back your curls.'

Vera took out the clip and gave it to him, watching as he bent the end into an L shape.

'Here,' he said. 'I reckon you can have a go at this.'

'Oh, I can't . . .'

'I'll bet you can,' Luca said. He slipped the pin into the keyhole, took her hand and pressed it over the grip. 'Go on,' he said. 'Feel for the place where the end of the pin becomes stuck.' He took his hand away and Vera was aware of him watching her.

She could do this, she thought. Ah, yes, there's the lumpy bit. She twisted the hair grip and discovered an opening in the hard piece inside the lock. Carefully she worked the grip round and then pulled.

'It's a piece of nut!'

'Well I never,' said Luca, peering at the tiny scrap of shell. 'I reckon you could find squirrels in your hut.'

Vera inserted the key, twisted it and felt it turn. The door opened and she gazed at her home.

'No squirrels,' Luca said. 'But I reckon you got a gift there for pickin' locks. I ain't never seen nobody do it as quick as that afore. Just remember, when you next pick a lock, that I taught you everything you know.' Then he carefully smoothed her curls back from her forehead and clipped them before winking at her and walking away, whistling.

Vera stared dumbly after him, then caught Nellie giving her a knowing look. Vera turned, going inside the hut.

It was about twelve feet by ten. Wallpapered boards covered

the metal walls and she could see how easy it would be for small animals to enter through the open ends of the corrugated tin roof.

The bed was made of wood and placed at the end of the hut. Next to the bed was a small table. There was one chair and shelves had been put up on the walls. Already they contained Rosa's old pots and pans, mugs and plates, which she'd brought down in previous years. An oil lamp hung from a wooden rafter and there were two rope lines strung across for drying clothes. Vera stood looking at what was to be her home for the next four weeks and couldn't help the big smile that inched its way across her face.

'All right then?' called Nellie as she came past.

Vera turned to her. 'I think I've died and gone to heaven,' she said. Nellie walked away laughing.

A few hours later Vera had scrubbed and cleaned with disinfectant and soap she'd found in a shoebox and hauled hers and James' stuff from the van to the hut. Rosa had told her there was a box beneath the bed with all sorts of stuff in it that she might find useful. A wind-up alarm clock that started ticking immediately, knives and forks and even a pot to wee in. Rosa had also given her a spirit stove that would boil a saucepan.

Vera made up a bed for herself and then started on the cot that was tucked in the corner. She scrubbed it clean and put in James' palliasse, then set it safely where she could see him when he slept.

There was a small shop on the farm that sold essentials. Vera knew the farm's hens had laid the eggs, the milk came from the cows, the butter was freshly churned and bread was baked daily by the farmer's wife. She bought food with Paddy's ten shilling note, which she still had after Rosa had steadfastly told her to 'stick it' when it was offered. Vera knew she was expected to provide food for James and herself during the day but in the evenings the gypsies would take turns in cooking a big meal for all.

Once everything had been sorted, Vera gazed happily around the hut. It was basic and small, but it was the first place that Vera could call her own.

A knocking sound was competing with the alarm. Vera staggered to the door.

'Early enough for you?' Luca stood in the doorway, filling it. He ran a hand through his curls.

'We knocked to make sure you was up.' Rosa stood at his side and put out her arms for James, who had slithered over to the doorway with wet pants and a huge smile. She scooped him up.

Outside it was misty. 'Luca, take yourself for a walk then come back in ten minutes. This gel needs a cuppa afore she gets dressed.' Luca gave Vera a grin and turned on his heels, whistling as he walked through the damp grass.

'Going to be a nice day,' said Rosa. Already she had lit the stove, set a pan of water on top and was wiping James' bottom, ready to dress him in the clothes that Vera had set out the previous night. Vera, dressed now in a full skirt and blouse tied round her middle, brushed her hair.

'I likes the way you done this place up, love,' Rosa added. 'It looks proper homely.'

'It's me first home,' said Vera proudly. 'Me an' James is gonna be happy in this little hut.' She poured tea into two mugs and stirred in condensed milk.

'Don't waste the rest of the boiling water, Vera. Got an empty bottle?' Vera produced a clean bottle with a screw top lid. 'Good, pour the rest of the water in there with some tea leaves and a couple of spoons of milk. We'll be needin' all the drinks we can get when the sun comes up.'

A knock echoed and Vera opened the door to Luca.

'Ready then?'

As they walked to the hop garden, James on Luca's shoulders, Luca explained their duties. 'We work along tunnels or alleys of hops, a bin between us. I'll pick high, you pick low and Rosa can pick what's left. The boy'll be all right at our feet. He'll get dirty but we'll all watch he comes to no harm.'

Vera nodded then asked, 'Why are you picking high?'

'The vines grow to ten, twelve feet, sometimes more. I'll bend them and pull them down to your height. The hops are picked into a big bag-like container. Be careful you don't put in any leaves. The field foreman will come along and check every so often. When we've filled one bag, we go on to fill another. Each filled bag is marked against the name of Rosa Smith. We stop for a bite to eat and drink and usually Farmer Crawford blows a whistle about half past four.'

'Fair enough,' said Vera. She was determined to show both Rosa and Luca that she could earn her keep.

'Eat this,' said Luca, later that night. Vera pulled her coat around her so he wouldn't see the old nightdress she wore that had belonged to Rosa.

James lay in his cot, his arms stretched above his head. His face and arms had caught the sun, deepening his tan. It had been all Vera could do to get a soft-boiled egg and soldiers down him before he fell asleep after they'd staggered back to the hut.

'Thanks,' said Vera, taking the bowl of mutton stew. She'd already had a little sleep after washing herself all over with water carried from the stand pipe at the end of the row of huts. 'I never expected the first day to be so hard.'

'You'll get used to it.' Luca put the stew on the table and found a spoon in a drawer. 'Eat it while it's hot.'

Vera saw he had washed and put on a clean shirt. There were droplets of water nestling in his curly hair.

He sat beside her on the bed. His closeness made her heart beat faster so she moved to the table, drawing up the kitchen chair. Vera clutched her coat tighter around herself until hunger got the better of her and she began to eat.

When the last spoonful had gone down, she yawned.

'Set your alarm, have you?' he enquired.

Vera nodded. 'How's Rosa?' she asked.

'When I saw her just now she was getting ready to go up the pub.'

'Really?'

'Don't be so amazed; she's a tough old bird. And she likes a bit of a knees-up. I'd have willingly bought you a few drinks there if I'd thought you could cope with it. But I wouldn't advise the pub for you, not yet awhile. Your time will come, Vera, you'll see. A rosy apple like you is ripe for the picking.' He stood up. 'Bolt the door behind me. See you in the morning.'

Vera moved to see him out. He opened the hut door, turned again and before she could move away from him he kissed her lingeringly on the lips, then he slid out into the night. Vera, her lips tingling, watched him disappear into the darkness.

She would always be grateful to Luca for saving their lives. But did that entitle the man to think she was his property and could be kissed whenever he wanted? She put her fingers to her lips, feeling the kiss lingering there. Oh, why did she crave the attention he bestowed on her? And yes, she'd enjoyed his

166

stolen kiss. Could it be that she was falling in love with him? Love? Desire? Were they the same thing? She thought of Tim and realised how much she missed him.

On aching legs, Vera shot the bolt and got back into bed, knowing Esme, being as jealous as she was, would tear her eyes out if she knew what Luca had done. And that was another thing; where was Esme? And did Luca really cause havoc with the village girls?

Too tired to worry any more, Vera was asleep before her head reached the pillow.

Chapter 18

The flames from the wood fire were shooting heavenwards in the darkness and the heat was making Vera feel sleepy. James was asleep, sprawled in Nellie's arms, his eyelashes fanned across his cheeks and his face serene.

'I don't know why you won't dance with Luca, he's easily the best dancer on the encampment.' Nellie spoke quietly so as not to waken James.

Vera turned towards her friend. 'I'm tired after all the hop-pickin' we done today.'

'No one feels tired dancing,' Nellie insisted.

Vera's foot was tapping to the violin music the gypsies were making as the dancers whirled. Old women and men were swapping tales and nibbling at food prepared earlier and children ran in and out of the picked vines, screaming and laughing, excited to be allowed to stay up late.

Vera sat down on the dry grass. She didn't want to tell Nellie that she was out of her depth. She'd refused to dance with Luca because she didn't want anyone to see how much she craved to be in his arms. She was drawn to him and even now her eyes strayed towards him. He dwarfed the men around him and commanded attention with his dark presence. The force of his personality and his energy made the other male dancers seem uninspiring.

And then, from across the clearing, he looked at her and then he threw back his head and laughed. It was as though he knew exactly what she was thinking, that his arrogance would make happen whatever it was he wanted to happen.

Vera looked away, her heart beating fast. She knew she must leave the gypsies soon. She was well, and anxious to see her mother and Patsy. James needed to get to know his family and experience the love that they would shower upon him. So why was she still here?

Another week or so and the hop-picking would be over. Vera's wages went into Rosa's coffers and Rosa gave her money. Vera wanted for nothing.

The reason she'd stayed so long with the encampment was to be near Luca. Why then did she refuse his advances? Was it because he was the first man she'd had feelings for since Alfred Lovell had raped her? Was it because she was frightened to accept that she was falling in love with him?

'Vera, I will not take no for an answer.'

Before she could protest, Luca hauled her to her feet and led her into the sea of dancers. Vera could hear Nellie laughing at the brazenness of the man.

'I think about you very seriously,' he whispered into her hair. He was holding her so tightly Vera was sure he could feel her heart beating. She was afraid of the fire in her body. 'And I would like to know you better,' he said.

Vera felt the heat of his skin beneath his shirt and she could smell the musk of his body. She was shocked by the force of held back passion in him. She suddenly realised there was so much for them to find in each other. Vera, as the music stopped, was utterly lost in her discovery.

And then, to her surprise, holding her by the hand and

without speaking, Luca took her back to Nellie and the sleeping child.

'You two women will walk back to the huts with me,' he commanded.

Nellie nodded. Vera knew better than to disobey. Rosa might be the head of the gypsy clan but even she respected a man who dictated what a woman should do to keep safe in the dark of night. 'You will both wait,' he added.

Vera looked about her. Most of the dancers were leaving and many of the children had already gone. A woman was damping down the fire.

Nellie and she waited in silence and it wasn't long before Luca returned from where his friends were still gathered. He helped Nellie rise, still with the child in her arms. Then he put out a hand towards Vera.

He held her hand for a long time before Vera scrambled to her feet. She smoothed the grass from her long skirt.

'It was a good night, tonight.' Luca didn't wait for an answer but carried on speaking. 'It's a pity we are still working tomorrow.' He put his hand on Vera's shoulder. Her breathing quickened. No touch had ever stirred her before like his did. She looked at him. His face in the darkness was full of compassion, yet there was amusement there as well.

It wasn't long before the dark shadows ahead became the line of huts.

'Goodnight, Nellie.' Vera carefully took her still sleeping child from Nellie's arms and kissed her friend. Luca stood by, silent.

When the door of the hut had closed on Nellie, Luca moved on down the path towards Vera's hut. Vera struggled with James and the key. She was about to wish Luca goodnight when he kissed her. At first gently, then harder, almost as though he wanted to bruise her lips. She wanted to put her arms around him but she couldn't because James was clutched to her. She was being held at a distance from what she wanted and her desire for Luca was rising.

And then he stepped away from her. Leaving her feeling bereft. Luca didn't speak. He slid away into the night.

Vera pushed open the door to her hut and laid James in his cot. She went back and closed the door, but not before she'd stood on the step and searched in the darkness, wishing with all her heart that Luca would come back to her.

The glasses were refilled with the red wine. Luca pushed his dark curls away from his brow and laughed. 'So it makes me the winner again, does it?' He scooped the coins to his side of the table.

Miko groaned. 'Lucky at cards and lucky at love. That's not how it's supposed to be, Luca.'

Luca shrugged. 'Can I help it if I have all the good fortune?' He pushed the cards across the table to Miko. 'Want to see if you can win some of your money back?'

Miko began shuffling, then he placed the cards face down on the table and said, 'Cut.'

Luca divided the cards into two separate piles and Miko took them up and began to deal.

Afterwards, the cards dealt, Luca again drank deeply of the wine. Then he licked his lips, set down the glass and said, 'She's ripe for the plucking is our little gorgio.'

Miko looked up and glared. 'I dunno why you needs to add Vera to your list of conquests. She's a hard worker an' a nice enough girl an' most important of all your gran thinks the sun shines out of her backside. An' that babby puts new strength in Rosa's actions.'

'I'm going to have Vera because I can.' Luca's eyes narrowed. 'Besides, it isn't as though she's a virgin, is it? Soon I'll be wed to the girl I love, and I promised Esme, and myself, that I'd keep faith with her until the day I die and I meant every word.' He poured the remainder of the wine equally between the two glasses on the table, then looked round Miko's sparsely furnished hut, sniffing the musty air. 'If you brought a few more girls back to this hut, it might encourage you to make this place more homely.'

'I'm not like you, Luca. I like to think I know how to treat women properly. They're not just objects to fuck and throw away.'

'Aren't they, Miko?' Again Luca emptied his glass.

'You might believe so.' Miko drummed his fingers on the table. 'But what about your grandmother and her feelings? Don't you think of the shame Vera will have to endure when she finds out you wanted her for one thing only? Vera's shame will rebound on Rosa.'

Luca shook his head and his glossy curls bounced about his forehead. 'Miko, you forget. I am the old woman's kin, her true grandson. Rosa might care for Vera and her boy but I'm the heir. Of course, if you want my leavings after I've finished with Vera, you are more than welcome.' He got up and went to the cupboard near the bed. Bending down he took from it another bottle of home-made red wine and held it towards Miko. 'I'll give him his due, old Tom makes a tidy drop of plonk. Uncork this and let's get on with our game of cards.'

Vera couldn't sleep. She listened to James' heavy breathing and thought about Luca. The sheets were cool and tempting but an overwhelming desire grew inside her, drenching her with heat as she remembered Luca's kiss.

She ignored the little voice inside her that was telling her he belonged to Esme. Esme wasn't here and without her presence Luca had made his choice.

The trees above her hut dropped leaves that rustled on the roof. She could hear the snuffling of night creatures. Thoughts of Luca wouldn't leave her. Desire was beckoning to the pair of them, bringing cravings within her that would not be stilled. Luca was drawn to her and she to him.

The bar was full, warm and welcoming and filled with cigarette smoke.

'What did I tell you? The bugger's surrounded by women!' said Rosa.

It wasn't quite true, thought Vera. Luca was standing over an elderly woman, looking down at her rosy cheeks and curly grey hair and using his hands to describe something to her. Sitting at the woman's side was a man in his seventies with his eyes closed.

'Luca, you buyin' me a drink?' Rosa's voice cut through the noise and he raised his eyes. A grin spread over his face and he beckoned them over. Rosa pushed her way through the mob closely followed by Vera, who was trying to ignore the men's stares. Rosa sat down on the chair that Luca had rescued from a nearby table and Vera parked her bottom on a high stool.

'You'll have to have a short, Rosa, the pub's run out of ale.'

'Bloody war,' said Rosa. 'It's a good job I fancies a drop of gin, ain't it? And get a drop for our Vera, 'ere.'

Music could be heard above the din. 'Comin' in on a Wing and a Prayer', by the Song Spinners, had the pub's patrons singing along.

'He's building a rabbit hutch for me grandson,' explained the grey-haired woman as Luca made his way to the bar.

'Good with his hands, is our Luca,' said Rosa. 'But make the most of his talents, for when the 'ops are done we're back to Hampshire and the Titchfield Fair.'

'I'll say he's good. He fixed up our hen house a treat. That bloody fox'll find it hard to get in now.'

Rosa laughed. 'So that's where he's been slidin' off to at weekends.'

Vera looked towards the bar and saw Luca speaking earnestly with the landlord. It wasn't often she saw him dressed up. He was wearing corduroy trousers, a green shirt and a darker green waistcoat over the top. A red neckerchief was tied around his throat and his trilby was perched at a rakish angle over his shiny curls. He looked up and caught her smile. A shadow passed across his face before he smiled back at her.

On his return, Luca put a gin and orange in front of Vera and handed a large neat gin to Rosa.

'Ta, lad,' Rosa said.

Vera picked up her glass and sipped. The strong taste of the orange almost hid the gin's oiliness. 'Seems daft us picking hops for beer an' there ain't any beer for sale,' she said.

'Well, that's the war for you, love,' Rosa said.

Luca elbowed Vera. 'Drink up,' he said. 'I feel like a walk outside.'

Vera nodded nervously. She swallowed the rest of her drink and then Luca took her arm. 'Be back in a minute,' he said to Rosa. Rosa gave him a frosty stare.

Closing the door on the noise and smoke, Luca said, 'I can't go on like this, Vera.' He guided her over to a seat in the garden area behind the trees and sat down. Without meeting her eyes, he said quietly, 'You must know I want you.'

Vera closed her eyes and took a deep breath of the night air. Wasn't this what she'd wanted? To be alone with Luca and him telling her he cared for her? She wanted to be loved.

Not meeting his eyes, she said, 'When we're in company you hardly look at me.'

'I got Esme to think about. It's supposed to be my duty to marry her, whatever else my heart wants to do.'

'And what's that?' Feeling bolder, Vera looked at him. 'What does your heart tell you?'

'This.' And then he pulled her into his arms and kissed her. Vera kissed him back, opening her lips and allowing him to push his tongue into her mouth. Vera had imagined this moment but none of her fantasies compared to Luca actually touching her body. He shrugged himself out of his waistcoat and dropped his hat on to the earth. Then he began on his shirt. She was almost lying on the bench now and he was leaning over her. His fingers fumbled with her blouse buttons. And then he was kissing her breasts. The manly scent of him enveloped her as he pushed her back on the bench. He was hovering above her, unfastening his trousers and sweeping aside her underclothes. They were belly to belly now and she felt his hardness enter her. She wanted to draw him in so that he could never be free of her again. Vera could feel him breathing harder, moving faster and she curved her body up to meet him. And she was melting, dissolving and he was holding her so tight she felt he was crushing her. Then there was stillness. He slid away from her.

'I'm sorry.' His voice seemed far away.

'I'm not.' She nuzzled into his warm neck. He pulled away and started adjusting his clothes. 'I've never been in love before,' she said.

He stopped all movements and stared at her.

'Love? Who mentioned love?' He frowned then began his buttoning again. 'You'd better cover yourself. It wouldn't do for anyone to see us,' he said, not looking up. Vera pulled herself into a sitting position. He leaned towards her to help her button her blouse.

In that instant Vera knew how stupid she'd been to imagine this man was going to leave Esme. 'I can fasten it,' she said angrily. The aftermath was nothing like she'd expected it to be. 'You've just made love to me but it was the act itself you wanted, wasn't it, Luca, not me?'

He sighed. 'You know we can't be a couple.'

'So you've now said. But am I to believe you don't care for me at all?'

She waited for his answer. She wanted him to tell her he didn't really love Esme and that their arranged marriage was a sham, one that he didn't want to go through with.

'I'll come to your hut later,' was all he said.

How many times had she dreamed of him saying those very words and then of waking up beside him? But now she shook her head. 'No, I'm collecting James and I'm spending the rest of the evening on my own, thinking.'

Luca looked agitated. Angry even that things weren't going the way he wanted.

'If that's how you want it.' His eyes left her face and he bent down and picked up his hat, slipping it on.

'I do.' She ran her fingers through her hair then said, 'Tell Rosa I said goodnight.' He shrugged, turned and began walking away, back to the pub.

Vera got up from the seat, finished dressing herself and brushed her clothes down. She began walking back to the row of huts. The stars were bright and the air was still tinged with late-summer's warmth. The moon shone down with a silver light. But Vera hardly noticed this. Her mind was in turmoil. Tonight hadn't ended the way she'd wanted it to. She'd given herself to the man she desired but he was only interested in sex. She'd cheapened herself. She wondered if it was possible to make him see how much she loved him. Then perhaps he would realise that Esme would be a poor substitute. Would he change his feelings towards her? What a fool she'd been to let her heart rule her head.

Titchfield Fair was in full swing. Steam engines powered the gallopers and the gaudily painted carousel horses, and music blared from loudspeakers. At the far end of the large field, the Ferris wheel turned slowly. The chair-o-planes swung widely, its occupants screaming as much from fear as pleasure. Young children and their parents slid down the helter-skelter, there was candy floss and coconuts, and the smell of fried onions filled the air. Brightly painted circular stalls were dotted about on the green. Next to the dodgem cars was the penny slide.

Vera, in her tight skirt, high heels and frilly blouse, a warm shawl over her shoulders, handed out change so that pennies could be slid down the small wooden slides. If a penny fell within a marked square, the pitcher received the money marked on the board. A coin falling on a line was immediately retrieved by Vera and put into the leather bag at her waist.

'Come on,' she cried. 'Only a penny a go. Try your luck!'

She was happy; happier than she'd been in ages. The bad feelings between her and Luca had been swept away. When she had finished closing down the penny stall she would meet him. Vera hadn't been able to resist him after finding a note pushed beneath the door of her hut at the hop fields. It said he was sorry and loved being with her. And that he would try to break with Esme.

'Kisses, that's all you'll get until you're free,' she'd said.

'You let me make love to you before,' he'd argued. Vera had seen the downward curve of his mouth.

'Think how special it will be when it's just you and me and no Esme,' Vera had goaded him.

Working at the fair reminded her of Tim, who'd risen at dawn to labour hard so he could surprise her with rides at Walpole Park. She'd been very young then but she'd been loved, she knew that now.

Vera waved at Nellie, who was sitting on the steps of her van, rocking the handle of her old pram. Inside was baby Ella and leaning over the pram was James. Nellie waved back.

James was no longer a baby, but a beautiful little boy. Vera still slept in Rosa's van with him but was aware she had grown into a woman in the company of the gypsies.

It was dusk; the blackout was still in force so the rides would soon shut down.

There had been a welcome lull in Hitler's planes flying at night. Vera hated the daytime bombings. Sometimes there were no warnings. Vera often thought about the school in the south-east of England where German bombers had dropped their loads. Twenty-three schoolgirls had been killed. The children were waiting to watch a performance of *A Midsummer Night's Dream*. Most of the dead were aged between five and seven.

She thought again of Tim and how a bomb had cut short his life. Who knew what might have happened between them if there had been no war? She thought of Patsy and her mother and of how she missed them.

The music ceased and Vera began putting up the plywood boards on the outside of her stall. She heard the bumper cars roll to a halt and glanced over to see Luca talking to Esme. Jealousy rose in her. He had his hand on Esme's shoulder and was bending down to whisper in her ear. The look on his face told Vera how much he cared about Esme.

'Want a hand?' Nellie had already lifted a wooden panel and was holding it so Vera could fix it in place. 'It's no good you looking so miserable. He'll never belong to you, no matter how much you drop your drawers for 'im.'

Vera stopped what she was doing and frowned at Nellie. 'How do you know what I done?'

'Don't be a dinallo; everybody knows that you've prostituted yourself to get 'old of Luca. He only wanted you for what you got between your legs.'

'That's not true!' Inside she recoiled because Vera knew it was true.

Nellie put her hand on Vera's arm. 'Esme is a true gypsy. She understands her man. She and Luca have decided to marry soon.'

'No!' But even as she uttered the word, she knew Nellie wouldn't lie to her. She looked over to where Luca and Esme were still close together talking. 'Watch James for me,' she threw at Nellie before striding out across the cable-strewn fairground.

'I want a word with you,' Vera shot at Esme.

Esme turned her almond-shaped eyes towards Vera. 'You have nothing to say that I want to hear.' Her voice was calm, her tone nonchalant. Luca stepped back, fear etched across his face.

'So you're going to marry that man,' she tossed her head at Luca, 'even though he made love to me?'

Esme began to laugh. 'He never made love to you; he used you. We all know that. When we wed, his foolish ways stop. Young men need to sow wild oats; every woman understands that.' She turned her back on Vera but Vera could still hear her laughter.

By now a circle of gypsies had enclosed them and it was clear to Vera by their smirks whose side they were on.

'You should get paid for it next time, gorgio,' shouted a woman.

Vera's face burned with shame and then her anger overflowed. She tapped Esme on the shoulder.

'Don't you dismiss me like I don't matter,' Vera cried.

'But you don't matter,' replied Esme with a cruel smile.

Vera couldn't hold back any longer. She leaped at Esme, tugging at her long hair, tearing at her satin dress. Esme might have been taken unawares but she soon realised what was happening and grabbed hold of Vera's arm, twisting it. Vera kicked out and winded Esme, causing her to stagger and fall to the grass.

'Let me alone, you whore,' Esme said, then spat in Vera's face.

There was a sudden hush in the crowd then Vera felt a sharp shove from behind her.

'Leave her be!' Luca pushed Vera to the ground and sank on his knees beside Esme, burying his face in her hair. Vera heard him say, 'I'm so sorry, my love.' Esme was crying now, her arms about Luca's neck.

Vera scrambled up with all the dignity she could muster. Ignoring the cat-calls that followed her, she walked back to Rosa's caravan.

Rosa moved aside on the top step so Vera could enter the van.

Vera searched beneath the bed for her suitcase and threw it on the bed. Rosa shut the door behind her and faced Vera.

'This will pass,' she said.

Vera shook her head. 'I've been a fool. I've stayed at the encampment for longer than I should because I thought there could be something between Luca and me. I was wrong and now I'm being victimised for falling in love with him.' She took her clothes from the cupboard and then searched for James' garments and packed them in the case. A gentle knock on the door saw Nellie come in with James asleep in her arms.

'I can't stop her,' Rosa said to Nellie. Vera looked at them both with tears in her eyes.

Nellie laid the child on the bed. 'I'll miss you,' she said. 'You've become like a sister to me.'

'But you're true Romany and I'm not. I'll always be an outsider. Especially now.' She picked up one of Rosa's hands and kissed it, then held it to her cheek. 'I've let you down, Rosa. I'm sorry I've brought shame on you.' She touched her earrings. 'These will always be a reminder of the kindness you've shown me. Without you and Luca, James and I would have died. I've learned a great deal from you. But I must find my own family and make a proper home for James. It's time I left.' Vera steeled herself from crying.

'Do you have money?' Rosa asked.

'Yes.' It wasn't exactly a lie, she did have some money but not much. Probably enough to buy a train ticket back to Gosport. Surely when her mother saw James, her grandson, she would allow them to stay for a while until Vera was able to get a job and a place of her own. Maybe Patsy would know where there was work to be had.

Without speaking, Vera handed Nellie James' warm coat and went on filling the case while Nellie dressed him.

Vera could hardly bear to hug the two women before she picked up James and steadied him on her hip. She slung a cloth bag over her shoulder, lifted the case and went down the caravan steps. Alone once more.

Chapter 19

The train pulled in to Portsmouth Harbour station. Through the dirty windows looking out over the Solent, she could see the dockyard and Nelson's flagship HMS *Victory*. At first the scene before her looked as it always had until she noticed the bombsites where hotels had stood opposite the dockyard gates. As the door opened, Vera was jostled by the sailors who had been crammed into the train and who were going back to join their ships. Portsmouth and Gosport were training places for all the servicemen.

With James straddling her hip, Vera made her way to the station café. The feather in her red hat was bobbing about in the cold current of air and her high heels were clacking on the platform. A porter wolf-whistled after her. She smiled just as she'd smiled at the sailors who had struck up a conversation with her in the train carriage. It cost nothing to be friendly with people. She knew some of the servicemen wouldn't return from fighting for their country. At least let them remember the woman on the train who'd laughed at their cheeky chatter.

It was raining and the café's window was steamed up with condensation. She pushed at the door with her free hip and it opened to reveal a single customer: a red-haired man wearing a checked suit with a trilby pushed back from his forehead. He was reading the sports pages of a paper and at his feet was a sea of dog ends. He looked up and gave her an appraising smile.

Dropping her suitcase at a table Vera stepped up to the counter, still with James on her hip.

'Cup of tea please.' The elderly woman, dressed in a pinny with strands of frizzed hair peeping from a turban, smiled at her.

'I'll also have two sandwiches,' Vera added. 'And do you think you could heat me a cup of milk?'

'Not a problem, love. You sit down and I'll bring it over.'

Vera paid her, and went over to a table and sat down, allowing James to scramble on to a seat of his own. She smiled at James, who gave her a dribbly grin and wiped Rags across the table.

Moments later the woman appeared with a tray. Vera pounced on it hungrily.

As Vera ate, she considered her options. She wanted to catch a ferry boat to Gosport and go to her mother's house. But the fight at the gypsy camp had unnerved her and she needed to compose herself. Every time she thought about her affair with Luca, the shame made her flesh creep. She'd been stupid to ever think she could make him love her. What little money she'd had was nearly gone and no way was she going to turn up on her mother's doorstep like a common beggar.

There was also the possibility that her mother might turn her away and she'd be out in the dark night with nowhere for her and James to sleep. The best plan would be to get a cheap room here in Portsmouth for a while and somehow earn a bit of money before going to Gosport.

'I don't suppose you know of somewhere I could stay for a couple of days. A cheap boarding-house or a room I could rent, do you?' Vera asked the waitress.

'Trouble is, ducky, with people losing their homes with

the bombing, everyone's crowded in together. Rooms to let are few and far between.' She gazed at Vera. 'Is your husband following you on another train?'

Vera shook her head. 'I haven't got a husband,' she said.

'Then, my ducks, you're going to find it difficult to get lodging anywhere. Most people think you're wicked if you have a child out of wedlock. I couldn't care less; there's many a little stranger arrived in Pompey homes sired by the visiting sailors.'

Vera was suddenly aware that the man who'd been sitting near the window was now looking at her. He wandered over to her table.

'Excuse me, but I couldn't help overhearing that you're looking for a room. I run a boarding-house in Southsea and I've just the accommodation you might fancy. The kiddie'll be no bother.'

'How much will it cost me?'

'Nothing, if you're willing to do a few light duties. Nothing you can't manage.' He smiled at her.

Why not, Vera thought. A roof over her head, with James by her side.

'Well ... I don't want to be traipsing around in the rain with a kiddie under one arm and a suitcase on the other.'

'That's settled then. My car's around the corner near the dockyard gates. So when you're ready, we'll make a move. My name's Delfont Simpkins. Most people call me Del.'

'I'm Vera,' she said. It was a quick decision and she hoped it was a wise one. He looked all right, not like an axe murderer; but then she had no idea what an axe murderer was supposed to look like. He had a gold watch and a chain stretched across his chest. So it was obvious he wasn't short of a bob or two, and he had a car. And if she found she didn't like the job, she'd just leave.

Scooping a sleeping James into her arms, she followed him out into the night.

Del was leading, her suitcase in his hand, up a flight of wide stone steps to a large house with ample gardens in Southsea, set back from the beach on a tree-lined avenue. The rain had stopped but had been replaced by the fog that had rolled off the sea.

He gave a sharp couple of knocks on the oak door. A small door set within the main door was opened so the occupant of the house could see who was calling. Vera heard a lock being turned and then she was in the presence of a huge bald-headed man dressed in evening clothes.

'Hello, Howard,' Del said. 'This young woman has come to work for us. I'm putting her on the same floor as Jinny.' Music seeped out into the night: a Tommy Dorsey medley, melodious and gentle.

'Yes, Mr Simpkins.' The man moved aside so Vera could enter the vast hall. A sparkling glass chandelier hung from the high ceiling. There were black and white tiles beneath her feet, and around the edges of the great hallway, brocaded sofas with plump velvet cushions. Vera decided Del must be very well off to own such an opulent house.

She clutched James tightly. 'I'd like to put my boy to bed as soon as possible, please?'

Howard smiled at Vera, but there was something about him that made her flesh crawl.

'I'll show you to your room,' said Del. 'Howard stays here to admit friends or let them out.' He turned to Howard. 'Everything ready for later?'

'Of course.' The man gave a smile that was more like a sneer.

'We've some special visitors arriving soon to be entertained by the children. Perhaps one day your little one might learn a few tricks from the others.' He picked up her suitcase and Vera followed him up a huge staircase with a polished wood banister. Deep red flock wallpaper lined the staircase walls. Everything was so clean and shiny that Vera thought it would be easy work if she was going to be a cleaner.

'You're lucky this house has survived the bombing,' Vera said as they walked up the stairs then along a lighted landing that held several closed doors.

'It is rather nice, isn't it? But then it's Georgian and they knew how to design houses in those days.' He stopped outside a door and opened it to show a white bathroom suite complete with shower.

Vera gasped. She'd never seen anything like it and it was a world away from the tin bath her mother had in Alma Street that had to be filled with hot water from the copper.

'This is your bathroom and your bedroom is here.' Del opened another door and Vera could see a brass bed with a glacier-white counterpane and a wardrobe that she was sure was almost the same size as her bedroom back in her mother's house. Del set Vera's suitcase on a small table. 'Over there,' he waved towards a third door, 'is a kitchen. You'll find everything you need: refrigerator, sink, cooker and there's plenty of food in the cupboards so don't be afraid to help yourself. Howard replenishes daily.' He put his hand on her shoulder. 'You don't need to worry about the foods you consume, certainly not the ones you know are on ration. We have a different system here. I have friends who supply me.' He touched the side of his nose and winked at her.

Vera was beginning to think she was in heaven. 'You have guests, I suppose?'

'Oh, yes. On this floor there's three young women. You

share the kitchen with them. Upstairs there are four young ladies. Downstairs is where the other guests sleep when they pay to overnight with us, and of course the Games Room is downstairs where the children play.'

There was a brief silence while Vera digested the information then she asked, 'What time do you want me to start work cleaning in the morning?'

He looked blankly at her.

'The work I'm to do for my keep?' Vera added.

He laughed throatily. 'Oh! Don't worry too much the first day. Take it easy and get used to your surroundings. I'll be along to see you later and discuss what's expected of you, unless I get called away, of course. You needn't worry about money. I treat my employees well, as any of them will tell you. Talk to them, make friends with them; you'll find them a most agreeable crowd.' He looked her up and down.

Vera felt uneasy under his gaze. All she wanted to do now was to put James to bed. 'I'll try to do my best for you,' she said.

'I'm sure you will, dear. I'm sure you will.'

Vera watched him as he left and then firmly shut the door. She realised there was no inside lock.

Instead of bathing James, Vera decided to put him to straight to bed. She pulled back the white sheets and tucked him and Rags in. James moaned softly but didn't wake. Vera kissed his downy cheek.

'I love you,' she whispered and stood back to look at him. He had Patsy's long-lashed eyes and Patsy's blond hair. She never thought of him having any part of Alfred Lovell.

When she was sure he wasn't going to move and fall from the bed she took her nightdress from the case and went along to the bathroom. She stepped into the shower, relishing the feel of the hot water cascading over her body. She took down one of the four shampoo bottles lined on the bathroom shelf and washed her hair. Feeling fresh and smelling of Amami shampoo, Vera went back into the bedroom and over to the window, rubbing at her damp curls with a fluffy white towel.

There were bars running down the outside of the window. Vera dismissed it as a safety measure against thieves. After all, the house was so well furnished, there must be plenty of valuables about.

Once inside the sweet-smelling sheets Vera put her arm around her son. After listening to his even breathing for a while she felt herself growing drowsy.

Vera wasn't sure how long she was asleep before she woke suddenly. It was still dark. Someone, somewhere, was crying. There were no other sounds in the old house. She listened for a long time until the crying stopped.

Chapter 20

The next morning, Vera was roused by noises coming from the kitchen and the smell of warm toast.

'Hello,' said a young pretty woman to Vera as she pushed open the kitchen door. 'There's milk in the fridge, cereal and eggs for the kiddie.' Vera thought she must be about sixteen. Her blond hair was in disarray and it was obvious she'd not long tumbled from bed.

'Thanks,' Vera said. She went to the bread bin and took out a soft new loaf and cut three slices. 'I'm Vera. This is my little boy, James. What's your name?'

'Jinny.' The girl was now at the table buttering her toast. She had dark circles beneath her eyes and remnants of make-up clinging to her lips and face. 'Del suggested I chat to you later about what goes on here.'

'Fine,' said Vera, putting the bread under the grill. She turned to watch the slim girl in her expensive pink wrap. Suddenly Vera felt dowdy and out of place.

'I've already made a pot of tea,' said Jinny, looking up. 'Funny how even though there's enough food to feed an army, I nearly always eat toast for breakfast.'

Vera knew the girl was trying to be friendly even though it was clear she'd rather be on her own.

'Do you work here?' Vera asked.

'You could say that. There are four of us now up on this floor, but Liza and Sal have gone away for the weekend to a big house party. It's usually quiet. Except for when Nancy cries. I've never known Del make such a big fuss of a child. She doesn't want to be groomed, you see, but Del has great plans for her.' Jinny got up and took her plate over to the sink.

Why, wondered Vera, didn't Nancy want to look nice? 'Well, I'm here to clean up.'

'Oh, you'll do that all right. If nothing else, Del isn't stingy. The men are going to love the size of your knockers.'

'What?'

'You'll have them standing in line to fuck you,' Jinny said.

'Fuck me?' It was then Vera realised. 'This is a knockin' shop, ain't it? And you're a prossie?'

'What did you think I am? I'm swanning around in silk and talking about the money I make. But I'm not your everyday prostitute. I'm a hostess. I sleep with councillors, police officers and the Mayor of Pompey. But only if I want to.'

Vera was taken aback at her words. 'That might be all right for you, but I couldn't do it.'

'Probably not today or even tomorrow but maybe there'll come a time when you'll say, "I'll do it". Jinny picked up Vera's slice of uneaten toast, broke it in two and gave a chunk to James to chew on.

'I thought I was going to be a cleaner,' Vera said quietly.

'Is that the yarn he told you? Pick you up at the Guildhall, did he, or fresh in off the train? Or did he say you'll be paid well and able to buy pretty clothes? There's parties every night, you know,' she added.

'I don't want to go to parties; I've got James to look after. And I don't want to be a prossie!'

Jinny laughed and reached across the table to pat her hand.

'You sound like Nancy. The only reason Del doesn't break her in straight away is he'll get a lot of money from the first bloke to pop her cherry.'

'You mean she's a virgin?'

'Well, at twelve you don't expect much else, do you? She'd run away from home and Del picked her up in the penny arcade on Southsea pier.'

Vera was horrified. 'So she's being got ready for her first client then? The highest bidder?'

'Got it in one.'

'But doesn't she have any say in the matter?'

'Of course not. She has to be locked in until she accepts her fate.'

'What d'you mean, fate?'

'No one leaves these premises without Simpkins' say so, and of course Howard is at the front door and it's impossible to get out any other way as there's bars at all the windows. D'you know Simpkins got special permission to keep those bars when all other railing and iron fencing is going to help the war effort? Even to get to the back garden, the front door is the only way out.'

'I thought the bars were to repel intruders.' Vera suddenly felt panicked.

'Daftie! Cheer up. It's not a bad life. We don't entertain clients in our bedrooms as there are special rooms downstairs for that, there's plenty to eat, nice company, pretty clothes and the chance to show those clothes off at all the parties. We're allowed to go shopping every so often, with Simpkins in tow of course. And then there's the garden.'

'Garden?'

'Don't even think about trying to escape that way. There's a high wall with broken glass along the top. Del doesn't intend for any of us to leave. Oh, yes, we've also got two Anderson shelters for when the siren sounds.'

Jesus Christ, thought Vera, this wasn't some tinpot operation, this was the real deal. A posh brothel. And once again, just like at the Magdalene home, she'd become a prisoner.

'What about the girls who never come around to wanting to sleep with clients?'

Jinny shrugged. 'Drugs usually solve that problem. Once hooked, they'll do anything.' Jinny sighed. 'I'm going back to bed. My room's next to the bathroom if you need anything.'

Vera's head was spinning.

Noticing James had nodded off, she put him to bed for his morning nap and then wandered downstairs.

Howard sat on a chair near the front door reading the morning's paper. 'Leslie Howard on plane shot down by Germans', ran the headline.

Vera couldn't help herself. 'Oh!'

'On his way to Southern Ireland, he was. Always thought he was a bit of a ninny in *Gone With the Wind*.' He looked Vera up and down. 'Getting yourself acquainted with the delights of this place, are you, Vera?'

'I'm just looking around. I thought Del was coming to talk to me today.'

He laughed. His teeth were broken and uneven. And one ear looked as though it had got mashed at some time. Vera wondered if he'd been a fighter.

'If I know Jinny, she'll have told you all you need to know. Del's left early; he'll be back later as we've a party tonight for the American sailors in port and some of the regulars. Should be lively. Del won't expect you to come down as he's giving you time to become accustomed to what goes on here. But if you did make an appearance, you could do yourself a bit of good.'

Play along, she told herself. Don't make an enemy of him yet. 'You never know,' she said. 'I might.'

'Jinny'll lend you some clothes,' he said. He stared at her breasts. 'Might be a bit tight up top but you could leave the buttons undone.'

Vera decided to ignore him. She'd come downstairs with the intention of looking at the front door and its security devices. Although the main obstacle wasn't the lock but Howard.

'If Jinny likes it so much here and the other girls reckon it's a good place to work, how come you need to be on door duty?'

'Kids,' he said. 'The little buggers sometimes try to make a run for it.'

His words washed over Vera like icy water. 'Children?'

'Big money for sex with kids.'

Vera said nothing, her thoughts returning to Nancy. Howard picked up his newspaper again and turned the page. Vera caught the headline. 'Catholic Home Heartbreak'. Below in smaller letters, 'Staff Under Investigation'.

She couldn't help herself. 'Can I see that?' She took the paper and smoothed it straight so she could read the full article.

'Why are you so interested in the Magdalene home near Stratford?' Howard raised his piggy eyes to meet hers.

'I was there,' Vera said quietly.

After a while he said, 'Those dog-walkers must have had a shock finding the body of that abused girl. Apparently the nuns didn't realise she was missing but she managed to escape from the place only to bleed to death after falling from the wall surrounding the home. Did you know the girl?'

Vera shook her head and took a deep breath. 'At least all the girls have now been sent to other homes where they'll be safe. But I'm sorry a girl had to die for the adults to get their comeuppance.'

'This is just the tip of the iceberg, so the police say,' said Howard.

'And one day all this will come tumbling down, too.' Vera waved her arms about.

'That's where you're wrong, love: too many high-flyin' blokes in high-up places use this little goldmine.' He gave a dark smile.

Vera turned and made her way back upstairs, her head full of thoughts about Aileen. Was she well? Was her baby alive and safe?

Vera knew then she had to escape. Not just for herself but for James' sake. There was no way she was going to allow any harm to come to him.

As Vera walked along the landing, the sound of Nancy crying rent the air again. Vera nervously followed the sound, deciding she would try to speak to the young girl.

'Hello,' she called softly.

The crying stopped. Vera heard scrabbling noises and then a small voice asked, 'Who is it?'

'My name's Vera. I wanted to talk to you. How long have you been here?

'About three days.' Her voice was thick with tears. 'Are you something to do with that man Howard?'

'No!' Vera was indignant. 'I've been conned the same way you have.'

Silence reigned. And then, 'I wish I could go home. I wish I'd never run away.'

Vera pushed against the door. 'I can't get in,' she said.

'I'm so frightened,' the girl whispered from the other side.

Vera looked at the lock. An idea came to her.

'I'll come back,' she said, heading to her room.

James was still sleeping soundly. Vera foraged in her bag and found a hairgrip. She bent the end into a large L shape.

Back along the hallway she bent down and peered into the keyhole. 'I'm going to try to open this door,' Vera whispered. 'Please be quiet.'

She put the bent end of the hairgrip into the lock and began lifting the teeth. After three failed attempts she heard the click and the door swung open. Vera slipped inside and pulled the door closed.

'You're only a kid,' she couldn't help saying. The curly haired blonde threw herself into Vera's arms.

'Don't leave me. Don't lock the door on me again.'

Vera thought she'd never seen anything so pitiful in all her life as this child imprisoned against her will and crying for her mother.

'How did you open the door?'

'Never you mind,' said Vera. This lock had been easy but she was thinking of the oak door downstairs and its large, heavy key that Howard was in charge of. Vera knew a hairgrip wasn't going to open that door.

'Why did you run away from home?'

The girl frowned. 'I wanted to go to school with lipstick on. I found a tube in Mum's drawer. An' I was nearly out of the door when Dad saw me and said, "Get that muck off your face."

'I tried to stand my ground, telling him all the women were wearing make-up because Adolf Hitler hated it. He liked a scrubbed-face look and us women were keeping morale up by defying him.'

Vera said, 'I bet your dad didn't like that answer very much.'

'No. He said, "I'll give you two minutes to stop acting like a tart and to get yourself ready for school."

'I said, "You can't make me!"'

Vera sighed. 'I bet he took you to the sink and washed it off himself, am I right?'

Surprise flashed across the girl's face. 'How did you know that?'

'Because, my girl, your dad was right. There's plenty of time for you to act like a woman when you are one.'

Fresh tears welled in the girl's eyes. 'If only my dad was here now ...'

Vera pulled the girl close.

'Howard says I'm going to walk around without any clothes on in the lounge downstairs and men are going to bid for me. I'm to be sold to the highest bidder.'

'Not if I have anything to do with it, you aren't.' Vera thought about the old men who would be leering at this little girl and she remembered what had happened between her and Alfred.

'Where's your home, love?' Vera asked.

'Glastonbury,' said Nancy, starting to cry again. 'And I want to go home.'

'I'll come back later.' Vera put a finger to her lips. 'Not a word to anyone, promise? I have to lock your door again. It's got to look as though I haven't been here. You understand, don't you?'

Nancy nodded. 'Thank you,' she said.

Vera closed the door, knowing it would lock itself.

When she reached the kitchen she knew exactly what she was looking for. She found a flat metal skewer and some pliers in a toolbox in a cupboard and a long piece of thick wire that she couldn't bend. She lit the gas and laid the wire across the burner. When it was red hot, she used a tea towel to hold the end of it so she wouldn't burn her hands, and fashioned the glowing tip into a large L shape using the pliers.

All the time she was working, her heart was in her mouth knowing that someone might enter the kitchen and ask her what she was doing. When she was satisfied with the simple tool, she put it on the floor at the side of the oven to cool.

Vera gave a start when Jinny walked in. She hoped Jinny wouldn't notice the burning smell lingering.

She stared at the large brown carrier bag Jinny dumped on the table. Jinny tipped the contents on to the kitchen table. She shook out satin underwear and a slinky dress made of silk, high heels that were more than the regulation two inches and a marabou feather boa that Vera would have killed for.

'My gentlemen pay well for me,' she said. 'These pretty things were left with Howard.' She picked up the boa and swung it around her neck.

Vera let out an intake of breath. 'I'd forgotten such lovely clothes existed.'

'Right, I better go and finish getting ready. Some of the clients arrived early and Del likes it if we mingle.'

Jinny walked out and Vera was left to wonder if she had been told to come and flaunt her gifts under Vera's nose.

'Vera, I want you downstairs.'

Vera shrugged off Del's hand, which was shaking her shoulder. James was asleep on the bed beside her.

'I've been telling our guests about you and they want to meet you.'

'I'm no prostitute.'

'That's what makes you so desirable. You're fresh meat, darling.'

Vera jumped from the bed and looked frantically about her. She ran to the dressing table and picked up a silver-backed hairbrush to arm herself with.

'Nice to return to this place and discover my latest little flower has a bit of spirit about her,' said Del.

Vera saw on the chair a pile of clothes that hadn't been there when she'd got into bed.

'Pretty things for a voluptuous lady. Don't worry about the boy, Jinny's going to look in on him. Get dressed.'

'No,' said Vera.

'Oh, I think you will. And you'll come down and join the men if I say something bad might happen to your little one if you don't.'

'You wouldn't dare.' But Vera thought of the girl locked in her room and knew Del would do anything to be obeyed.

'I'll expect you ready in ten minutes. I'll come back to escort you down.' He looked at the hairbrush and laughed. 'And use that silly weapon to brush your curls with.' He swept out of the room.

Vera felt tears rising. She'd slept with Luca because she'd wanted to, because she thought she was in love with him. But she'd be damned if she'd let some fat, slimy unknown man touch her body so Del could be paid for it. She looked at James, his arm clutching Rags. No one was going to hurt her child, no one.

Vera picked up the clothes. She shook out a pink silk night-dress. The feel of it was soft against her skin. There was a garter belt, a pair of tiny lace knickers, a brassiere and a pair of finest sheer nylons. High-heeled pink satin mules trimmed with marabou completed the outfit.

Again Vera looked at her sleeping child. Then she tugged

off her cotton nightdress and dressed herself in the revealing outfit.

True to his word, Del quietly opened the door. 'You look a treat, Vera,' he said. He took her arm and led her out of the bedroom. As they passed Jinny's room, he opened it and said, 'Watch the kid.'

Down the stairway Vera walked, every step making her feel more nauseous.

Del led her into a room that seemed full of plush furniture and gold paint and piano music. The air was steeped in cigar smoke from the men lounging on the velvet furniture. Old men, Vera noted, but expensively dressed. Scantily dressed girls that Vera hadn't seen before were draped over the men and fondling them.

Del pushed her into the centre of the room. 'Here we are, gentlemen: my latest acquisition. Isn't she gorgeous?'

The men turned from their partners and began looking her up and down with agreeable murmurings. Vera felt like a piece of meat on a butcher's slab. She saw she'd upset a couple of the girls, who pouted at her with annoyance.

'Vera is the raffle prize for Sunday night, which means the more tickets you buy the more chance you have of being the first to win her favours.'

Sunday? Today was Friday. So perhaps that meant she wasn't actually going to start whoring for Del for another couple of days.

Vera looked at Del, who said, 'Walk round the room. Let the punters get a gander at those lovely breasts.'

Vera didn't move.

'She's a little shy, gents.' Del put his hand firmly under her elbow and paraded her, stopping at each of the men's chairs so she could be pawed. Vera thought she was going to spew and it was only the thought of what Del might do to James that helped her to bear their wrinkled hands on her intimate parts.

Del pushed away one over-eager man. 'Come off it, gents. Enough is enough. We don't want Vera shop-soiled before the winner gets his hands on her, do we?' He led Vera to the door and then whispered, 'Now you know what the deal is. After these punters have told their mates and the word's got about, I should get a decent price for your first time. We'll have a bit of a party and you can draw the winning ticket yourself. After that, it'll be business as usual for you. So go back upstairs and prepare yourself for your new line of work, darlin'.'

Vera flew up the stairs and fell on the bed, trying not to cry as she curled next to James' warm body.

Later that night, Vera set about gathering together her and James' belongings, as many as she knew she'd be able to carry in her large shoulder bag. She pushed the suitcase beneath the bed and then lay down with James, waiting until she heard Jinny's door close and her high heels clatter down the stairs.

Vera went along to Nancy's room and, using the hairgrip, opened the door. 'Grab your stuff,' she hissed. 'We're going to try and get out of here.' Vera was praying that when Luca told her she had a gift for picking locks, it hadn't been a lie.

Nancy put down the comic she'd been reading. Her face split into a nervous smile. 'How?'

'I don't know yet but you've got to do everything I say, okay?' The girl nodded and began stuffing clothes in a satchel. She turned and stared at James, peeping from behind Vera's skirts and dragging Rags on the floor. 'You've got a baby,' said Nancy.

'You got a problem with that?' snapped Vera, nerves getting the better of her.

'Oh, no, he's lovely,' said Nancy.

'Just as well you like James because I'm gonna need your help with him.'

Vera made sure the landing was clear then crept downstairs with the girl behind her and James in her arms. She paused and put her finger to her lips as she saw Howard snoozing in his chair. She walked very quietly, urging Nancy to do the same, and then hid James and Nancy behind the floor-length velvet curtain.

Vera planned to get Howard away from the door by causing a disturbance of some kind to make him leave his post. She was shaking with fright. What if it didn't work? She needed him away from the door so she could get at the lock.

As if her prayers had been answered, at that moment the siren went. Its shrill sound sent fear into Vera's heart to melt with her gratitude.

Howard leaped to his feet. Vera ducked behind a red velvet Queen Anne chair. He made for the door that led to a part of the house she hadn't yet explored. Vera guessed he was going to get the children. She listened to his heavy footsteps and stayed where she was. Within seconds Howard was back, pulling a dark-haired girl by the hand.

'Go and round up the children,' he shouted. 'I'll get the little ones.'

Nancy poked her head from around the curtain and ducked back when Vera glared at her. The noise outside had increased. There were several thunderous explosions and voices shouting and screaming. Somewhere a fire engine bell was clanging and there was the sound of gunfire overhead.

The hall was empty. Vera knew it was now or never.

'Stay there even if you have to put a hand over James' mouth to keep him quiet,' she whispered urgently to Nancy.

Vera raced towards the front door and dropped to her

knees. She sent up a silent prayer. 'Please, please, let me do this right.' Into the keyhole went the flat piece of metal. Vera forced herself to concentrate and inserted the L-shaped tool. Her hand was shaking so much she had to remove the tool and count slowly to five before she inserted the rod again. This time she gave the lock her full attention. The sound of children panicking and screaming was getting closer.

Vera turned the handle.

Nothing.

Her heart plummeted. If she didn't turn the lock, Howard would discover them. Her fate and that of Nancy would be sealed.

'Bugger,' she swore.

Just then loud footsteps echoed on a stone floor.

'Get back.' Vera issued the command to Nancy, who was peeking round the curtain, a terrified look on her face. Vera rolled to the safety of a chair with a gold-threaded throw that not only covered the chair but reached the carpet. She crouched there thinking and watching as a heavy-set man ran across the room and disappeared through a rear door.

Vera's brain was working overtime. The door lock obviously had more levers to align. She took a deep breath, left her hiding place and began again, counting the clicks inside the lock. Five. Six. Jesus, how many more? Seven. She wiggled the metal wand. Click!

Her heart leaped.

Vera turned the handle and the door opened.

Footsteps and voices were raised as people began to descend the stairs.

'C'mon,' Vera cried, and grabbed her bag and James and, with Nancy following, ran down the steps beyond the open door and into the cordite-filled, noisy night.

Chapter 21

'I got you this far, girly, and I'll think of a way to get you home. Now eat your Spam sarnie and be thankful.'

Vera mollified Nancy then began feeding James with bits of meat and bread while he sat on a chair in the Bath transport café. The boy was fretful.

Vera tried to distract him by hiding Rags beneath the table, then asking James, 'Where's Rags gone?'

'Gone.' James' voice echoed hers. 'Rags gone.'

The child looked expectantly at Vera, who quickly produced the toy from beneath the table, saying, 'Here he is. Here's Rags.' And James forgot about grizzling and laughed his infectious giggle as he saw his beloved toy again.

'There's been a man in here looking for you.' The old man in a dirty apron who'd just served her now hovered near. 'Bloke in a check suit,' added the man.

'No, can't have been looking for me,' Vera said firmly. Her heart plummeted. How had Del found them?

Vera supposed it was possible that Del believed they would make their way to Portsmouth Town station and catch any train that was travelling remotely near Nancy's home. The air raid had halted the train service and that delay could have given Del time to search the surrounding area.

The man shuffled away. Vera looked at Nancy. 'Right, we'd better make tracks. And fast.'

'He's gonna get me.' Nancy's eyes were full of tears.

'Not if I have anything to do with it,' Vera hissed. Their best bet was to hitch a lift the rest of the way to Glastonbury. Vera looked around the room where truck drivers were eating huge breakfasts. Cigarette smoke hung in the air and a juke-box in the corner played a Frank Sinatra tune. Vera sighed.

'You look down in the dumps, love. Anything I can do to help?'

Vera looked up. Standing there was a man who seemed to tower over her, wearing a wool overcoat and thick trousers. His eyes lingered on her breasts. Vera pulled her coat across as best she could. She made a split-second decision.

'We need a lift to Glastonbury. I don't suppose you're going that way?' She let her coat fall open. 'Damage on the train lines got us stranded here.'

'I'm going as far as Street but I'm leaving now. I've got a schedule to keep.' Vera felt his eyes on her again.

'Street's not far from me mum and dad's place,' whispered Nancy.

'Well?' the man asked impatiently.

They left the warmth of the café and followed him to a covered lorry parked on a grassy verge.

'You'll all have to be up front with me. I'm transporting furniture from Winchester to Street. It's too dangerous for you to be in the back. If I wasn't on a deadline, I'd take you all the way into Glastonbury.'

He had an accent that Vera didn't recognise.

Vera climbed in and slid along the bench next to the driver's seat and settled James on her lap. Nancy sat down beside her.

'Get some sleep, Nancy,' she said. Nancy leaned her head

against Vera's shoulder. Vera gazed around the cab. There was a picture of a woman stuck to the dashboard. She was thin with dark eyes.

'Your wife?' Vera asked as the lorry started moving.

The man nodded and said, 'That was taken before she got ill.'

For a while the talk between them was stilted. He introduced himself as Don. Vera didn't talk about Del or being locked up in the house in Southsea. Just that she was taking the girl home but hadn't realised how expensive everything was when there were three of them to feed.

He listened carefully.

'Tell me about your wife,' Vera asked, taking off her hat and stowing it on the seat behind her.

He put a hand up and touched the photo. 'That's my Marlene. I love her to bits. But she's very ill, six months maybe and then ...'

Vera could see how upset he was.

'Cancer,' he added.

For a while again there was silence. She watched dark countryside flash by, sometimes she saw outlines of houses. The time seemed to stand still.

'How about the boy's father?'

'He doesn't have a proper father,' said Vera. The words were out before Vera had time to think.

'So you don't have feelings for the man?'

Vera took a deep breath. 'I was raped.'

Don said nothing. The silence was punctuated by a sleepy grunt from Nancy.

'You're a very lovely young woman. But I'm sure you don't need me to tell you that.' Don glanced at her, his eyes once more raking over her breasts. 'My wife loves me but she can't do it any more.'

Vera knew exactly where this was leading. She glared at him angrily and pulled James closer to her.

'I'm going to have to charge you for this trip. There's three of you, you know,' Don said.

'But I don't have any spare cash.' Vera began to feel uneasy.

'You can pay me in kind.'

His words sent chills through her body.

'If I said no, I suppose you'll stop this lorry and put us all down on the grass verge?'

'Afraid so.'

Vera felt the tears prickle the backs of her eyes. After everything she'd escaped from, here she was once again: at the mercy of a man. Her reply came out like a shot from a gun. 'I might have a baby and not be married but I don't go around bedding strange men!' She stared at him and he shifted his gaze back to the road.

Vera thought quickly. She needed at least three pounds to get Nancy home to Glastonbury and then enough money for her return ticket back on the train to Portsmouth Harbour. Even with a couple of meals thrown in, five pounds should cover it. But could she bear to have this man crawling all over her? Vera shuddered. If Don wanted to have sex with her, would she be able to make him pay *her*?

'Five pounds,' she said, fighting back the urge to cry. 'And you take us to Street like you promised.' She was selling her body, just like a proper prossie. No, she argued with herself, she was doing this because she could decide for herself. This time there was no Del Simpkins forcing her, but he *was* somewhere out on the road stalking her.

She glanced at Don who grinned at her. 'It's a deal,' he said.

'Can I have the money first?'

'Of course, just as soon as I park along this lane.'

When the lorry had pulled over, Don took his overcoat from behind the seat. Leaving James and Nancy cuddled together, Vera slid past the steering wheel and Don helped her down from the warm cab.

It was a starry night and there was no wind. Vera took a deep breath.

He put down the coat on the grass and took out his wallet, extracting a note that he gave to her. 'C'mon, Princess,' he said.

She looked at the note. 'This is a tenner. I got no change.'

'It's for you. Don't you ever sell yourself short, Vera.' He smiled. 'C'mon, get them knickers off.' He sank down on the coat and made room for her. Vera closed her eyes tightly and tried to think of how relieved she'd be to get Nancy safely home again with her parents. She made herself ignore his fumblings, grunts and groans as his body slid on top of hers.

Afterwards, 'That was wonderful,' he said. 'I don't think, in the past, you've been treated right, Vera.'

'Probably not,' she said, glad it had been over with so quickly. 'Thanks for the extra money.'

'You've made me feel like a new man.'

'Would you really have left us at the side of the road?'

'You'll never know, will you, Vera?' he said.

Vera slipped from him and gathered up her clothes. 'You've got a deadline to keep and I must get that girl home to her parents,' she said with no emotion in her voice. Don sorted out his clothing.

The two in the cab hadn't moved and it wasn't long before Vera, on the road again, her head on Nancy's shoulder, felt herself drifting into an uneasy sleep.

It was light when Don stopped near the train station.

James was already awake and staring about him. His movements caused Nancy to open her eyes.

'Where are we?' Nancy asked sleepily.

'Ready for the last stage of our journey, I hope.' Vera leaned over and kissed the pair of them.

Don pulled over to where a railway bridge towered into the mist.

'I'm stopping here because across that bridge there's a station café that opens early. You'll be needing something hot to line your stomachs and there's a couple of hours to go yet before Street comes alive with buses.'

He turned off the engine and helped them down from the cab. Vera turned back. 'Oh,' she said, 'I forgot me hat.'

Don foraged around on the seat and came up with the red felt hat. Miraculously, the feather wasn't broken. He passed it to her.

'Thank you,' said Vera quietly, jamming her hat on and swinging James on to her hip.

Over the bridge Vera could see the two platforms of Street Station and their huge canopies. She could smell fried food and gravitated towards the small café. She ordered their breakfasts and pulled out the ten pound note to pay.

'Where did you get that?' Nancy eyed the money.

'Ask me no questions and I'll tell you no lies,' said Vera, as they settled at a table by the window. Outside, the town was waking up. A train was already disgorging passengers and buses had started lining up on the road near the bridge.

Suddenly Vera's heart constricted. 'My God!'

'What's the matter?' asked Nancy.

Vera peered through the net curtain. 'Nancy, I can't believe it.'

'What?'

'Del! I don't know how he managed it, but he's here.'

He was walking up and down by the entrance to the station.

'Why would he follow us all this way?' Nancy leaned across Vera to look out of the window. Vera could feel the girl trembling.

'He'd do anything to get you back. You're costing him a lot of money.'

'I don't want to go back to Southsea and that dreadful house!' Nancy cried, looking frantic.

'You two all right?' the waitress called over.

'Do you have a telephone?' It was time for the police to be involved, thought Vera.

'The lines came down in the last raid.'

'Is there a back way out of here?'

'Yes. Just go through there. There's a path that leads along the top of the railway embankment. The bus station's there.'

Vera wondered if she could trust the waitress and decided she had no alternative. 'There's a man who means to harm us. If a bloke in a check suit comes in here, will you tell him you haven't seen us?'

The waitress looked at James and he grinned at her.

'Yes, of course. Go through the kitchen.'

Nancy struggled with the bags while Vera carried James. It had started to rain and the grass was slippery as Vera led the way over scrubland.

'Vera, I'm scared.'

'It'll be all right,' Vera said with more confidence than she felt.

She turned and looked back in the direction they'd come

from and realised with horror that Del had spotted them. He was already scrambling down to the lines, sliding on the wet undergrowth in an attempt to climb up the side nearest to them.

'Run faster!' shouted Vera.

Nancy looked petrified.

They ran as best they could, bags bumping against legs. After a while Vera stopped to catch her breath and chanced another look around. Del was nowhere in sight.

Vera spun frantically around. 'Come on, we've got to keep going.' She pushed Nancy ahead of her.

'Not so fast.' Del Simpkins' voice seemed to come from no-where. He jumped out from behind an overgrown blackberry bush with a fierce expression on his face.

'Leave the bags and run, Nancy!' Vera saw the girl hesitate so she shouted, 'Go!'

Nancy ran towards the banking at the side of the track. Then she stumbled and fell. Del was already at her side and hauled her up. 'I've invested time and money in you, you little cow,' he shouted into her face.

Nancy leaped at him, her hands and fists pummelling his body, pushing him away. Del lost his footing and toppled backwards. Vera watched as he hurtled to the bottom of the steep bank. He tried to stand up but then fell heavily across the rails, lying with his head on the line, quite still.

'Is he dead?' Nancy's whispered voice broke the silence. Vera pushed James into Nancy's arms, ignoring the boy's protests.

'Keep him safe.'

Vera slithered down the bank. One look at Del and Vera knew he was dead. She thought quickly. This wasn't something Nancy would want to live with for the rest of her life. If the girl thought she'd caused this man's death, it would colour her whole future. She made a show of taking his pulse and then gave a thumbs-up sign to Nancy. It took great exertion to pull his body clear of the line he'd hit with force. The side of his head was a bloodied mess. Vera left him and began climbing up the bank towards Nancy.

'Did I kill him?'

Vera scooped James back into her arms. 'Takes more than a slide down a bank to get rid of him.' She thought of the gaping head wound. 'When he wakes up, he'll have a terrible headache. He'll come round and stagger back to the station café if someone doesn't find him first. The most important thing is to get you home. C'mon, let's get a bus and get away from here.'

Glastonbury Tor was a magical place. Vera, holding her son's hand, stood transfixed, staring at the lush, rolling countryside that surrounded the tower on the hill. As they walked through the town, Vera tried to forget all that had happened. She gazed in wonder at the abbey's crumbling walls, the pretty shops and gardens with bright flowers, all with hardly a sign of bomb damage. And as they walked, Nancy talked some more about the argument that had led to her running away.

In a small street at the rear of the main road, Nancy led her to a cottage tucked away in a garden of flowers.

'This is my house,' she said. There were tears in Nancy's eyes and she put her hand in Vera's as though drawing strength from her. 'What if they don't want to know me any more?'

'Don't be daft,' Vera said softly.

'You knock,' Nancy said. Vera stared at the shining brass door knocker in the shape of a lion's head and then gave it a loud bang.

When the door opened, Nancy stood uncertainly on the

threshold for a moment then threw herself into the arms of the pale woman standing there. Vera smiled.

Astonishment turned quickly to joy.

'Joe, Joe! Our baby's home!'

Chapter 22

Vera, clutching James, leaned against a hoarding at the bottom of Alma Street. Across the main road, where once stood a row of small terraced houses, another ragged gap showed where Hitler's planes had dropped their bombs. Now grass and willow herb grew unchecked.

As much as she'd loved the rolling fields of Glastonbury, she knew she was a town girl who was more at home with the market's bustle, the crowded pubs and the different accents of the soldiers and sailors who visited the town of Gosport.

Standing on the corner, Vera stared up at the door of number fourteen. Would her mother welcome her with open arms just as Nancy's mother had? It seemed a long time since her mother had sent her away. Vera knew she was no longer the same girl who had left this place. Memories came flooding back: the air raids, playing in the street, and of course Tim. And Alfred, Angela too, all gone now. She nuzzled her face into James' neck.

'This is where I grew up, my little one.'

'Mama,' he gurgled and put up his hand to her lips.

'This is where Nanny and Auntie Patsy live.' She kissed his podgy fingers.

Vera felt in her pocket and her hand found the tissue paper. She had a present for her mother: a silver cross and chain she'd bought in Glastonbury. She'd wished she could have spent more on the gift but hoped her mother would like it.

'It's now or never,' she said to James. Slowly she walked over and knocked on the door. After a while the door opened and a young woman stood there wearing a flowered pinny. A grubby-faced child peeped out from behind her knees.

'Yes?'

Vera stared at the woman, unable to speak. Who was this stranger in her mother's house?

'I've come to see my mum and my sister, Patsy.'

'You must be Vera. Come in.' The woman looked flustered as she stepped aside and allowed Vera to walk down the hall. The wallpaper was different, pink roses on a cream background. Vera walked through to the kitchen. Somehow the room looked bigger and brighter with children's toys scattered about on the floor and a vase of flowers on the table. Through the window she saw, on the washing line, blowing in the breeze, white terry-towelling nappies and bedsheets.

'Would you like a cup of tea?' the woman asked gently.

Lost in her thoughts, Vera didn't hear her. Perhaps they'd moved away, Patsy and her mother. And they wouldn't have been able to contact her to tell her at the Magdalene house after she'd escaped.

'It's just made,' the woman said, pointing to the teapot.

Vera nodded dumbly. The woman came back from the scullery with a piece of cake and a glass of orange for James. He was sitting on the floor happily playing with the other boy.

'Mama, boy,' James said importantly.

'Yes, sweetheart,' said Vera.

The woman sat down opposite her, unsure of where to look.

'My mum, my sister? Where are they? And how do you know my name?'

Somehow, Vera knew even as she asked the question what the woman's answer was going to be.

'I'm sorry to tell you your sister was killed in an air raid and your mother died about six months ago from pneumonia. The landlord cleared the house. My husband and I moved in a couple of months ago.'

The tears ran unchecked down Vera's face. The woman went over to a drawer in the sideboard and took out a fresh handkerchief that she pressed into Vera's hands.

'Thank you,' said Vera, blowing her nose then dabbing at her eyes. Why had she stayed away for so long? Why had she allowed a stupid passion for a gypsy lad to keep her away from her family? What a fool she'd been; if only she'd come sooner. The woman's voice broke into her thoughts.

'The landlord. He's kept some of the stuff in store in case you wanted it.'

Vera slowly nodded. She felt numb. Her sister and her mum were gone. She had never felt so alone.

'Do you know any more about what happened? Was Patsy still living here at the time?' She sniffed and wiped her nose again.

'Oh, yes, I was informed of everything by Mrs Williams at number twenty-three. But are you sure you're in a fit state to hear it?'

'I have to know,' Vera whispered.

The woman nodded. 'Patsy had gone to a dance in the town with some of her friends.' The woman paused. 'The hall took a direct hit. If it's any consolation, she wouldn't have felt a thing.'

Vera felt as though she was going to faint, even though she was sitting down. She took a deep, shuddering breath and then gave a quick nod to the woman to continue.

'Apparently your mother had become ill but wouldn't stay away from the church. Patsy's death had hit her hard,' the woman said. 'She became very forgetful and disorientated. The only way she could cope was to drag herself down to the church to clean. Every day she went. Wouldn't be persuaded otherwise. The neighbours looked out for her as best they could but they'd find her in all sorts of places. One day she was found in the allotments. Been there all night. That's how come she got sick in her body as well as her mind. It was over very quickly. Pneumonia's like that. Anns Hill Cemetery, they're both there.'

It had never occurred to Vera that her mother and Patsy wouldn't be here. She dabbed at her eyes. The woman leaned forward and clasped Vera's hands.

'There's something else,' she said. From behind an elephant ornament on the mantelpiece she took a crumpled letter.

'This is for you. Sorry it got a bit grubby. It was amongst your mother's stuff and has your name on it. The landlord reckoned one day you'd come here.'

The envelope bore her mother's writing and she put it in her pocket.

It was then, through the window, she spied the cat asleep on the top of the dustbin lid.

'That orange cat.'

'He was here when we came and doesn't seem to want to leave. Sleeps on the bed mostly. We call him Red. My lad worships him.'

Vera smiled, despite her pain. So Mogs had survived. It was true then that cats had nine lives.

'Can I go and stroke him?'

Feeling a little more in charge of herself, she went through to the scullery and out of the back door.

She put her hand on Mogs' fur. He woke, looked at her and started purring. Vera tickled him behind his ears. She thought of Tim and of how the cat and he were always together. Memories of Tim knocking on her window and bringing her fish and chips swam into her mind. Vera looked up and a lump formed as she saw what used to be her bedroom window. She remembered Patsy giving her nylons and chocolate so she could buy Angela's friendship and then she imagined her mother walking briskly towards the house, the Blakeys on the heels of her shoes clicking away like taps from a hammer.

But there was nothing left for her in Alma Street now. Fetching James, she made her goodbyes. Then, after the woman had closed the front door, Vera took one last look at the outside of her childhood home and walked away.

When she reached the bottom of the street Vera couldn't contain herself any longer. She shakily opened the letter from her mother. There were just five words.

'Dear Vera, I'm sorry, Mum.'

Vera was still crying as she boarded the Provincial bus to town.

'C'mon sweetheart,' Vera said, holding tightly to James' hand as they crossed the road towards the Dive café.

It had started to rain and James was grizzling. She helped him down the steep entrance steps.

'I saw the card in the papershop window askin' for a waitress.' Vera gave the man a smile. She was conscious that she looked bedraggled.

'Done this job before?' The man stopped buttering currant buns and looked her up and down. Vera was hungry and the food made her mouth water.

'I can soon learn.' She tried another smile. The man spoke

again but James was crying in full flow now and Vera couldn't hear what he was saying. 'Oh, lovey,' she said, picking him up and surveying his runny nose and tear-streaked cheeks.

'You got someone to care for the boy?' The man tore off a piece of kitchen roll and handed it to her. Vera wiped James' nose.

'I'll find someone.'

He looked at her hands. 'No weddin' ring means you ain't married. I can't hire you. You'll give this place a bad name.'

A raindrop dripped from her hair and Vera wiped it away. She was too dispirited to argue. She turned and, clutching James close, climbed the stone steps out into the rain again.

The rain was like needles piercing her face as she walked back down Mumby Road. In her purse was just enough money for a cheap bed and breakfast. With James straddling her hip, Vera searched the closed doors and windows for a 'Vacancies' sign.

Dusk was falling now. She smiled at James, who had screamed himself to sleep. Tomorrow things would look better, especially if they had a warm bed to sleep in tonight.

Halfway down Mumby Road Vera saw the blue-painted door with the sign above it announcing 'Bed and Breakfast'. With trepidation she pressed the buzzer. After a few moments the door opened to reveal a middle-aged woman with lipstick spilling into the creases around her lips. The woman was thin and pale with dyed red hair. She reminded Vera of a Swan Vesta match.

'Yes?' There was no smile from the woman, neither did she invite Vera inside out of the rain. The smell of boiled cabbage swept over Vera.

'Have you a vacancy for tonight?'

The woman looked at James then stared at Vera. 'You'll be

wanting a double bed for you and your husband and a cot for the child?'

'Just a bed for me and my son.'

The woman's eyes bored into her. 'This is a respectable lodging house. I don't take in unmarried mothers.' The door slammed in Vera's face.

Vera stood in the rain, now close to tears. The dusk had turned to darkness and Vera shivered. Then she straightened herself and walked back the way she'd come towards the ferry and the Porthole fish and chip shop.

Vera made herself comfortable in a booth and ordered fish and chips for herself and a fishcake for James, who had woken up.

'Oh, and a cup of strong tea and a glass of orange,' she added.

It was warm and cosy inside the café and Vera made sure James ate his fill. She glanced at the blackout curtains. She could hear the heavy rain still pelting down outside.

Vera sat until the fish shop closed.

Where was she going to sleep tonight? It hadn't occurred to her that she wouldn't be staying in her childhood home in Alma Street. And there was little point in trying for a room in a pub or hotel; now she and James had eaten she didn't have enough money. Anyway, they had all closed. It was dark and the deluge had settled in for the night.

With James in her arms she walked across to the ferry gardens.

The *Vadne* ferry boat was tied off the pontoon to bollards. Across the strip of water dividing Gosport from Portsmouth she could just make out the tall masts of the *Victory*. Vera looked around her. She could see no one else braving the rain.

She and James were quite alone. She walked down the ramp that led to the squat vessel.

Carefully, Vera stepped aboard. The lock on the downstairs cabin door was broken so she stealthily made her way down the wooden steps into the dark interior.

She froze. She could hear snoring. A strong smell of body odour was coming from a bundle of rags lying across one of the slatted seats. She realised she wasn't the only visitor. Her foot kicked against a bottle and it rolled noisily.

'Got a bedmate, 'ave I?' The man's voice was gravelly. The bundle sat up. 'Got a babby with you an' all,' he added sourly.

'I'm sorry to disturb you; we need to get out of the rain.' Vera's heart was beating fast.

'Don't we all, girly. Got anything to drink?'

Vera shook her head. 'No,' she whispered.

The man settled himself back down. 'Me name's Ted an' I shan't hurt either of you. Used to visitors, I am. If you're kippin' 'ere, better get some shut-eye quick. The *Vadne* sails across to Pompey at five in the morning. You don't want to be 'ere when the skipper arrives.'

Vera began to relax. She'd found shelter and she and James weren't hungry. Vera settled James against her body and closed her eyes. Thoughts of her mother, Patsy and Tim floated in and out of her mind. She fought back tears, vowing to stay strong for James' sake. But soon her tiredness overwhelmed her and the sound of the lapping waves against the boat lulled her to sleep.

Vera woke when she heard the man saying in a sing-song voice, 'Walky round the garden, like a teddy bear.'

Her heart was pounding as James cried, 'Do it, do it!'

'What's going on?' Vera cried, rolling from the slatted

bench, James no longer safely by her side. Her eyes pierced the gloom for her child.

James was standing, leaning in towards the old man, who was tickling him!

The man held on tightly to the boy so he wouldn't fall and said, 'Sorry to wake you, girly, but your lad likes to play games, doesn't he?' Vera breathed a sigh of relief that was shattered when the man said, 'Lucky I wasn't a sleeping beauty like you. This kiddie could have made short work of those steps and been on deck in no time. If us two was both asleep, we wouldn't have heard the splash and likely his little body would have washed up on Stokes Bay beach.'

Vera snatched up her boy into her arms. She held him so tightly James gasped, 'Mummy hurt.'

Vera set him down again and James made a grab for the man's unkempt beard.

'No, James,' she chided. The man grinned but held on to James' chubby hand. Vera realised everything the man said was true: James could be floating in the harbour if this man hadn't taken the trouble to keep her son amused while she slept. But what kind of mother did that make her that her only shelter for her child was sharing a ferry-boat cabin with a vagrant?

'I want to thank you,' Vera said sheepishly. 'I shouldn't have nodded off.'

Vera hauled James on to her lap after sitting down next to the man. Looking at him she realised he wasn't as old as she'd first thought.

'You must have had a rough day to sleep as soon as your head touched the seating.'

Vera nodded. She had no reason to unburden herself to this man, who surely had his own problems.

'I guess we all got problems,' she said.

'Not me, not now,' the man replied.

Vera smiled at him. 'Then I wish you'd tell me the secret of how to get rid of all my problems,' she said.

'Do what I did, girly. Run away. Leave 'em behind.' He sat up and scratched inside his coat. Disturbed, a waft of stale air escaped from his clothing.

'Whatever do you mean?'

'It happened like this: I had a nice little house and two fine boys and a trim wife. I went off to the war and saw some pretty nasty goings-on. I got shot in me leg and it went real bad. But I was one of the lucky ones, for on the twenty-seventh of May I was evacuated from Dunkirk.' He paused, while Vera settled James into a more comfortable position. 'Operation Dynamo it was called and eventually three hundred thousand French and British men were brought across the Channel to safety in all manner of boats.'

'I never knew,' said Vera.

The man scrutinised her. ''Appen you had your own problems,' he said kindly.

'What happened about your leg?' Vera steered him away from talking about her.

'Oh, that. I was in hospital and lucky to get out with both me legs, so I was told. You know, I never 'ad a sniff of a visitor all the time the doctors was making me well. Twenty miles away was me house and family and not once did I get a visit.'

Vera frowned. 'Perhaps they'd been bombed out.'

'Bombed out, be buggered,' he snapped. 'I took a bus home and found my missus living with a bloody farm boy who didn't even go to war!'

'God,' said Vera. 'What did you do?'

'Nothing.'

'Nothing?'

'What'd be the point? She was pregnant with his kiddie. I didn't even wait for my boys to come home from school. I just walked away from me house, me wife, me kids.'

Vera was silent while she thought about his words. 'I could understand you leaving your wife but don't you miss your children? Don't you ever wonder how they are?' She glanced down at her sleeping child. 'I couldn't leave James,' she said quietly.

'And that's why you got problems, girly. You may not realise it but that child is a millstone round your neck and you aren't showing your love for him by draggin' him through the streets when he should be in a proper bedroom at nights.'

Vera was upset by the man's words. 'An' you think you've got a good life, do you?'

He began to laugh then. A rumbling sound that made his whole body shake.

'I'm an alky. I'm on me uppers. I got nothing. Nowhere to live or sleep and I begs for a bite to eat. But, girly, I'm doin' it to myself and only myself. I ain't hurtin' no one else.'

Vera picked up James. Her conversation with this man was at an end. She walked to the other side of the cabin and sat down, her thoughts in a turmoil. She digested his words. Every word he had spoken was the truth. Vera realised this man's life could be hers, and if she lost her determination to find a job and make some money she could end up as lost as he was. Much as she loved James she was not being a good mother to him. But that didn't mean she was going to sit on her arse and do nothing about it. No, definitely not.

Vera walked past Blundell's furniture store and the pet shop. When she reached the Fox, next door to Bert's café, she noticed the piece of cardboard stuck in the window. *Wanted. Live-in barmaid. Apply within.*

Vera hoisted James up on her hip and wiped his nose. He had developed a cough. She steadied her heavy bag over her shoulder and pushed open the pub door. Chatter stopped. Someone wolf-whistled.

Vera knew it wasn't the done thing for a woman to enter a pub on her own. Only tarts did that. Determined, she took a deep breath and said to the man behind the bar, 'Can I see the manager?'

The large man was red-faced and immediately his eyes dropped to her breasts. He gave her a sickly smile. 'You're talking to him.'

'I've come about the job,' Vera said.

'Have you had any experience?'

Vera nodded. How hard can it be to pull a pint? she thought.

'Where did you work before?'

'Glastonbury,' Vera lied quickly.

'I take it you want to live in? Where's your husband?'

'I don't have one,' she said, staring him straight in the eyes.

He nodded. Vera could see he was thinking about it. She decided to make a stand. 'How much are you paying?'

He finished polishing a glass and looked at her from under bushy blond brows. 'You get lodging, meals, and I'll pay you what you're worth.'

'So you're offering me the job?' Her heart lifted.

'No, I'm giving you a week's trial,' he said.

The man's oily grin made her uneasy but Vera was desperate. It would mean a roof over her head, food and money, plus she could look around for something better in her spare time.

'If you want, you can start tomorrow,' he said. He stared at her breasts again. 'Your room is at the top. I'll come up and pitch up a cot for the lad. The kitchen's through there if you fancy a cup of tea. I live here but I'm on my own and need help.'

'Fair enough,' she said. Across the bar she could see two old men playing shove ha'penny. A dartboard was fixed to the wall opposite.

'Usual hours,' he said. 'Ten till two then six till ten. I expect you to be on call for cleaning and cellar work and you get Sundays off.'

'Fine,' Vera said. 'Can I see the room?'

He didn't answer her; instead he called into the crowd, 'Charlie!'

A small man shuffled up to the counter. He had yellow hair and teeth like tombstones. 'Look after the bar for a minute, will you, mate?' The man moved towards the end of the bar and lifted the wooden hatchway.

The manager turned towards her. 'What's your name?'

'Vera.' Again his eyes had fallen to her breasts. Vera felt uncomfortable beneath his scrutiny.

'Mine's Mike. Mike Carmichael.'

Vera nodded. She followed Mike up two flights of stairs. She could smell the body odour coming off him.

The room was clean, large and airy and faced Murphy's the Ironmongers. The double bed was covered with a patchwork quilt and a rag rug was on the floor. There was a wardrobe, dressing table and a chair.

'Functional and clean,' he said. Vera badly wanted to curl up on the bed and sleep.

'I'll get the kiddie's cot out of the shed, give it a wipe over and bring it up. The cot belonged to me own kiddie so I know it's all right. Make yourself at home.'

James started coughing and Vera picked him up and wiped his nose.

True to Mike's word he was back in no time and proceeded to put the cot together.

'Where d'you want it. Near your bed?'

She nodded and then said, 'It's very kind of you.'

'I don't have any cot blankets but you'll find plenty of blankets in the wardrobe. Help yourself to whatever you need from the kitchen,' he said before disappearing back downstairs into the noise and cigarette smoke below.

She made up the cot with James helping her. He insisted on climbing in to try it. When Vera had unpacked her large shoulder bag, she turned round to find him already asleep, Rags in his arms.

Down in the kitchen she made herself a sandwich and a cup of tea and then found the bathroom and had a strip wash. She got into bed and thought about all she'd lost, her mother and sister, and she began to cry quietly, trying hard not to wake James. She should have been there to look after her mother. She would never forgive herself for that.

But now she had to think about her son. She hated herself for dragging him all over the country when he needed stability and a decent home. She needed to focus on their future.

But what would happen when she went behind the bar and Mike Carmichael realised she knew sod all about the bar trade?

Chapter 23

Vera was downstairs by half past seven the next morning. She and James had been fed, and despite his waking in the night and coughing, he was now settled in the pram that Vera had found at the bottom of the stairs. It wasn't top of the range but was clean and plenty big enough for James. Mike had even cushioned it with a pillow and left a folded cream blanket over the handles. He was in the bar washing ashtrays.

'Did you sleep well?'

'Fine thanks,' she replied. 'And thank you for the pram. It'll certainly make my life easier.'

'Just off the bar next to the kitchen is a sitting room. It's close enough for you to hear the lad if he cries and I can make up a wooden gate so he can't get out. We could clear the room of any hazards. He could play quite happily in there.' Another clean ashtray was piled on top of the others. 'Come and have a look.'

Vera followed him to a room that didn't look as though it was used much. During her lunch break she could give it a good going over.

'I think it'll be ideal,' Vera said with a smile.

'Have you toys we can put in here to make it more like a playroom?'

Vera shook her head. 'James has only got Rags, his bunny. But he loves wooden spoons and saucepan lids.'

Mike put his hand in his pocket and took out a pound note.

'Take this and run into the market and see what you can find.'

'Oh, I couldn't.'

'I insist.' He narrowed his eyes and pushed the crumpled note into her hand.

James had fallen asleep in the pram. Vera ran upstairs and grabbed her hat and coat. All her clothes were getting shabby now as she'd had to leave most of them in her suitcase at the whorehouse in Southsea. She thought of the few items of underwear and James' tiny trousers and shirt that she'd washed this morning and hung over the wooden clothes rack hanging from the ceiling in the kitchen. Mike had told her to make herself at home, and if there was one thing she couldn't abide it was dirt.

Rushing downstairs, she pushed the pram out on to the pavement.

'When you get back, come straight into the bar,' called Mike. 'And undo that top blouse button. You might up me sales with that figure of yours.'

Vera stepped smartly past the caff. She didn't look back at Mike, who she knew was watching her. Just when she was beginning to think he was a genuinely kind man, he came out with some grubby remark, but for the sake of a bed and food for James and herself, Vera knew it was better to keep on the good side of Mike and ignore his lewdness.

In the market she bought a wooden train and some bricks in a cart that James could push about. It would help him with his walking, she thought. Vera worried about how quiet he was. He seemed to take everything in and think a lot.

Walking back through the crowds with the traders calling out, trying to sell their goods, Vera was glad she was home in Gosport once more. But as she passed Walpole Park she remembered walking through the fairground with Tim and how happy she'd been. Afterwards they'd sat near the creek. Tim showed her how he could make a daisy-chain necklace and he'd slipped it over her head. But it was no good thinking of the past and what might have been, she told herself.

When she got back, she settled James in his playroom with his new toys and stepped into the bar to begin work. The place was already full of men, who suddenly gave wolf whistles and then started clapping. Vera felt a flurry of nerves in the pit of her stomach.

'Here she is everyone, our Vera.' Mike looked at her proudly and Vera felt herself blush. She forced a smile and crossed her fingers behind her.

Her first customer wanted a Forest Brown. Nervously Vera found a half-pint glass and took the top off the bottle using the opener set in the wood of the bar. Thank God she could pour it without it frothing all over the place. The price had been chalked on the shelf so she took the man's money and opened the drawer of the till and counted out the right change to him. Feeling pleased, she went up and down behind the bar familiarising herself with everything.

Vera watched as Mike took a pint glass and stuck it under the Brickwoods beer pump. He gave a strong pull on the pump and the brown liquid flowed in the glass. She could manage that, she was sure. Then she saw him pour a whisky without using the measure, which he drunk straight back.

The bar was becoming warm and fuggy with cigarette smoke and body heat. The Mills Brothers' 'Paper Doll' could just be heard above the noise.

A seaman shouted, 'When you're ready, love.' Vera smiled at the man in the navy blue suit with the white piping. His large white collar hung neatly over his shoulders.

'Yes?' She went towards him. 'What can I get you?'

'A rum and black, please.' He had twinkling blue eyes and a southern accent.

Right, thought Vera. She knew what rum was and Guinness was the only black drink that came to mind. She put the pint glass beneath the Guinness tap and waited for ever for the beer to fill and settle. Then she tipped the rum into it and put it on the counter in front of the man.

His forehead furrowed. 'What's this? I asked for a rum and black.'

'Rum and Guinness,' she replied.

He started to laugh. 'It's easy to see you're no barmaid. Quick, pour it down the sink before Mike sees what you've done. He's funny about wastage.'

Vera, one eye on Mike still chatting with his back to her, poured the drink away.

'Now, love,' said the man, 'I want a rum and blackcurrant juice. Have you got blackcurrant?'

Vera looked along the back of the bar and there was a half-full bottle of juice next to a bottle of orange. She took it to him and asked how much he wanted in the glass of rum.

'I'm glad Mike's managed to get as many drinks as he can off the black market. There's still empty shelves in other pubs,' he said to her quietly. He put some coins on the counter and winked. 'You'll soon get used to it,' he said.

Mike came over. 'Are you all right, Vera?'

'Course she's all right,' said the sailor.

Vera turned away to pull a pint for an old man, but was surprised when Mike said, 'It's time you went and looked in on James.' Vera sensed that Mike didn't like her talking and laughing with the sailor.

'I checked on him earlier,' Vera said, her voice like cracked ice.

Suddenly the siren went, and following it the roar of planes overhead and guns firing.

'Where's the nearest shelter?' Vera asked frantically.

'There's one at the end of Bemisters Lane but you use our Morrison.' Mike had to shout for the noise was at full pitch in the bar. 'It's in the kitchen covered by a makeshift table,' he yelled above the pandemonium.

'Are you coming?' Vera asked, already rushing to the door.

'What and leave this lot to loot me bar? Business as usual here, my girl.' As if to prove his point he poured himself another whisky and downed it in one.

Vera ran into the back where James was. Scooping him up she went into the hall and made her way to the kitchen. She passed the door to the bar and saw it was mostly empty as the customers piled into the street outside, gawping heavenwards.

'You get the bastards!' one cried.

Casting a backwards glance at the kitchen, Vera went to see what they were shouting at.

'Move over a bit so Vera and the boy can see.' Mike made a space for her and lifted James and set him on his shoulders.

Planes were chasing each other at high speed in a wild battle over Gosport and Portsmouth. Vera could hear the noise of distant firing coming from the aircraft but there was no sound of anti-aircraft guns at ground level.

'Come on, Boyo, you got the bloody huns on the run!' shouted someone. Vera was spellbound. She looked down the street to see other inhabitants poking their heads out to watch the dogfight between the RAF boys and the posse of German fighters.

'Fuck me, he's got 'im!' cried someone else.

A German plane, smoke belching, flew seawards. The sky was as blue as baby's ribbon but now black plumes were being tossed by the wind.

The crowds were still cheering when another German plane was hit, and followed the first towards the southern shores.

Vera wondered how far they'd get towards home.

The other enemy fighter planes seemed to lose enthusiasm for one by one they disappeared. Eventually the sky above was emptied of its roaring noise and silver flashes.

'I need a bleedin' pint after that little lot,' Vera heard a man say as everyone walked back inside.

Vera took James back to the sitting room where he was soon playing contentedly. Back in the bar, she was rushed off her feet serving those who'd hung around to replay the action they'd just witnessed. But above the rowdy din, Vera could vaguely hear the conversation of two men at the bar and she almost dropped a pint of beer when she realised who they were talking about.

'The coppers ain't caught that bleeder Del Simpkins.'

'That's not what I hear. Seems they found him down near Wells. Dead.'

'So he definitely won't be goin' to trial for them kiddies, then.'

'Don't make no difference now.'

'Well, if he was killed, the authorities should be clappin' their hands. He won't ruin no more kiddies' lives, will he?'

Vera couldn't eavesdrop any longer for fear of being caught out so she moved down the bar. But what she'd heard made her feel better about Simpkins' death. Maybe, she thought, she'd sleep easier at night now.

Mike rang a small ship's bell and shouted, 'Come on, let's be 'aving you.'

Vera collected up all the dirty ashtrays. Then after the glasses were clean and dried, she polished the bar top and then began sweeping the floor.

When Mike had finished counting up the takings and put the float back for the evening session, he said, 'We've had a good morning; better than usual. I've got no complaints about you so far but you didn't need to lie to me. It's obvious you've never done this sort of work before but you're learning quickly and I'm happy to keep you on.'

Vera couldn't help grinning. A proper job! And she wouldn't have to drag James around the streets any more looking for a bed. She wondered if he'd been coughing while she'd been working in the bar.

'Thanks,' she said. 'You don't know what this means to me.'

'There is one thing,' Mike said. 'I've heard quite a few customers offer you a drink this morning and you've refused them.'

Vera nodded and pushed the hair out of her eyes. 'If I drank all them drinks I'd be sick as a dog and lying on the floor now.'

'Well, it's part of a barmaid's perks, love. When you're asked if you'd like a drink you say, "Yes please". You take money for a cheap drink so as not to be greedy and then you puts a bottle top on the counter at the back of the bar. If at the end of the shift you've got a lot of bottle tops, I gives you the money for them.'

'Fancy that,' Vera said.

Then Mike came very close to her and put his hands on her shoulders. 'Now look, Vera, I've not just come up the Solent in a bucket. You're not a *good* barmaid, not yet. But you will be.' His body odour made her wrinkle her nose. There was still sleepy dust in the corners of his eyes and his false teeth moved when he spoke. His eyes fell to her breasts. 'Perhaps we can work things out between us.'

Vera's heart was beating fast. She didn't reply; instead she moved away and said, 'I think I can hear James.'

Mike watched her as she walked from the bar.

James had fallen asleep on the carpet. There were two trails of green snot beneath his nose and he was breathing heavily. When she picked him up, he had lines on his face. She took him upstairs and laid him in his cot. 'Poor little mite,' she whispered. 'I love you so much and I'm trying my hardest to be a good mum.' Tears filled her eyes as she gazed down at him. She wondered if she'd done the wrong thing in wanting to look after James herself. If she'd handed him over to the nuns for adoption, there was every possibility that he could be living in a fine big house now, with a room of his own filled with toys and loved by a mummy and a daddy who would bring him up right and see he went to the best schools. And then maybe go on to university and make something of his life. But instead they were living in a dingy pub and Vera had to leave her son on his own for much of the day if she was to keep a roof over their heads. 'One day I'll get us a place of our own,' Vera vowed.

After a week, Vera had more than learned the ropes. Now she was tapping and changing barrels down in the cellar. The customers liked her and she gave as good as she got to the cheeky ones and their lewd remarks.

Her pile of bottle tops grew each day and Vera was able to take James into the market to buy him new clothes. He seemed to have lost weight recently and he still had his cough.

The only fly in the ointment was Mike and his roving hands. He was always squeezing past her and taking the opportunity to fondle her bottom, or brush against her breasts with his hands or arms.

'Give us a kiss, Vera,' he said one night when they were washing up glasses. There was only Ron Wilkes in the bar, drinking up his mild. Mike had cornered her between the sink and the end of the bar.

'Give over, Mike. You know I'm not interested.'

He backed away from her as though he'd been slapped and his face turned nasty as he sneered, 'You got a kid. He weren't no immaculate conception. You ain't married, so you been givin' it away for free. Why don't you give me some?' His breath stank of fags and whisky as he loomed over her. 'I gives you a roof over your head an' a job an' I reckon I should get a bit more in return, don't you?'

One of his hands gripped her breast, squeezing it hard. She winced with the pain but managed to give an almighty shove in the region of his beer belly and Mike stumbled away from her. His hands spread out to stop himself from falling and knocked against the gin optic. The liquid sprayed out across him. The look of utter surprise on his face made Vera laugh.

'I don't give it away for free an' even if I did you wouldn't be getting' any.'

A rumble of laughter came from Ron. He was known as the town gossip, and Vera knew it would be all over the pub tomorrow that she'd bested Mike. She threw the tea towel at Mike. 'You can do your own bleedin' dryin' up.'

She stalked off to her room. Although she'd stuck up for herself, it felt like a shallow victory. For Vera knew that men like Mike refused to take no for an answer. If she'd been by herself she would have walked away from Mike and his pub right then. But not now she was a mother.

Without this job, they'd be on the streets again. Vera sighed as she crawled into bed, wondering if a day would come when she'd no longer be at the mercy of a man.

Chapter 24

Vera was almost asleep when she thought she heard the door creaking open. In the cot next to her bed James was sleeping, his breathing laboured, his chubby arm thrown above his head. The room was in darkness, illuminated only by the dull glow from the streetlamp.

Then she heard footsteps.

The feather quilt was roughly pulled from her body and the side of the bed complained as Mike climbed in.

'Get off me!' Using her knees, Vera shoved him to the floor. 'Get out of my room!'

Mike got up off the floor and lunged towards her across the bed. 'I don't think so, Vera. You've been flaunting it long enough!'

Vera jumped out of the bed.

Mike slid across the quilt and made a grab. His hands were on her flesh. Again she gave an almighty shove and he reeled backwards. Vera ran for the door just as Mike grabbed at her nightdress, feeling it tear away from her body. She reached the door but Mike was quicker and he slammed it shut.

'No you fuckin' don't.' His voice was low, determined.

James had woken and was crying and coughing. Vera ran towards the cot, her arms outstretched to pick up her child.

'You're not getting away this time.' Mike followed and

pushed her to the floor. James was now standing in his cot screaming. Vera kicked out at Mike but missed. He was all over her as he grabbed one of her flailing arms and yanked it above her head. Something seemed to snap inside her shoulder.

'Owww!' Vera screamed, the pain like nothing she'd experienced before. Her arm was completely useless, hanging at her side like it didn't belong to her. Vera thought she might pass out from the excruciating agony. 'Bastard,' she cried.

He hit her across the mouth and her jaw shuddered. 'Shut up, bitch.'

Vera knew if she didn't get away, he would either rape or kill her. With a renewed effort, she kicked out and her foot connected with his balls. He screamed with pain, doubling up.

Vera made towards the door, half staggering, half crawling, her arm swinging uselessly as she somehow got to the bottom of the stairs. Agonising moments were lost as she fumbled trying to slide back the heavy front-door bolt. And all the time, she was screaming inside, torn between wanting to get back to her child and getting help. What if Mike stopped James screaming by hurting him?

And then the bolt slid and her body's force against it sent her stumbling out on to the wet pavement to collide with a man.

'No! No!' Vera beat at him with her one good hand.

'Stop it!' His words were sharp, commanding.

Exhausted, Vera ceased her relentless hammering and sobbed, 'My boy's in there! Please save him. Please get him out of there.'

The man held her at arm's length and stared at her. She was suddenly aware of her near nakedness.

'Come with me,' he commanded, dragging her along the street a few paces and thumping open a door next to the Fox.

There was a dim light and a flight of stairs facing her. Vera stopped in the hallway.

'But my boy! My boy's back there!'

Quietly, he said, 'I'll sort it.' And then he pushed her further in and closed the door behind him. She heard the lock click in place.

Vera sank to the wooden floor. There was no way she could have carried James with only one good arm. But she shouldn't have left him. And now all she could do was wait until this stranger came back. After a few minutes, Vera could stand it no longer. She had to get her child. With difficulty she stood upright and tried to turn the latch. Her whole body was aflame with pain.

And then the door banged open and in swept the man with a struggling James in his arms.

Vera almost collapsed with relief. He carefully passed her the child and waited while Vera, using her one good arm, fiercely hugged James to her.

'Get in the caff. It's warmer in there.' He pushed gently in the small of her back, guiding her into a room full of Formica-topped tables and scratched wooden chairs. He looked at the boy. James had two green lines of snot running from his nose to his mouth. His eyes were encrusted with sleepy dust and his skin was waxy looking. 'That child's ill,' the man cried. 'He needs a doctor.' Vera wiped James' nose with the torn hem of her nightdress then she looked at the man. The blackout curtains were drawn at the windows. Vera was about to thank the man for rescuing them when the door closed and she was on her own with James.

James nuzzled into her and Vera held him to her, searching for signs of abuse. He was unwell. A throaty cough bubbled in his chest. Hiccups showed he'd been screaming. Vera rocked him against her then watched his eyes flutter and close and felt his heart beating in time to hers. 'I'm sorry,' she said, 'I'm sorry.' Tears were streaming down her cheeks.

Vera looked at the café clock, an old station timepiece ticking grumpily away on the wall. It was half past three. She wondered where the man had gone. What had she done, allowing herself to be taken in by this stranger? Suppose he was another rapist? Vera shivered. James was warm against her skin as she tried to cover herself with the remnants of her nightgown. She suddenly felt very tired but didn't want to fall asleep in a strange place and leave herself and James vulnerable.

Vera decided she would leave as soon as it was light and make her way towards the hospital so they could look at her arm and check out her son. Perhaps when the man returned she could ask him if she could borrow a coat.

The door thundered open. 'Come on, let's get you into bed.'

Vera's eyes flew open. She tightened her hold on sleeping James.

'Sorry, not the best words to say,' the man said softly.

Vera focused on the man in front of her. He had a tied bundle at his feet and poking from it she saw one of James' romper suits.

'James' clothes? And mine?'

'Well, they won't look good on me.'

He bent down and extracted her dressing-gown and put it on the chair next to her.

Vera smiled. It seemed her face had almost forgotten how to smile. The man made to take the disgruntled child from her arm and immediately Vera froze and clutched James more tightly. Then she carefully settled him on the chair.

The man went to the sink and drew some water from the kettle which was already on the gas. He poured the warm water into an enamel bowl. Then he refilled the kettle and set it back on the flame. He tore a tea towel in two and brought the bowl to her.

'I'm thinking you'd like to wash the stink of him off yourself.' He motioned towards next door.

Vera nodded.

'Okay then, I'll either go outside the room or keep my back to you.'

Vera nodded again. She found her voice. 'He didn't get what he wanted.'

The man didn't say anything. He soaped the rag using carbolic soap and passed it to Vera who began carefully wiping her face, smoothing slowly over the cuts and scratches that she didn't know existed until the pain jabbed at her.

The kettle began to whistle and the man went back behind the counter and made tea.

He was about five foot nine with blond hair swept straight back from his forehead. His face was chiselled, marred only by a scar that ran from his forehead down through his left eyebrow and ended at the top of his cheekbone.

As though he could feel her staring at him he looked up, smiled and said, 'Battle scar. He came off worst, though.'

Vera looked away and carried on washing herself. Considerately the man kept his back towards her, making a show of setting out cups and saucers and rattling cutlery.

'You can turn round now,' Vera said quietly. She'd watched him carefully in case he took a sneaky peek at her but he had kept his promise. James mumbled in his sleep.

Vera watched as he poured the thick dark liquid into two cups and then opened a fridge and took out a long-necked bottle of sterilised milk.

'I don't take sugar,' Vera said, conscious of using up his ration.

'You do now. Good for shock.' He stirred in two heaped spoonfuls.

'I heard the noise,' he said. 'I know what the bugger's like. He's conned more women than a rogue market trader. He won't touch you again. Probably won't open tomorrow, either.'

'He frightened me to death.' Vera felt the tears rise and was powerless to stop them spilling over. 'I don't know what he's done to my arm.'

'Drink this, then we'll get your arm sorted.'

Vera took the cup gratefully. Her hand was shaking and she tried to keep it from spilling by drinking quickly. A sudden thought struck her and her heart tightened with worry. 'A patchwork rabbit! Did you find it?'

He grinned at her. 'A very grubby patchwork rabbit lies in the bundle.'

She heaved a sigh of relief. 'My James loves that old thing.'

'Are you Vera?'

Sniffing, she handed him back the cup and nodded.

'I've heard nothing but good reports about you. Mike's customers like you. Spirited lass, they reckon.'

Vera knew she was blushing.

'I'm Bert. This is my caff and above it are rooms I sometimes let out. It's not posh but it is clean. And I don't allow any hanky panky in here. In case you're wondering, no, I don't come from around here. London, originally. But this is where I'll stay now.' He stared at her. 'Ready to let me loose on your arm?'

'Do you know what's wrong with it?'

'It's been pulled from its socket.'

Panic rose within her. 'Are you going to hurt me?'

'Only for a little while.'

'Perhaps a doctor would be better?'

'He'll do the same as I will. Don't worry, I've done more than my share of this and worse before I was shoved out of the army. Come and sit over here.'

Vera eased herself off the chair and walked painfully to where he was making space.

'Needs a bit of room.' He smiled at her. The smile didn't make her feel better. 'Sit down and try to relax.'

'You got to be joking!'

'You got a sense of humour after all.' He pointed at her dressing-gown. 'I need this off the shoulder.'

With her shoulder bare and sitting with him at the back of her, she felt him gently run his hands over her back and neck. She was just thinking how soft his touch was when he gave an almighty wrench at the top of her arm.

'Jesus Christ!' The pain shot straight along her nerve ends and made her head swim.

'You'll be all right now,' he said, lifting her dressing-gown back over her shoulder.

Vera wiggled her fingers. Amazed that she could. Her shoulder felt sore as hell but at least it was now back in place.

Going to a drawer behind the counter, Bert took out a white tea cloth and tied it as a support for her arm.

'Thank you,' she said.

'It's all right. Now we need to get you and the kiddie to bed. I'll carry him.'

He picked up James. 'This little boy isn't right,' he said. 'He's very hot.' Vera didn't speak but followed him up the long flight of stairs that smelled of disinfectant. Eventually he stopped outside a door and kicked it open. Inside was a rumpled bed. It was probably the bed he had crawled out of, Vera thought.

As if reading her thoughts, Bert said, 'Yes, it's my bed but I don't think either of us is in a bed-making mood and it's clean and warm. Sleep here with your little one. I'll take one of the other rooms.'

Vera eyed the bed gratefully. Carefully Bert laid James on the sheet. The boy stretched but didn't wake. Bert turned towards the door.

'I'll go down now and bring up your stuff. Afterwards, if you feel the need, the key is in the back of the door. But I'll not harm either of you, you needn't worry about that. I'll also phone the doctor to look at your little one. I've felt his forehead, he's burning up.'

Vera climbed in beside James. Bert was right, James' body felt as though it was on fire. The doctor would come soon. The pain in her shoulder had eased to a dull ache. Vera relaxed and closed her eyes.

James' crying woke Vera. His breathing was a strangled sound and his face was red with the effort of screaming. Vera cuddled him close, noting the snotty marks on the pillow and on her nightgown. Holding him tightly she ran to the door and opened it.

'Bert!' Vera cried. 'Bert, come quickly.' She had no idea which room he was in. All she knew was that she needed Bert. Needed him to see what a state her James was in.

'Bert!' Vera called again. Footsteps echoed on the stairs and Bert emerged, tying the cord round the waist of his brown wool dressing-gown.

'It's James. He's very sick.' And James chose that moment

to prove it by opening his mouth and gushing a spume of vomit over Vera's nightdress.

'We must keep him warm,' Bert said. 'Take him back into the bedroom and clean him and yourself up. There's water in the jug. I'll phone again for Doctor Dillinger.'

'James is very sick, isn't he?'

'Yes, I think your child is ill, and sometimes Doctor Dillinger isn't in the best of health either.' Bert held out his hands in a hopeless gesture. 'But if the doctor can come straight away, he will.'

Vera washed and dried her son all over but his body quickly shone with the sheen of fresh sweat. And all the time she wiped his skin he was either crying or vomiting. Eventually Vera was able to roll him in clean sheeting, and sit beside him, watching him.

'Please, please don't die, my angel,' she whispered. She held on to his small hand, wishing she could take away his sickness.

Bert came back into the room and stood beside her looking down at the child. In his hand he held a cup of water. 'I think we should try to get a drop to drink inside him. He's de-hydrated, poor little mite.' He tipped the cup towards James' lips but the child couldn't make the effort to swallow and the liquid ran down his neck into the sheeting.

Vera wanted to cry, to scream with frustration because she could do nothing for her little one, but she resisted; what good would it do?

And just when Vera felt she could stand it no more a loud knocking sound rent the air. Bert rushed down the stairs. A mumble of voices reached Vera's ears and the doctor had, at last, arrived.

*

'This child has bronchitis.' Doctor Dillinger stank of whisky. His hair was long and matted and his eyes were bloodshot. Vera moved back a few steps to escape the unwashed smell that emanated from him. Amazingly, his hands, with their slender fingers, were immaculately clean. He turned and faced Vera. 'Get plenty of fluids inside him, plenty of rest and make up some honey and lemon to ease his sore throat.'

'Does that mean he's going to live?'

'If you look after him properly, of course he'll live.'

Vera sank down on the side of the bed and covered her eyes with her hands. Her tears went unchecked.

Bert went over to the chest of drawers and took a bottle of whisky from the bottom drawer. From his pocket he took a note. The whisky and the money were handed to Doctor Dillinger, who, without another word, swept from the room.

'Now before you open your mouth, Vera, I want you to know that the doctor got struck off a few years back for helping a prostitute he couldn't save. He took to the hard stuff but I'd trust my life to that man and so would many other Gosport citizens.'

'So he asks no questions?'

'More importantly, he keeps his mouth shut. Now, while I make up some honey and lemon, why don't you keep James company? It's been a hell of a night for all of us, from getting you and the kiddie out of the Fox to finding out your lad is ill.'

Vera climbed back into bed with her listless son. She put her arms around him. She was worn out. She'd thought her boy was going to die, and it was her fault because she was dragging him around the country in all weathers without the prospect of a proper home. She knew now her love wasn't enough to keep James alive.

All through the rest of the night James was coughing and being sick. Bert was at her side with compresses for James' forehead to cool him down.

'It's my fault,' she cried. 'He was going to die because I dragged him around in the rain.'

James, his chest wheezing, finally slept. Vera wept.

Chapter 25

'Vera, that child needs a proper home,' Bert said, standing awkwardly in her bedroom doorway a few days later.

'You're not tellin' me anything I don't know, Bert.' She wasn't angry with him for speaking his mind. But Vera didn't want to hear the truth.

'I could work for you and live here,' she said.

'I can't afford to pay anyone wages to work in the caff. I used all the money I had buying this place. I need to make it a going concern before I start handing out jobs.' He put down a tray containing a plate of sandwiches and a mug of tea and milk for the boy and sat beside her on the edge of the bed.

'And who is minding the caff now then?'

'Lily. She's a good friend of mine. Not that it's really any of your business.'

Vera looked at James fast asleep.

'Vera?'

'Yes?'

'Don't jump down me throat when I approach you with this. But I know this couple who had a little girl killed in the Blitz. She was caught in a shower of glass from a shop window when they were running towards the air-raid shelter. The wife can't have any more children.'

'That's really sad. I know how she must feel, not bein' able to have any more kiddies.' She looked at Bert. It was as though he was expecting her to say something else. 'Why you tellin' me this? You think maybe they would look after James while I worked?'

'More than that, Vera. They could give your boy everything you can't.'

His words stunned her. It seemed to her as though she was gasping for breath without making a sound. Then she rounded on him.

'What d'you mean? How dare you say I don't look after my child!' Vera's voice had risen almost to a scream. 'I love him!'

Bert put his hands on her shoulders. 'I didn't say you don't love him. I didn't say he's not the most important person in your life but I am saying with all the prejudice of being an unmarried mother, it's a tough world to bring up a child in if you haven't got a man behind you.'

'I don't need or want a man,' Vera said fiercely. 'Only my boy.' She pushed his hands away from her.

'Have you any qualifications for a job?'

Vera hung her head.

'Any relatives who could help you out?'

Vera didn't look up. Her mother and Patsy had been her only family and now they were gone.

'As soon as you tell any new boss you're not wed, what's going to happen?'

Vera sighed. 'They'll say I'm disgusting for having a child out of wedlock an' I won't get no sniff of that job.'

'Society looks down on the people who need help most. But that's not the end of it. Another reason work is hard to find is that wounded men are being sent home from the war. Those that can work want their jobs back and they take priority over women.'

'War ain't over yet,' Vera said sullenly.

'I bet it won't be long though and things ain't goin' to change overnight to a land of plenty and jobs for all. This country's got to get back on its feet.'

'Leave me alone,' Vera said. 'Get out an' leave me alone!'

He went out and softly closed the door. With tears sliding down her cheeks, she climbed into bed and held James tightly until she fell asleep.

In the morning Vera washed James and dressed him in clean clothes. All night long she'd been thinking about what Bert had told her and she was determined to prove him wrong. She was going to pay him back for all the meals he'd given her and James. She was owed money from Mike but she had no intention of asking him for it. And the little money she had left would have to do for bus fares.

With James at her side, pale after his illness, Vera crept downstairs and out of the side door, her high heels clattering on the pavement.

Down through the market she strode, ignoring the wolf whistles that followed her. The sun was warm and she was full of confidence. She held her head high and clutched James' hand with Rags dragging on the dusty street. She revelled in the bustle and smells and the sounds of people as they strolled or milled around a stall. At the clothes stall she stopped and rifled along a rail of dated dresses until the man had finished serving a customer.

He was obviously expecting another sale as he looked surprised when she asked, 'Do you need someone to help you out?'

'Barely makes enough to feed the wife an' kids, love. I can't afford no staff. Besides, I 'as to get up at three in all weathers and erect this cast-iron frame of the stall. Ain't no job for a little thing like you.'

He turned away to serve a customer. Vera waited until he'd finished then started again.

'I'm good with customers an' I can add up real fast. No mistakes either.' She put on her hopeful face and pulled James away from the dresses that he was playing with.

'Jesus Christ!' he shouted at her. 'You still 'ere? I told you no!'

Disentangling James, Vera grabbed his hand and walked quickly away.

In Woolworths she asked to see the manager. She was escorted down to the end of the store. Shoppers jostled her but the girls behind the counters looked smart in their green overalls and chatted easily to customers. She was left on her own for a while until the manager appeared.

She was a tall, thin woman who looked to Vera as though she could do with a decent meal. She also acted as though Vera had interrupted her and she needed to return quickly to her office.

'I'm looking for work,' said Vera.

The woman looked her up and down. 'Have you served behind a counter before?'

'I've worked behind the bar in a pub and I've taken charge of the coin stall at the fair. I'm good with money.'

'Do you have references?'

Vera was stuck for words. References? She'd never get one off Rosa even supposing she knew where her people were camped. And what kind of reference was she likely to get from Mike at the Fox? Suddenly, she realised James was no longer at her side. Her eyes found him at the same moment the man-ageress's did. Just as he was undoing the wrapper from a fruit

252

bonbon he'd taken off the sweet display. He paused to look at them and to have a raspy cough.

'I'm so sorry.' Vera swept him up. 'I haven't got any references.' James put the sweet into his mouth. 'Do references really matter?'

The woman didn't answer her but simply walked away, her thin straight back showing her disdain.

'I suppose that's no, then.' Vera made her way to the exit, stopping to wipe James' sticky mouth, feeling heartened by the lovely smile he gave her.

Next she walked down Bemisters Lane to the Sunlight Laundry. The laundry was huge, built of Gosport red brick, and the entrance loomed uninvitingly. Vera was suddenly reminded of the laundry at the home for unmarried girls. She stepped into the small entrance and knocked on the glass panel. The music to *Worker's Playtime* was trilling out through loudspeakers.

The panel slid back and a man wearing small round spectacles peered out at her. 'Come for a job, 'ave you?'

Vera nodded.

'Always wanting gals. Come through 'ere.' He opened a door and Vera, holding her son's hand, stepped inside a small room with two chairs in it. 'I'll get Mrs Pink.'

After a few moments another door opened and a large woman in a tweedy suit entered.

'Sit down, girl.'

Vera sat.

'Ever worked in a laundry before?'

Vera nodded.

'Where?'

'Magdalene Home for Girls.'

The woman narrowed her eyes then stared at James.

'I suppose this is the end result of your stay there.'

'If you mean is this my son then the answer is yes.'

The woman looked at Vera's left hand. 'Not married yet, I see?'

Vera shook her head. She knew this was probably her last chance. 'I need a job so I can get a place for the two of us. I don't have any family who could take us in. I'll work hard.'

'You have a babysitter for the child?'

'Not yet but as soon as I get my first week's money ...'

'I'm sorry. You'll be too much of a risk if the child was ill, and he doesn't look too well, if you ask me. Or what happens if the sitter lets you down? We need young women we can rely on. Goodbye,' the woman said curtly before she left through the door at the back.

Vera shouted desperately, 'I could bring him with me.' But even as she uttered those words she knew how ridiculous they sounded. How could she keep an eye on James and work at the same time, especially in such dangerous surroundings with all the steaming water, bleaches and heating equipment?

Vera, tears in her eyes, walked slowly out of the laundry and back up Bemisters Lane. James was in her arms now and she hid her face in his coat to stop herself from crying.

'Don't cry, Mum-mum,' James said.

His words made her cry harder.

Dare she go back to the caff and once more impose on Bert's kindness? She had to go back to collect her things anyway. She gave a sigh as she walked down North Street, James clutched to her body.

She pushed open the main door of the caff and approached the counter. He was cooking sausages, the smell of which made her mouth water. Vera lifted the hatch and, pulling James after her, said, 'I've been thinking ...'

And then she stopped, her mouth open in awe.

Sitting on a stool with nyloned legs neatly crossed and hair the colour of ripe corn was a woman Vera had never seen before.

Bert turned from the spitting frying pan and gently pushed Vera back towards the hatch.

'I can't 'ave a little dot like this,' he nodded towards James, 'round this side. Suppose he gets splashed with hot fat.'

Vera was at a loss what to say to this beautiful stranger and was surprised when the woman smiled at James and then turned her flawless smile on Vera.

Bert looked up from the bread he was now scraping with margarine; wiping his hands on his apron he came over and said, 'Vera this is Lily, Lily this is Vera.'

Vera was tongue-tied. From her pert little black veiled hat to her shiny black patent high heels, Lily was the epitome of glamour.

'Hello,' they both said at the same time, and Lily laughed a deep, sexy laugh.

Vera stared hard at Lily's long red nails that matched perfectly the colour of her lipstick. She was so dumbstruck it took all her willpower to say to Bert, 'Can I have a word with you about what we was talking about last night? In private, like?'

'Course. Lily can look after the place for five minutes while you and I go out the back.'

Lily nodded. 'Get off the pair of you,' she said. 'Won't be the first time I've fried up a bit of bacon.' She slid off the stool with graceful ease. Bert made his way to the back kitchen and Vera followed, her hand in James'.

'We won't be disturbed here,' he said. Vera could hear the juke box playing and the muffled sound of the customers in the caff talking while they ate.

She sat James on the floor and pulled out some pot lids and spoons for him to play with. She took a deep breath. 'I been thinking about that couple you told me about.'

'Oh, yes?'

'Nice people are they?'

'You won't find better,' he said.

'Nice home?'

'And a car.'

'It don't matter about no cars; tell me about them.'

He paused and stared at her. 'You know what you're doing, Vera?'

'Yes, I'm asking you about a couple of people you know, right?'

James was merrily banging away on a lid with a wooden spoon. Rags was stuffed in a saucepan.

Vera looked at Bert. His face seemed full of sorrow.

'I already told you they'd lost their little Annie, didn't I? Well, a month or so back, Petal, that's the missus, lost her dad. Mind you, he was ninety-six. Petal was left the family home, a little cottage on a nice piece of land out Sussex way. They're poor people but Sid's got a job waiting for him at a nearby farm. He can turn his hand to anything, that man. Anyway, they'll be off soon, away from all the bleedin' bombs fallin' down here.'

'Well, I've been thinkin',' Vera began uncertainly. 'Thinkin' about that couple you was talkin' about ... An' I been thinkin' about meself and how I'm at rock bottom now. I been trying for a job this morning but you was right all along. No one's going to help an unmarried mother with no place to live. This morning I've been made to feel like I'm dogshit on the bottom of everyone's shoes.'

'Don't put yourself down.'

'Well, it's true. You're the only bloke in Gosport what's shown me any kindness without jumpin' all over me. But even you 'as to draw the line somewhere. I ain't a charity case. But you see, I came down from Glastonbury with high hopes of meself in a little place with James playin' with his toys. But that was dashed immediately.' Vera opened her red bag and pulled out her purse. The coins totalled sixteen shillings. 'Me and my boy ain't gonna get very far on that, are we?' She didn't wait for Bert to say anything but continued. 'I ain't a mother, I can't provide for him.'

Vera felt the pressure of his hands on hers. She looked into his face, her vision blurry with unshed tears.

'Let's go an' talk to this couple you knows.' Vera wiped her eyes.

'You're sure?' Bert asked softly.

Vera nodded. 'I got to think what's best for him.'

Bert sat looking at her for what seemed an eternity. 'Are you sure about this?'

Vera could only nod, her throat thick with emotion. She hugged James to her, breathing in his familiar scent.

Bert took off his apron, hung it over the newel post, ran his hand through his hair then opened the side door and together they stepped out on to the pavement.

Chapter 26

Bert didn't ask if she wanted him to carry James. It was as though he already knew she might be carrying her son for the last time.

The market was in full swing, the noise deafening, with vendors trying to sell their wares and shouting louder than the next stallholder. But Vera walked through unseeing. So many things were rushing around in her brain like fairground horses, rapidly going nowhere.

Bert had slipped on the coat Vera had seen hanging on the back of the door and he looked unusually smart. His hand was underneath her elbow, guiding her, for she had no idea where he was taking her.

He steered her towards the ferry where a boat had just disgorged its passengers. He walked her past the floating bridge, its huge chains clanking, then down Beach Street with the boatyards smelling of sawdust and pitch, and the bombsites where enemy planes had done their damage.

With each step Vera's heart grew heavier.

Beyond Trinity Church stood three small wooden cottages.

'It's the middle one,' Bert said. 'The one with the pretty garden.'

At the garden gate Vera's feet faltered. There was no reason why she couldn't turn and walk away, she knew this. She looked down at James, asleep in her arms. But she had to do the best for her boy. He needed a decent home.

'Are you all right?' Bert asked.

'Yes,' Vera managed.

Bert used the shining brass door-knocker to announce their presence. Vera noted the net curtains at the mullioned windows were snowy white.

After a few moments the door opened and a rosy-cheeked woman of about forty, with a floral pinny wrapped around her ample body, stood in front of them.

'Hello Bert,' she said, reaching up to his height and kissing his cheek. 'Come on in. You must have smelled the lemon cake that's just come out the oven.' To Vera she said, 'Hello, dear.' She eyed the sleeping James and smiled. 'He won't cause no trouble, will he? Sparked out, he is.'

Vera stepped inside the house and the smell of baking surrounded her.

'Petal, I'd like you to meet Vera.'

'Pleased to meet any friend of Bert's,' she said with a warm smile, leading them into a small living room and pointing to the sofa. Two comfortable chairs flanked it. 'Sit down,' she said. Looking at James, she asked, 'And who is this little love then?'

'That's James,' Bert said.

Vera was thankful that Bert had answered for her because there was now a lump in her throat stopping any sound from escaping. Just then James woke up.

Petal looked at him and said, 'Want some juice and cake?' She didn't wait for an answer but bustled off with Bert behind her.

Vera looked around. A fire burned in the grate, there was a patterned carpet over polished floorboards and the room seemed clean and cosy with a scrubbed table and chairs set in the middle of it. And in the corner was a bookcase chock-a-block with popular reading and classics.

Vera settled James in the corner of the sofa. He was properly awake now and trying to get down to explore. She took her compact from her bag and gave it to him to play with. He liked seeing his reflection in the small mirror.

'Me, me,' he exclaimed. Vera could hear Bert and Petal talking together in what she supposed was the kitchen.

Vera's heart was pounding. She'd known when she'd left the caff that she was about to give her child away for his own well-being. And as soon as she'd seen Petal she knew she would be good to her boy and come to love him as her own. But James was a part of her and Vera didn't know how she could go on without her little boy at her side. She could walk out of this house right now and no one would blame her. But then what? Her and James on the move again? No, the boy needed stability. In her mind's eye she could see him running across the fields in the sunlight, happy and without cares. Running towards a cottage where Petal was waiting in a white pinny and smelling of the scones she'd just baked. Perhaps there'd be a dog at his side. Later, much later, her boy, Petal's boy, would go to college and perhaps on to university. He would study hard and make something of his life. Not get stuck on this old merry-go-round of existence that she, his birth mother, couldn't stop. She stared down at James, reached towards his tousled hair and ran her fingers through its softness. 'I love you,' she murmured.

It wasn't long before Bert and Petal returned with a tray of tea and cake. Petal handed a cup half full of orange juice to James and he slurped it straight back, giving her the empty cup. An orange moustache adorned his upper lip.

'My, you were thirsty. Can I give him some cake?' Petal deferred to Vera, who nodded.

'Like cake,' James said. Cake in hand, he ate contentedly and clutched Rags to him.

Petal surprised Vera by coming straight to the point after she'd given everyone tea and cake. 'Bert says you need someone to look after him?'

Before Vera had time to open her mouth, she heard the front door latch click and a man's gravelly voice call out, 'Where's my Petal, where's my flower?'

Petal coloured up and said in a rushed voice, 'Excuse me, that's my Sid. He's a daft love.' Then she rushed into the hall and Vera heard muted voices. She looked at Bert sitting on the other end of the sofa and he gave a half smile and hastily swallowed a piece of cake.

Then he said, 'Wouldn't think they been married twenty years, would you?

Everything went suddenly quiet as a tall thin man wearing glasses entered the living room. His work clothes were dusty.

'How do you do?' he said to Vera with a nod. Then he went forward to shake hands with Bert. 'All right, Bert?'

'Couldn't be better,' Bert replied. 'This is Vera, and that's her little boy.' The man's eyes twinkled at James and the crumb-laden sofa. 'Proper boy, then?'

Vera nodded. 'I'll clean it up.'

'No. I like to see a kiddie eat well.'

'You'll have to excuse Sid's dirty clothes but he's working at Haslar, for a local builder, rebuilding the sea wall. Been with the firm for fifteen years, he has.' Vera could hear the pride in Petal's voice.

The man went through to the kitchen and Vera could hear

him washing his hands. He'd taken off his coat by the time he came in seconds later.

'Always better to eat cake when me hands are clean,' he said. Then he looked at James, who was studying him. 'And what have you got to say about it, little 'un?' James grinned at him.

'James is not a great talker. A good walker, but he's always been a silent boy,' Vera said.

'Well then,' said Sid. 'I expect he thinks a lot. That's right, isn't it?' And he tickled James and made him laugh.

'Well, do you want him or not?' Vera blurted out without thinking.

There was a lull as if everyone was afraid to speak.

'You have to tell me now, else me and James is leaving.' Vera shakily stood up.

'But don't you want to know more about us? This is a huge decision to make, you know?' Petal had moved towards her and had slipped her hand through Vera's arm.

Vera looked at her. 'All *you* needs to know is I love him so much me heart breaks looking at him. But sooner or later he's gonna come to grief with me. If it wasn't for Bert, I reckon the both of us might be dead now.'

Bert was staring at her. She could see the glisten of tears in his eyes.

The woman sat down in the middle of the sofa, pulling Vera down with her, and clasped Vera's hands.

Vera stared straight into Petal's blue eyes and said firmly, 'I'll want no more contact with him, do you understand? He must never know his real mother gave him away. You two must be his proper parents. In case you're wondering about his father, I was raped at fourteen and the man went abroad. He knows nothing of his son.' Vera paused and looked at the shocked faces about her. 'But,' Vera stressed the word, 'when

262

I get employment, and I will, I want you to promise to take the money I shall send you. This money will be for James' education. I promise I will never try to find you.' Vera's legs were still shaking.

There was a long hush in the room. Petal was the first to speak. 'Are you sure about this, dear? What if you change your mind? I couldn't bear to take him for my own then have to give him up.'

'I'll sign a paper.'

'There's no need for that and I doubt it would hold much water.' Sid was thoughtful. 'Has Bert told you of our position? That Petal can't have any more children and that we lost our little girl?'

Vera nodded. She wanted to tell him she couldn't have another child either as she'd been sterilised by the nuns but she kept quiet.

'Bert told me all I need to know and I've already seen enough to know you'll treat my boy good.' Vera wiped a tear away before it fell. 'And I heard Bert telling you about me and what happened at the Fox. So it's up to you.'

'Come and see the rest of the house, dear.' Petal rose and grabbed Vera's arm and took her through into the hall where coats overflowed on a coat stand and a red patterned carpet ran up the stairs. Vera followed Petal up and stood in front of an empty room.

'This will be his bedroom. We cleared Annie's stuff and put it in the attic. Well, I couldn't just throw her belongings out, could I? Though people said I should. We'll go down to Court's and buy him a bed tomorrow. One he can grow into. He'll like having his own room.' Petal looked at Vera. 'I'll keep him safe and warm and take him to church and Sid will show him how to make stuff and play football.'

Vera looked about the room, imagining her son growing up here with this couple. Then remembered he wouldn't grow up here as they'd be moving soon.

'Bert told me you're going to live in the county?'

'A better life for us all,' Petal said.

Over the other side of the stairway, the door was opened to their room. She could see a big, squishy bed and bright curtains: a comfortable room for a couple who had a lot of love to give and a great deal of love between them.

At the bottom of the stairs Vera turned once more into the sitting room.

'Don't you want to ask questions?' Sid was standing, moving from one foot to the other. Vera shook her head. 'I've seen enough and I trust Bert. All that remains now is for you to agree to my terms.'

Sid crossed the room and stood next to his wife.

'I'll agree to anything to have that little love for my own,' Petal said quickly.

Vera hesitated. 'I'd like it if you could send me photographs from time to time. Send them care of Bert but I promise on my mother's and sister's graves that I'll never bother you.'

Vera went to the sofa and picked up her boy, who was busily engaged on his second piece of cake. Vera, aware that this would be the last time she would hold him, kissed his dark curls and then handed him over to Petal. James held fast to Rags and looked at Vera, squirming to get back into her arms.

'Have a wonderful life, my little one,' Vera said. Then she turned, looked at Bert, who rose to follow her, went into the hall, opened the front door and walked out into the sunshine without looking back. Ringing in her ears was James crying, 'Mum-mum.'

Vera knew in her heart that she'd done the right thing. But

it didn't make it any easier, and she forced herself to keep on walking and not turn back. Her sobbing was loud, the tears streaming down her face. She started to run and didn't stop until she was out of breath and could run no more. She realised she was sobbing for herself, and that was useless and selfish.

An arm slid across her shoulder.

'Whew!' Bert said, finally catching up with her. 'I've not run so fast for years. You've done the right thing, you know that, don't you?'

'Yes, Bert, but I don't want to ever talk of this again.'

'Right,' he answered, giving her shoulder a squeeze.

'I'd like it if tonight you'd take round to her James' clothes and his birth certificate and stuff. Though she might want to change his name by deed poll to her last name.'

'It's all right,' Bert said soothingly. 'I'll do all that. Don't you worry yourself.'

Vera stopped walking and faced him. 'There's something else. I know you can't give me a proper job but could I work for you part time in the caff, in exchange for a room? I'll get myself a proper job soon.'

'Of course you can.'

'In that case, can I have the top room with the two windows?'

He looked at her and frowned. 'It's a lot of stairs to climb.'

'That's why I want it. I'll be completely alone up there.'

Now Bert was smiling at her. 'You're a funny woman. But you can furnish the room with bits from the shed. Have a look down there and see what you can find. I'll give you the rest of today to do that.'

Vera nodded, glad to have something to keep her busy and stop her thinking about what she'd just done.

Chapter 27

Vera washed herself all over. She thought how lucky she was to have a sink in her room along with a gas stove. The oven was so grease encrusted that at first she didn't want to touch it. It hadn't been used for years and it took two buckets of hot water that she trudged up the stairs with to get it scrubbed clean.

Everything around her was scoured and shining. All the furniture she'd dragged up and down the stairs gleamed with as much elbow grease as she'd been able to muster. Even the windows sparkled. Vera had stayed up late in the night cleaning her new surroundings, fearful of falling asleep and dreaming of James.

Yesterday was the worst day of her life. The day she gave her child away. Vera pushed the thoughts from her mind. She had to pull herself together if she was going to get through her first shift in the caff. *Pull herself together, yes.* She wondered how many times she'd experience a repetition of last night's fiasco. James was crying and Vera had slid from her warm bed to attend to him. At first she didn't understand why he wasn't in the room with her. Then her senses had returned and she remembered her child was with Petal. Vera had sobbed herself back to sleep.

She looked in the speckled oval mirror then scrubbed at

the block of mascara and applied it to her lashes. She was determined to present a happy face to Bert's customers.

There was still stuff she needed, such as curtains, sheets and rugs, but she was confident that once she'd got a job she'd be able to afford some from the market. After she'd made sure Petal got her money for James, of course.

Slipping on her high-heeled peep-toe shoes and giving herself a last glance in the dressing table mirror, Vera pulled the door closed and locked it.

As she clattered down the stairs and passed the back kitchen, she spotted the pans and wooden spoons James had been playing with less than twenty-four hours ago.

Stop it, she told herself firmly, as she rushed through to the caff.

'I guess I'll still have to carry on cooking.' Bert blew out his cheeks but there was a twinkle in his eye. 'You're costing me a fortune in burned bacon.'

'Never said I could cook, but I makes a lovely cuppa tea, don't I?' Vera looked at him and smiled. She was tired and her feet were killing her. It was now one o'clock in the morning and the customers were beginning to thin out.

Though exhausted, Vera liked her new job and enjoyed chatting to the customers. But every so often she caught Bert staring at her with a sad smile on his face before he looked quickly away.

When finally the last customer had gone and the juke box was unplugged, Vera said, 'I ain't leavin' any of this dirty crockery for the morning. An' all them ashtrays got to be washed; they stink the place out. I've seen a galvanised bucket and a mop in that cupboard in the hall that don't look like it's been used much.' She put her hand over her mouth. 'I don't mean you ain't been keepin' this place clean, you 'ave, but I can make it sparkle.'

'If that's what you wants, Vera,' he said with a smile.

'I'll soon have this place shipshape,' she said.

He nodded his assent and finished cashing up then bade her goodnight.

Vera worked until the early hours, trying hard not to think about James.

Exhausted, she climbed up the stairs to the top floor. She unlocked her door, happy to find everything was just as she'd left it. It had been such a long time since she'd had a place she could call her own. This was only one room, but it was *her* room.

She washed herself, cleaned her teeth and put on a pair of Bert's pyjamas that he said she could keep. She turned off the light and went to the window, pulling back the blackout cloth.

The stars were twinkling and in the light from the moon she could see an aircraft carrier moored up in Portsmouth Dockyard. The water in the harbour was still, like glass. Vera thought she'd never seen anything so beautiful in all her life. She lifted the bottom sash window to let some air in, closed the curtains and got into bed.

Despite her tiredness, it took a long time for sleep to come.

When Vera woke in the morning, she wasn't alone.

Two unblinking yellow eyes stared at her from the bottom of her bed. Then a noise like wood sawing started up and the mackerel-coloured cat began walking fearlessly towards her, its tail stuck straight up in the air like the mast of a ship.

'Hey,' Vera said, 'where have you come from?' The answer was a soft head butt against her arm.

She stroked behind the male cat's ears as he settled down on the blanket at her chest.

She peered at him. 'You are such a pretty boy, aren't you? Oh, my God, you're full of fleas!' She could see a flea crawling across the cat's ear, then it hopped on to the blanket.

She threw back the covers and ran out the door and down the stairs to where Bert had already opened up the caff and was attending to his early crowd.

'Psst! Bert, Bert, come here!' She couldn't enter the caff in his pyjamas. He left what he was doing and came over.

'You made a lovely job of this place last night.'

'Bert, you got any Keating's powder?' Vera interrupted.

'Why? You lousy, love?'

'Not me, this cat what's in my room!'

'Tabby? Oh, don't bother with him, love, he's covered in fleas!'

Vera stood and looked at the man as though she could kill him.

Bert continued. 'He comes and goes. I feed him sometimes when I see him. There's a tin of newfangled cat food under the sink. I got a few tins off an American soldier. And there's some Keating's powder under the sink as well.'

Vera stalked off. Bert called, 'Don't get too attached to the little bleeder; he don't like nobody much!'

Vera went back upstairs, fully armed with food, a drop of milk in a bottle, two saucers and the large canister of flea powder.

The cat was now curled up on her pillow, asleep.

Half an hour later the room was covered in grey dust and Vera was sneezing. The cat looked at her warily, swishing his tail angrily.

'I'm not sure which of us won that battle.' Vera washed her

hands and arms, scrubbing at the cat scratches where he'd resisted being held, and sneezed again. 'So don't bleeding sulk!'

Then she served up the cat food and poured the milk. She
looked at the name on the tin.

'I don't know what your name is but I'm callin' you Kibbles.
Eat your food, drink your milk and the window's open so you
can bugger off when you wants.'

Vera, knowing she'd now have to clean her room all over
again later on, got herself ready and went down to help Bert.

The next few days passed in a blur of early mornings and late
nights, aching feet and tired limbs. Work took the edge off
her wound of sadness but she knew it would take for ever to
scar over.

Gradually Vera came to accept that Kibbles had made his
home with her. She never closed the window, so he could
come and go at will. And she took comfort from his night-
time purring. He looked at her with his big yellow eyes as
though he knew all her secrets and she loved him for it. And
when customers left her a few pence as a tip, she paid a visit
to Ted's fish stall at the market for treats for *her* cat, as she'd
come to think of him.

Then came the day she became friends with Lily.

'You done that sausage sandwich yet?'

Vera plonked the plate down on the counter in front of
Bert so hard the sandwich jumped

'You're getting a lairy cow, our Vera.' But he laughed when
he said it.

The caff was full. There'd been talk of the war ending soon
and everyone was in good spirits. Vera looked at the lads
hanging around the juke box in their sharp demob suits and

the girls clinging on to their boyfriends as though if they let them go for one moment they'd disappear into thin air. Many of them were not much older than her. It felt like a long time since she'd been so carefree.

The door opened then and in sauntered the vision. Vera watched dumbstruck as Lily sashayed across the caff and perched herself on a stool against the counter.

'All right, Lil?' Various people greeted the woman and she smiled at each of them, showing her white, even teeth.

'Cup of tea, please, Vera.'

Vera turned to the large tea urn and poured her a cup. The very same urn that was now silver coloured instead of dirty black. Vera had spent a whole evening polishing it up.

'Sugar, milk?'

Lily nodded and took from her handbag a black suede purse as Vera put the tea in front of her.

'Put your money away, Lily. The day I start charging you for tea is the day hell freezes over.' Bert gave Lily a huge wink.

Lily laughed.

Vera couldn't help staring at the woman. She was wearing a tight red suit with a short peplum that emphasised her slim waist, and a red fox fur was casually slung across one shoulder. Vera stared at its glass eyes. There was a tiny pillbox hat perched to one side of her head with a net veil that didn't quite reach her eyes. Lily put her purse back in her handbag on the counter in front of her and Vera saw her nails were long and scarlet. Vera wanted to hide her own hands, which were rough and sore from the scrubbing.

'My, you've cleaned this place up since the last time I was in.'

'Not me, Lily.' Bert put his arm loosely on Vera's shoulder. 'This one's the woman who can't stand a bit of dirt and clutter.'

271

Lily laughed. 'Bloody good for her.'

Vera marvelled at her clear skin, pencilled, arched brows, long eyelashes and red, red lips.

'You've not been in lately?' Bert enquired.

'No, I got taken to Littlehampton to see this bloke's yacht an' then we stayed up there for a few days.'

Vera served another customer and began wiping the counter top. Fancy being invited on to a yacht. A spate of customers stopped her daydreaming.

'Bert,' Vera called. 'Henry and his missus want a couple of all-day breakfasts. You want me to start 'em?'

Bert appeared magically at her side. 'You go and talk to Lily, I'll do the cooking. Don't want you burning the place down, do I?' He gave her arm a squeeze and pushed her towards Lily.

'So, where do you come from?' Lily asked her.

'I was born here in Gosport,' Vera said.

'Ah, Gosport's been good to me.' Lily had a low, husky tone that made Vera think her own voice sounded squeaky. It was then Vera realised Lily was a lot older than she'd first thought. Maybe in her forties, but her slim body and the way she'd expertly applied her make-up disguised her age.

'How long have you known Bert?' Vera asked.

'For ever. The fact you're working and living here means Bert obviously trusts you. But we all got skeletons in the cupboards, haven't we?'

Vera nodded, unsure of what to say.

'I was with him the night he got shot,' Lily added.

'Shot?'

It was all over the *Evening News*, dear. But of course they never got the full story. I got Doc Dillinger to sort him out, no questions asked, of course.'

Now Vera could see why Doctor Dillinger was so well

thought of, even if he didn't have a legal practice.

'He'd come down to Gosport after a girl, the silly bugger, and the jealous husband didn't like it.'

'But the woman stayed with Bert?'

'No. She had a kiddie so she went back with her bloke but Bert never went back to his old manor in London. You can trust Bert; he's a good bloke. His one failing is he'll go on hoping his woman will come in one day and say she finally wants to be with him.'

'Do you reckon that'll happen?'

Lily shook her head. 'No. Eddie and Kenny, the woman's kids, are her life, no matter how many beatings her old man gives her. Kenny is Bert's boy. Of course the lad don't know, no more than her old man. But one day Bert reckons the lad will come to him.'

'That's a very sad story, Lily.' Vera reached for her handkerchief, thinking of her own son.

'Trouble is, girly, it ain't no story and sometimes life is bloody hard.'

Lily slid off the stool and straightened her clothes. Then she looked at Vera and asked, 'Do you like dancing?'

'I went once with me sister when she was alive. I liked it fine then.'

'Well, I love dancing. What about me and you pop over to the Portsmouth Pally, you know, the dance hall near Southsea, sometime?' Lily had an expectant look on her face.

'What, you'd really go out with me?'

'What's the matter, you got two heads or something?' Lily laughed and Bert looked up from his frying pan.

'What are you two hatching up?'

In unison, Lily and Vera said, 'Nothing.' Then they looked at each other and laughed.

'I'd like that,' said Vera.

'Good.' Then Lily sighed. 'I suppose I'd better get back to work if I wants the tenancy of the Anglesey Hotel. And money to tide me over the sale.'

Vera stared at her. Even she knew the Anglesey Hotel was in Alverstoke, and it cost an arm and a leg to live there.

'You gonna buy it?'

'I've got a decent chance. I've done a few favours here and there so I'm reaping the benefits now. The present tenant moves out in two months and hopefully I'll be the next one moving in. Then I'm retiring. Except for the hotel and bar work, of course.'

The words fell out of Vera's mouth before she had a chance to check them. 'You must be made of money?'

Lily gave her a quizzical look. 'No, dearie. I 'ad nothin' when I started. Same as you, I was. In fact, you remind me of me when I was younger. I started working, saved me money. I give good value, respect the punters, and myself. And I look after meself.' Lily leaned towards her and whispered, 'There's many that don't.'

Vera stared at her until at last the penny dropped.

Lily must have seen it in her eyes for she whispered, 'That's right, darling. I'm a prostitute.'

Chapter 28

'I'm off then.' Vera, wearing a tight black skirt and jacket and red frilly blouse, glanced at herself in the mirror, satisfied that the cheeky red feathered hat was at just the right angle.

Bert looked her up and down. 'Very nice, but you goin' to be able to walk in them high heels?'

'Lily gave me these. I'd sooner change the whole bleedin' outfit than not wear 'em.'

Bert put his hands up in mock horror. 'I only asked.'

No one had put any money in the juke box, so Bert had the radio on.

'Cor, listen to that, Vera. President Roosevelt's dead. What a bloody shame he never lived to see the end of the war.'

'That's a blow,' Vera said. 'At least he didn't die like those poor buggers in them German concentration camps. When me and Lily went to see Betty Grable in *Coney Island*, I couldn't believe what I was seeing in the Pathé News. They showed us bad stuff you couldn't dream of. Lily cried.'

'Soft-hearted, is Lily.'

Vera shook her head, trying to dislodge the atrocities she'd seen on the screen and to bring herself back to the present.

''Ere, you sure I look all right?' She turned full circle.

Bert gave her a Pompey thumbs-up sign. 'You look smashing. Now get going, and good luck.'

Vera took a deep breath and went out of the side door and across the road to Murphy's the Ironmongers.

It seemed to her that there was hardly any place for an assistant to stand. The shop was packed with all manner of stuff from tea sets to drainpipes and slates, and it smelled of candle grease and herbs.

The owner was small, round and cuddly. He looked at her over his oval gold-rimmed glasses and asked, 'Well, love, what do you know about ironmongery?'

'Nothin', that's what I've come to learn.'

'I need someone who can saw planks of wood, someone who knows what all the different nails are for.'

'I can learn,' Vera said.

He sighed and looked at her swelling breasts.

'I'm sorry, dear. If I hired you today my wife would fire you tomorrow. You're much too pretty for me to employ. The blokes that come in here would forget to buy and never want to leave.'

Vera sighed and turned on her heels without another word. She saw Bert watching her from his caff window. She scowled at him and he reversed his Pompey sign to thumbs down.

Vera carried on up the road, towards the fire station and into Mumby Road. At Weevil Lane she turned towards the armament depot, walking as quickly and carefully over the cobbles as she could.

When she reached the armaments factory and she saw how big it was and how spread out, Vera gasped. To think her sister Patsy had worked here for years and Vera never knew where it was as it was entirely hidden from the main road. It was well guarded by a high fence so Vera approached the main gate and waved at the man on duty there.

'I want to ask about a job,' she said. 'Where do I go?'

The morose man shook his head. 'Don't think you'll be lucky, ducks, they're laying off.' But he pointed her in the right direction towards the inside of the red brick building and she knocked on the door that proclaimed 'Office'.

'Come in.'

A large man, who looked as though he could barely fit in the chair he was squashed into, said, 'Yes?'

'I'm after a job.' There was a chair by the table in front of him but he didn't ask her to sit down.

'Nothing, I'm afraid. We're cutting down.'

'Why's that? There's still a war on.'

'Yes and a couple of years ago I'd have taken you on like a shot but not for much longer now Hitler knows he's on the run. We've promised our men jobs to come back to after the war and we've got to stick to that.'

Vera wanted to argue with him but she knew it wouldn't do any good so she turned on her heels and walked out.

She was almost at the gate when three women passed her. Despite their headscarves Vera could see the orange staining on the front of their hair and their yellowed faces. And she was reminded of Patsy, who was always trying to disguise the orange colour of her fringe. Vera sniffed and wiped her hand across her eyes. There were times when she missed her sister so much.

Vera walked back to the town. Everywhere she tried, cafés, factories, shops, the answer was negative.

In the paper-shop window, she saw an advertisement for a cleaner. That sort of work had been good enough for her mother, so why couldn't she apply? After all, she'd just scrubbed Bert's café from top to bottom, hadn't she?

The sun was high in the sky so Vera took a walk out to Park Road. The house was set in its own grounds and the gardens were immaculate. Vera pulled the chain to the bell and heard it ring through the house. She was just about to try again when the door opened and a woman in a severe black dress, who looked like she was sucking a lemon, opened the door.

'I've come about the cleaning job,' Vera said, smiling brightly. The woman merely looked her up and down and said, 'I can see by the look of you that the only things you've ever polished are your nails. No, you won't do!' The door was firmly shut in Vera's face.

It was late afternoon when she arrived back at the caff, tired and dejected.

'Any luck?' Bert asked.

Vera shook her head and climbed on to a stool by the counter. A loud wolf whistle rent the air. The curly-haired man in the corner was looking at her.

'You're a right stunner, today, Vera,' he shouted.

Vera ignored him and started stirring the tea that Bert had poured for her.

'I've got to find a job, Bert,' she whispered. 'I promised I'd send money to Petal for my little boy.'

'She understands,' he said. 'Vera, that woman knows you can't run before you can walk. Have you seen James since?'

Vera shook her head. 'I'll keep my promise. But I'm not saying how many times I've wanted to walk round there in the hopes I could catch a glimpse of him. I never 'ave,' she added. 'I've managed to stop meself. I won't go back on my word.'

Vera finished her tea but before she began the climb upstairs to her room, Bert reminded her that Lily was coming round that night especially to see her.

'I'll send her up to you, shall I?'

Vera brightened. Lily was going to show her how to dress. The dance Lily had invited her to was planned for Saturday night but Vera had moaned that she'd nothing suitable to wear. She didn't want to tell Lily that, beside her, she felt scruffy.

Vera found Kibbles asleep on the bed. She stroked his silky fur and curled up next to him.

She must have fallen asleep, as a loud knock on the door made her start. Bleary eyed, she stumbled to the door and opened it.

'Thank Christ for that. This lot's breaking me bleeding arms.'

Vera could hardly see Lily for all the packages she was carrying. Lily staggered into the room and threw them all on the bed. Kibbles flew out of the window.

Lily's perfume filled the room as she looked about and said, 'Not a bad little gaff, this.' Then she too plonked herself down on the bed. 'I got wonderful news, Vera. The Anglesey Hotel is *mine*!'

Vera threw her arms around her, genuinely happy that her friend's wish had come true.

'Have you signed the contract?'

Lily nodded. 'Today and I'm picking up the keys soon.' She gave a huge contented sigh. 'So, I've been through my wardrobe and brought you some of my clothes that aren't suitable for me to wear in my new role as an Alverstoke hotelier. I'll 'ave to be all twinsets and pearls now! But tonight we're going to dress you up for Saturday night, make-up an' all, and I got a little proposition to make to you.'

'Proposition? I got nothin', Lily. In fact I ain't even got the price of the entrance to the dance yet, let alone the boat and bus fares.'

'Forget all about that. I've got money, so it'll be my treat.'

'Oh, Lil, I couldn't.' Vera was beginning to think she would soon be in everyone's debt.

'Shut up and listen to what I'm offering you.' Vera sat up straight. 'I have a pitch down town. It's the best pitch and I've fought off the other prossies to keep it. I also have a room; well, it's like a little flat really, over the Porthole café, that's furnished very nicely. I never take anyone back to my own home. My home is private. It's my sanctuary, bit like this room is for you.' Lily waved her hand expansively. Vera realised her mouth had fallen open, so she closed it. 'There's my maid, Mae, who's getting on a bit but can still pack a punch if needs be. Always have a maid and a telephone; it stops the johns gettin' too frisky if that's not what *you* want. I'll tell you straight, I've only been slapped once and that was when I was pickin' up blokes outside the Guildhall in Portsmouth. I was very young at the time and new to the game but I soon learned! And, of course, the more high class you are, the better class of customers you can attract. I want you to take it all. I'll put the word about and so you'll have some of my established clients. What do you say?'

Vera looked at her in astonishment. Hadn't she run away from a brothel in Southsea to escape the sexual attentions of dirty old men?

But Lily was her own boss. She hadn't slept with men she didn't want. And there'd been no pimp like Del Simpkins taking her money.

'I ... I've not had a great deal of experience.'

'The johns won't know that! Half of them just want a quick fuck.'

'If I jump at this chance to make meself some money, I still don't have enough money for the maid, the flat ...'

'But I'll bankroll you for that. I've money left over now.

You can pay me back after you've paid some to the bank for your little boy.' Vera could see that too late Lily realised what she'd said.

'How do you know about that?' Vera's voice was cold as ice.

Lily sighed. 'I don't know the ins and outs. But it don't take a blind man to see you ain't got your boy with you no more an' you're working yourself to death trying to forget something. Then I overheard you say something about a bank account, to Bert. Well, I knew it wasn't any good me interrogating Bert. He's tighter than a duck's arse. I just put two and two together. I reckon you need money pretty bad so I'm offering you my old job in the hopes that it serves you as good as it's served me.'

Old job? Lily was expecting her to jump at the chance of sleeping with strange men? All Vera's sexual encounters so far had ended with her being hurt. Did Lily expect her to enjoy being at the mercy of men?

Vera was trying to take all her words in when Lily sighed and said very quietly, 'I'm sorry if I've offended you, overstepped the mark, like. I never meant you any harm.' Lily moved closer to Vera and took one of her workworn hands in hers. Vera suddenly thought of her sister, Patsy, and the presents she'd brought home, the record players, the nylons, the food. Now Vera knew how Patsy had paid for the gifts. With her body. She'd prostituted herself. But did that make Vera think badly of Patsy? Of course not.

'I don't know, Lily. It's not the sort of work I envisaged.'

'So you don't want to be your own boss, work your own hours? Why, you'll be able to buy your own place and have money for James' education.'

Lily paused then frowned. Vera was quiet, thinking over all that Lily had said. And what was the alternative? Vera had tried for so many jobs and been turned down. At least by being a prostitute she could be her own boss. Vera slowly nodded.

Lily looked at Vera and threw her arms around her. 'Oh, it's so lovely to have a woman friend,' she said.

'Don't you have friends?'

'Men, yes. You'll find women will steer clear of you. Some wives will be happy that their old men bother them less frequently but they won't know it's because he's visiting you. Housewives will be jealous of you because I'm going to make you so gorgeous, you'll turn heads wherever you go. Other prossies will hate you because you've got the best pitch in Gosport. But you've got a lovely personality that when you are lucky enough to make friends, it will be for ever, like me and Bert. Still want to be a prossie?'

'If I can make money to send my boy through college, I'll do anything.'

'Atta girl!' said Lily. 'Now, does that stove work?'

'Sure does,' said Vera, full of fresh ambition.

'Well, make us a cuppa then, an' we'll start on titivating you up a bit!'

Later, Vera sat in front of the mirror, the empty mugs on the draining board. She'd tried to look at the clothes in the bags but Lily had slapped her hands away. 'Don't bleedin' touch, Vera! Now turn round.'

'But I want to see what you're doing.'

'And I don't want you to see until I'm finished with you. Then I'm goin' to explain everything so you'll be able to do it all yourself.'

Vera sat quite still and felt Lily's hands smoothing her face and neck with something that smelled nice. Then Lily was patting at her eyes, pressing on her eyelids. Vera wanted to open her eyes and see if she could catch a glimpse of what was going on but Lily kept turning her away from the mirror.

Then she heard Lily turn the gas on and the pop of the flames as she lit the burner.

Minutes later she realised Lily was curling her hair with heated tongs.

'Open your mouth,' commanded Lily and Vera felt lipstick being applied. 'Blot.' Vera pressed her lips on paper. 'Feet up in the air.' Vera did as she was told, as Lily got to work on her toenails. 'You got pretty feet,' said Lily. 'You should show them off in strappy shoes. Right, hands.'

'Can I open me eyes now?'

'I think so.'

Vera turned round and looked in the mirror. Then she shook her head to make sure it was her.

'For Gawd's sake, say something!' cried Lily.

Her dark curls framed her face, a face with a flawless complexion. Her nails were painted the same shade as her toenails and exactly matched the colour of her lipstick. But it was her eyes. Pencilled brows, long eyelashes and shaded to perfection.

'I ain't never gonna manage to put them eyelashes on straight meself. I remind me of someone.'

'Hedy Lamarr, the film star.'

'I-I can't get over it. I look so glamorous.'

'I wouldn't be givin' you my pitch if you looked like the back of a bus, would I? I got my reputation to worry about!'

'Shall I go down and show Bert?'

'Not in them clothes. I know just the sort of gear that you like and I know how I can dress you up to look a million dollars.' She began rummaging in the bags, eventually coming out with a black suit with a belted waist. Then she sorted through another bag, taking out a red silk blouse with ruffles down the front. 'This was a favourite of mine,' Lil said, holding up the suit, 'but I put on a few pounds and now the skirt doesn't look right on me. Nylons,' she muttered. A pair of stockings in a box emerged. 'Bloody good job we take the same shoe size.' From yet another bag came a pair of black suede ankle-strap shoes. 'Now go over there and get dressed and this time I promise I won't look until you're ready.'

Vera took off her own clothes, which until now she'd thought suited her, and, careful of the nylons, dressed herself in Lily's cast-offs.

When she'd buckled up the shoes, she said, 'Ready now.'

Vera could see by Lily's smiling face that she was pleased with the transformation and when she looked in the mirror, she looked, well, gorgeous!

'Now you can go and show off to Bert!'

Chapter 29

'I've had a word with Doctor Dillinger, he's always looked after me, an' he's willing to keep an eye on you.'

Vera looked at the Gosport pontoon growing smaller as the ferry boat wove its way across the strip of water to Portsmouth. She loved the smell of the murky green sea and the feel of the warm May breeze ruffling her hair.

'Well, I ain't likely to get pregnant, am I?'

'No, you silly cow, but you could catch all manner of diseases if you don't make the blokes wear a johnny.'

'Do I buy them or do I expect the men to have them?'

Lily gave an exasperated sigh and opened her handbag. 'You buy 'em an you make sure you don't ever run out of 'em. You can't trust blokes to think ahead. Look.' Nestling inside her suede bag were several condoms.

'We're going to a dance, ain't we? I didn't think this was a business trip!'

The answer she got from Lily was a big grin.

At Portsmouth Hard they caught a bus to Grove Road where the dance hall was. Vera saw other girls dressed for dancing but thought that none equalled them. Lily wore a tightly fitting dress of flowered cotton and a large red rose in her hair. Vera wore a plain yellow dress that fitted her body like a second skin and a yellow flower in her hair.

Once inside the ballroom, Vera was entranced by the big band. All the musicians were dressed in white suits and the music was fantastically loud. The air was full of cigarette smoke and a heady mix of perfumes. The band was playing a quickstep and she hardly had time to look around before she was whisked away by a man dressed in Air Force blue. With the crowded dance floor and the noise she couldn't hear a word he said to her but when the dance finished, he took her back to the small table and two chairs Lily had managed to bag.

The music changed its beat to a boogie-woogie and Vera sat and looked around the opulent hall, with its white and gold-painted walls and a beautiful silver ball twirling high on the ceiling, so that the light inside the hall flickered like stars.

Then she noticed a crowd gathering around a couple of dancers. The mass of people were clapping and shouting good-naturedly. Vera made her way to the throng and squeezed through to see who was dancing, amazed that it was a black American soldier and Lily. The crowd were cheering them on as he picked her up, threw her first one side of his body and then the other side and then she slid between his legs and, jumping up, began moving again to the fast beat as he twirled her around. Vera was mesmerised.

When the music stopped, Lily came back to the table, thanked her escort and sat down heavily on a chair. Vera pushed a glass of orange juice towards her.

'I expect you need that drink. Where did you learn to dance like that?'

'I just love dancing. But I haven't had anyone to come along with me. You just don't know what it means to have a friend to go with.'

Suddenly the band stopped playing and the manager, a short, bald man in a dinner suit, strode on to the stage. He grabbed the microphone and said, 'The BBC Home Service has just announced that hostilities with Germany will end tomorrow, Victory in Europe Day, and there will be two days holiday. The war with Germany is over!'

Whatever he was saying next was drowned out by the cheering and the whooping voices. Then the men and girls were stampeding around the ballroom, kissing each other and throwing their arms about complete strangers.

Lily threw her arms around Vera and said, 'Thank God it's over!'

Then Lily was torn away from her, swept off her feet and carried out of the door. Vera was kissed, and kissed some more, by men and women alike and jostled around the dance floor.

It was over, she thought, over. Tomorrow she would put Union Jack flags out in the café. She knew there would still be fighting out in the Far East and the Japanese wouldn't give in, but for now there was victory in Europe.

After a while the band started playing again and Vera seemed to dance one dance after another. There weren't so many people in the ballroom now as some had gone outside to party in the streets. Eventually Lily came back.

'Where have you been?' Vera asked.

Lily just grinned at her. 'Tell you later,' she said, then, 'Me and you are going down to Hardway to do a bit of business in the morning.'

Both of them brushed aside requests to see them home by hopeful men and they had to run to catch the last ferry boat across to Gosport at eleven o'clock. Standing by the funnel to keep out of the stiff breeze, Lily opened her purse and gave Vera three pairs of nylons.

'Where did you get these?' Vera knew she hadn't taken them with her.

Lily was smiling all over her face. 'Off that American soldier.' And momentarily Vera was taken back in time to the Connaught Hall and her sister warning her never to go outside with any men. Yet Patsy did and always came back with treats.

'You never!'

'I did!'

'So that's why you had them johnnies in your bag?'

'I know I've given it up, really I have. But that was just for old times' sake!'

Vera started laughing. 'The war might be over but rationing will still be in place. Next time we come to the dance I might just come round the back with you.' Slipping her arm through Lily's, Vera said, 'You know, I've really enjoyed meself tonight.'

'So have I,' Lily said. 'You're not worried about Monday, are you?'

'The first day on the job? Of course, I'm scared stiff.'

'Well, don't be. Mae's promised to work for you and Clarence will be one of your first customers. All you do with him is tie him up, blindfold him, gag him and lock him in the hall cupboard for a few hours. Just don't forget he's there and go home and leave him like I did one night.'

'Jesus, what happened?'

'He paid me double,' Lily replied with an impish grin.

On the dot of nine the next morning Lily was sitting on a stool in Bert's caff waiting when Vera rushed down the stairs.

'Don't forget you'll be working tonight to make up for the time you've been gallivanting,' warned Bert, waving a tea towel at her.

'Oh, Bert, don't be such a killjoy! Next week I hope to

be paying you rent and I'll still take a turn in the caff!' Vera waltzed up behind him and planted a kiss on the back of his neck. 'I'll be back in double quick time to start dollin' the place up with Union Jacks.'

'Gerroff!' he laughed.

'You're a little love—' Vera began.

Lily said, 'For Christ's sake, let's get going!'

At the ferry they caught the Provincial bus to Brockhurst and began walking towards Elson. Every house they saw had bunting up to celebrate VE Day.

Hardway was barricaded to stop sightseers. A guard approached them and when he saw Lily, he said, 'I'm still not supposed to let anyone past except residents but I reckon you've done more'n enough to help the war effort, our Lily.'

Vera saw Lily give him a devastating smile as he allowed them past the barrier.

The nearer they walked towards Hardway's newly built landing ramp leading down into the sea, the more vehicles they saw lined up along the roads.

'What's all this, then?' Vera asked.

'Hardway's a sheltered location and near enough to Gosport town centre, without going through it, to accommodate the huge landing tanks that were part of Operation Overlord. All these vehicles,' Lily waved her hand towards the jeeps and machinery in trailers and the ambulances, 'and all manner of people and troops in their trucks embarked and disembarked here. Winston Churchill, Field Marshall Montgomery and our King George visited and then thousands of troops poured into Gosport. That was last year. Now, the war in Europe might be over, but there are still medical and surgical equipment needing transportation overseas and men who have to be brought back to dear old Blighty, so my little Vera, you could be making a fortune.'

Vera looked puzzled.

'It's not a cup of tea the men want when they reach England's shores, Vera, it's a woman.' Vera gave a hearty laugh.

Just then a head popped out of the doorway of a wooden building and a man in a blue knitted sweater and wellington boots called, 'Lily, come over here and say hello.'

Lily grinned at Vera. 'Come on, I'll introduce you to some of the lads. These are the workers, the blokes what gets their 'ands dirty, the other part of the services who sometimes know what's goin' on in the forces before the bleedin' high-ups do.'

Lily sashayed over to the long hut and stepped inside and Vera followed. Half a dozen men were drinking tea out of tin mugs and sitting on beds while they read newspapers. The cigarette smoke could be cut with a knife.

'This young lady takes over from me, boys, so you know where to go for a good time.' Vera laughed at her. It always amazed her that Lily could be so frank about things.

It wasn't long before the men and the two women were giggling and talking about Lily and her exit from the world of prostitution and her move as proprietor of the Anglesey Hotel.

'The German prisoners of war landed here, didn't they, gentlemen?' Lily continued. 'They marched under guard through Elson to the holding camp situated in Mill Lane. Some of them went directly to the railway station in Spring Garden Lane and on to other holding camps elsewhere.'

'What about the ones who were injured?' Vera asked.

'This is England, ducky. We patched 'em up and looked after them a damn sight better than our men were treated.'

Lily's voice grew hard. Vera knew she was remembering the atrocities she'd seen on the Pathé News.

'This site will still be in service as long as we have boys to bring home from overseas,' said a tall thin man. 'The war's ended, Vera, but it's not over yet.'

'Quite so,' Lily said. 'War's only the beginning. Afterwards comes the clearing up.' She put her tin mug on the wooden table and stood up. 'Well, lads, I hope you'll pass the word around that our Vera has taken over my place in Gosport town.' Plenty of nodding and smiling went on as Lily made her way to the door and the two women began picking their way over the cobbles that ran the length of Green Lane. Vera stopped, turned and looked back at the ships moored in the grey green water.

'Them blokes'll spread the word around for you, Vera, and I'll get me share of new customers in the hotel bar. Personal service, that's what we've just been giving. Advertising our wares.' Lily was quiet for a while, then she said brightly, 'I've got the key to the Anglesey Hotel so I'm going to have a proper look now it's empty. You can come if you want.'

'Yeah! But then I'd better get my skates on and get back to the caff before Bert blows a gasket!' She paused. 'Thanks for that introduction, Lily.'

Lily smiled at her. 'I'm determined to make a huge success of this venture, Vera. I came to Gosport with nothing when I was fifteen and now I've bought one of the most prestigious buildings in the area. Not on a mortgage, either – I pay cash on the nail for what I want, well, they can be a bit funny about giving mortgages to women on their own, can't they?' Lily tossed back her hair. 'The next thing is to give the place a coat of paint, bit of an uplift, and hire staff. And if you're wondering why I didn't offer you a job, it's because I only want good part-timers and their money will be nowhere near the amount you can earn.' She looked wistful. 'But I sometimes have dreams that it'll all go arse upwards.'

Vera pulled her round so Lily was facing her. 'You are silly. How can it go wrong when you're such an excellent business-woman? You will make a success of this, I know you will.'

Vera stood on the corner by the taxi rank. It was a warm night but she was shivering with apprehension. She'd met Mae, a monkey of a woman, small and very fierce, definitely from gypsy stock, thought Vera. The flat was immaculately clean because Mae wouldn't let anyone clean it except herself.

There were two bedrooms; one very tiny that Mae slept in as she lived in the flat full time, and the second bedroom was for 'business'. It was lavishly furnished with plenty of gilt and white furniture and chiffon scarves thrown across table lamps to diffuse the bright lights.

Mae was also in charge of Lily's appointment book, now Vera's, so Vera literally took over where Lily left off.

It was decided that while a client was being entertained that Mae would sit next to the telephone in the hall, ostensibly to take messages but also to guard Vera should anything unto-ward happen. Vera was a little afraid of Mae but trusted her completely, as had Lily. Mae would also handle the money.

'Excuse me, ma'am, but are you in business?'

Vera's heart started banging against her ribs. 'I could be. What are you looking for?'

He blushed. Dressed in white with his jaunty round hat perched well back on his carroty hair, Vera could see he was hardly more than a boy.

'What part of America do you come from?'

'Ohio, miss.'

No doubt he was from one of the American ships berthed at Portsmouth, she thought. So she told him her price and that she had somewhere they could go. He agreed and she slipped her arm through his and together they crossed the road, where Vera pushed a bell next to the brightly painted door to let Mae know she was on her way. They climbed the stairs. Soft music was coming from the flat as the door opened.

'Money up front,' said Mae.

Vera went into the bedroom and after a while the young man followed. Something told her he was just as nervous as she was. He was all fingers and thumbs getting his clothes off and Vera felt so sorry for him that she asked, 'Is this your first time?'

His wholesome face turned towards her and he said, 'Yes, ma'am.'

Vera took one look at his freckled body and his cornflower-blue eyes and said with the tenderness she truly felt, 'Come here, I'll give you something to remember and to brag about to your mates.'

Her first client went away more than satisfied.

Vera didn't go back to her pitch immediately. True to her word, Lily had told Clarence about Vera and she had the pleasure of shutting him in the cupboard in the hall. She was getting dressed then undressed as one client followed another. One client simply wanted her to talk to him while she was dressed as a waitress with a very short skirt and no knickers. Every so often she had to bend over in front of him and pick up a piece of cutlery. Not once did he touch her.

By two o'clock in the morning, there were no more clients.

Mae was in the kitchen making cups of cocoa. 'You want me to cook you something to eat?'

Vera shook her head. 'I think I could sleep standing up,' she said.

Mae pointed to a pile of bank notes on the table. 'Those are yours.'

Vera hadn't seen so much money for ages. In her head she had already started calculating how much she needed to put by for the rent on the flat and its outgoings, Mae's wages, rent for Bert and some aside to begin paying Lily back. Most importantly, she needed to give some to Bert to start paying into the bank for James' future.

Mae surprised her by walking over to the kitchen drawer to produce a tea caddy and an exercise book. 'I've begun the same as I did for Miss Lily.' She opened the tea caddy to show Vera's notes nestling inside. Then she opened the exercise book and showed the columns of figures she'd started. 'This book shows the monies you need to put aside for essentials, rent, electricity, gas. I've taken it all out, not all of it of course, but enough so that at the end of the month bills will always be paid. Miss Lily was a stickler for paying her way. Now, if you don't want me to carry on with this, say so. That money on the table is a bit like your own wages.'

'But surely that's too much money for me? What about your wages?'

'I told you, you got nothin' to worry about. I'll look after you same as I did at the beginning for Miss Lily. Though Miss Lily got so good with sorting her own finances that she's now an astute businesswoman.'

Vera thought of Lily paying cash for the Anglesey Hotel. She had obviously saved most of her own money while Mae looked after the day-to-day expenses. Vera picked up Mae and swung her around.

'You're a bloody marvel, Mae, that's what you are.'

Mae looked flustered and frowned as Vera put her down, but Vera was sure she saw a twinkle in her eye.

Vera thought of the change in herself. She was now a woman determined to be every bit as astute as Lily. One day she would own her own massage parlour and have a stream of clients visiting her girls. But she'd do it all on her own terms. Never would she be dependent on anyone again.

Chapter 30

'Vera, open this door at once!' The knocking reached a crescendo.

Kibbles, disliking the noise, escaped through the open window. Vera tied her black silk dressing-gown around her, padded barefoot across the room and let Lily march in, bringing with her a cloud of perfume. Vera stared sleepily at her immaculately dressed friend, who pushed an envelope into her hands.

'Bert said to give you this.'

Vera's heart jumped as she recognised the writing on the envelope. Whatever Lily wanted, Vera needed to get her out of her room quickly so she could open the precious letter. Vera slipped the envelope into her dressing-gown pocket and grumbled. 'What on earth do you want at this time in the morning?'

'It's eleven o'clock and you should be out in the fresh air enjoying the countryside, or at least mooching through the market. I can't stay long.' Lily shook the kettle to see if it held enough water for tea and then lit the gas.

'Make yourself at home, why don't you?' Vera said. She ran her fingers through her wayward curls. 'I didn't get home till two and I'm tired.'

'You'll soon perk up when I tell you my news.' Lily winked at her and let a smile spread across her face.

Vera tutted. She emptied the tea leaves into the sink tidy and, after rinsing the teapot, pulled two mugs from the top cupboard. Then, waiting for the kettle to boil, she sat down at the small table and motioned Lily to join her.

'Come on then, tell me why you're here.'

'I got a couple of blokes staying at the Anglesey, been with me about a month now, and one of them wants to meet you.'

Vera looked at Lily as though she was mad. 'Ain't hard to find me, is it? If I'm not at me pitch, I'm at the flat. Or here.' She glared at Lily. 'Trying to get some sleep, that's if my best friend will let me!'

Lily ignored Vera's taunt and smoothed her blond hair away from her face. 'This man's not a possible client.'

Vera frowned. 'All men are possible clients,' she said. Lily was shaking her head. The kettle started its mournful call and Vera reluctantly rose and made tea. After enjoying the first mouthful, she smiled at Lily.

'What's his name?'

'So you are interested.' Lily put her mug back on the table. 'Richard,' she said. 'Richard Merryweather. He's been staying at the hotel until the paperwork's completed on a house he's buying.'

'Never 'eard of him,' said Vera.

'Course not, you haven't met him yet. He and his friend want to take us both to Goodwood.'

'Goodwood? What's that?'

'Well, you won't find out if you don't go, will you?'

Vera said, 'Sometimes, Lily, you can be so infuriating.' She pursed her lips and looked thoughtful. 'But I could do with a day out.'

'I'll tell him you'll come, then.' Lily pushed her empty mug to the centre of the table, got up and made her way to the door.

Vera looked at her retreating figure. 'Lily?'

Lily turned. 'What?'

Vera laughed. 'I'll be looking forward to it,' she said.

The moment Vera heard Lily's high heels clatter down the stairs she climbed back in bed. Kibbles, now sitting on her pillow, stared at her with his all-knowing eyes and began purring.

'Let's see what Petal's sent, shall we, precious?' A friendly head butt was her cat's reply before she tore open the envelope. Out slipped a single photograph. Vera held it up and peered eagerly, her stomach full of butterflies.

The serious little boy stared back at her. Dark curls peeped from beneath a school cap. His tie was awry and one side of his shirt collar was winging heavenwards.

'You are so beautiful it hurts me to look at you,' she said to her son's image. 'So very beautiful.'

On 18th September the Rolls-Royce Silver Wraith paused outside the side door of Bert's café. Vera, who had been watching out of the window for the car's arrival, ran down the stairs.

Customers gawped as a tall dark-haired man opened the rear door, allowing Vera to slip inside to where Lily sat grinning at her friend as though her face would split in two at any minute.

The blond man with the moustache sitting in the front passenger seat turned his head to smile, then said, 'I'm so glad you could make it.'

Vera decided she liked his upper-class tones. Lily squeezed Vera's hand as the driver's door slammed.

Before the dark-haired man accelerated the car he said, 'Vera, I'm Marcus Selby, this is my good friend Richard Merryweather.'

'I'm Lily and this is my best friend, Vera,' chirped Lily. Marcus laughed. 'I know who you are, Lily.'

'Hello,' said Vera. She could see by the way Marcus held Lily's eyes just a moment too long that if they were to be paired up she would be Richard's partner. And she didn't mind that one bit.

She could tell by Richard's slight shoulders beneath his charcoal-grey jacket that he hadn't an ounce of fat on him. He seemed shy and looked away every time she caught him looking at her. Vera decided it was going to be a very interesting day indeed.

The car purred through the town and out into the countryside. After a while, Vera could see the spire of Chichester Cathedral drawing closer. Fields and farms dotted the landscape and some trees, in the process of shedding their leaves, still held their autumn colours of red and gold.

'I'd forgotten how pretty it is when you get away from the towns,' Vera said. She crossed her nylon-clad legs and peered hopefully through the gleaming windows of the car.

'Ever been to Goodwood before?' Richard asked. 'Most tracks closed down during the war and this is the grand re-opening for the circuit.'

Both Vera and Lily shook their heads.

'Richard used to drive,' interrupted Marcus. 'And won a few races.'

'Really?' Lily sounded curious.

'It's a scenic place, nestling as it does by the foot of the South Downs.' Richard hesitated as though he had said enough and then grew silent.

He obviously didn't want to talk about his car racing and Vera was convinced she'd heard a hint of sadness in his voice. At least he wasn't one of those men always bragging about his accomplishments, she thought, and that made her warm to him all the more.

Marcus began to talk of one of his childhood experiences, which resulted in all four of them giggling like children. Both men appeared to be good company so Vera relaxed and began to enjoy herself.

The entrance to Goodwood was busy with colourful vendors, their patrons and vehicles queuing to enter the grounds.

'So many people,' marvelled Vera.

'Estimated number is fifteen thousand spectators,' said Marcus. 'And if no one's got cold feet there should be over eighty drivers.'

Vera could just make out the size of the Goodwood circuit. People were standing alongside the fence encircling the track. Some visitors were sitting on the bonnets of cars, some had brought picnic tables and were seated around, laughing and talking.

The Rolls-Royce climbed to a hillock and then stopped. 'Here, I think,' said Marcus. He didn't wait for a reply but exited the car and walked round to open its boot.

Lily opened her door and tumbled out crying, 'I can help. I'll set out the picnic stuff.' She hauled a large wicker basket from the back of the car and set it on the grass.

Vera got out, glad to stretch her legs, and went to see if she could help, as the large boot seemed to be packed solid with stuff. She paused in amazement as Marcus lifted out a wheelchair.

Vera looked at Lily, who smiled back hesitantly. Once the lightweight wheelchair was unfolded, Vera watched as Marcus wheeled it round to the front of the car.

Richard was lifted into the chair and Marcus asked, 'Okay?' Richard nodded, then looked anxiously at Vera.

Marcus stood up straight, glanced at his watch and said, 'We've got more than half an hour before the Bristol sporting saloon appears with the Duke and Duchess of Richmond to officially open the track. What say you and I,' he looked at Lily, 'take a walk and look at some of the cars before they go hurtling around the track?'

Lily nodded, then looked at Vera. 'You'll be all right, won't you?'

'Of course,' said Vera. But she was wondering why Lily hadn't explained about Richard and his inability to walk. Not that it made any difference, he was a nice man and she wanted to get to know him. Which was, she decided, precisely why Marcus and Lily were going for a walk and leaving them together.

She watched her friend and Marcus walk away and saw Lily slip her hand into Marcus's. Vera stood in front of the wheelchair and asked Richard, 'Do you want to go anywhere or shall we stay here and talk?'

'Here, I think.'

Vera took a blue blanket from the car's boot and spread it on the grass at Richard's feet. She sat down and lifted her face to the surprisingly warm sun.

'This feels nice,' she said. 'I love the warmth.' Then she stared into his blue eyes. 'Do you want to tell me how this happened?' She waved towards the chair.

'I'd rather tell you how long it's taken me to pluck up the courage to ask you out.'

Vera didn't know what to say. His reply had been totally unexpected. Was he serious or was it some kind of sick joke? She decided honesty was the best policy. After all, what had she to be ashamed of?

'You don't have to ask for my company. Men pay for it. You do know I'm a whore?'

He raised his eyebrows. 'When I first saw you, you weren't.

But I was in no fit state to become involved with anyone then. Let alone a girl I saw on the dance floor, the day it was announced that we had victory in Europe.'

Vera gasped. This man *was* completely serious. 'But that was years ago. And the first dance Lily and I ever went to together,' she said.

'And I was a broken man feeling sorry for myself; sitting in a corner. You've no idea how I cringe when I remember my self-pity.'

Vera thought about other men she had met since the war. Men shattered in mind and body, who had come to her for comfort. So why was this man any different?

'Well, it's very nice to meet you now, Mr Merryweather,' she said, trying to keep her tone light.

'Likewise, Vera.' There was a smile waiting to happen at the corner of his lips.

'So?' Vera asked.

Now he frowned. Vera wanted him to talk. But remembering how he had deflected the conversation away from himself in the car, she realised it wasn't going to be easy.

'So I hoped you'd tell me how come you're in a wheelchair?'

Richard let out a long sigh. 'It's a similar war story to others you've probably heard. I flew a spitfire but I was shot down by a Messerschmitt and fell out of the sky near the aerodrome at Biggin Hill. A posse of kids found me and raised the alarm. When I eventually came to in the local hospital I was told I'd never walk again. I'm paralysed from the waist down.'

'You're lucky to be alive.'

'I didn't think so at the time.' He looked down at the grass. 'And now I've been dealt a double blow. I have a tumour. The doctors can't operate and some days I'm such a bastard to everyone around me that I want to end it all. But then

I remember I probably won't see the year out, so it doesn't matter.'

'You mustn't talk like that,' Vera said, grabbing at his hand.

There were tears in his eyes but he stared straight at her and said. 'It's the truth. After I saw you at that dance, which was my first foray out into the big wide world after the crash, I never stopped talking about you. It's taken me a long time to learn to live again without all the self-pity. In a way the tumour has convinced me I only have the one life to live. Marcus suggested I put myself out of my misery and meet you. So that's how come we're on this picnic today. I begged Lily not to say anything until I'd spoken to you first.' He raised his eyes heavenwards. 'You've no idea what a hard job that was, with her being your friend.'

Vera laughed. 'I know what she's like. But she's also the best keeper of secrets ever.'

'So I've found out. Vera, if we never meet again after today, at least I'll have the satisfaction of knowing I summoned enough courage to meet you.'

Vera opened her mouth to speak but her words were lost in the midst of a huge squeal from Lily as Marcus chased her over the grass towards them. She collapsed on to the blanket.

'This place is enormous,' Lily said, puffing and panting with the exertions of running. 'And cars are lining up at the start point for the first race.'

'This used to be Westhampnett airfield during the war,' said Richard. Vera silently cursed Lily for her untimely return. Just then a fanfare rose and the crowd began cheering. 'Royalty's coming,' Richard quipped as the couple in the car began their tour around the racing circuit. Vera looked at him and he smiled back at her with the bluest eyes she'd ever seen. Warmth spread through Vera's body.

Marcus opened the picnic hamper and spread out a white tablecloth on the grass. Next came the champagne flutes, and Lily giggled as the cork exploded from the bottle.

'You've thought of everything,' announced Vera looking at the mountain of salad, the cooked chicken and the pastries. Even the serviettes had been folded into napkin rings.

Marcus didn't ask Richard what he wanted to eat. He simply piled a plate high with food and handed it to him along with a knife and fork. Vera thought they made a good team with Marcus anticipating Richard's needs. Richard accepted the ministrations from Marcus with such aplomb that Vera knew they cared a great deal for each other.

Amazingly, Vera didn't realise how hungry she was until she saw that she'd eaten everything on her plate.

Marcus put down his empty plate. He made to refill Richard's glass but Richard put his hand over the rim and said, 'Old chap, I need to visit the bar to buy more champers, do you mind? I think there's time before the first race.'

'Not at all,' Marcus said. 'You two girls carry on without us for a while.'

Marcus released the brake to the wheelchair and began strolling towards the clubhouse, dodging between the sight-seers and picnickers.

When the two men had been swallowed up in the crowd, Lily said, 'That was for your benefit, you know.'

Vera looked confused. She put down the piece of shortcake she was about to bite into and asked, 'What was?'

'Richard giving us the opportunity to talk,' said Lily.

'Richard told me about—'

Lily interrupted her, 'He won't tell you everything because he doesn't want to scare you off and he doesn't want pity.'

'Pity's the last thing he'll get from me.'

'Good. That's what I told him. I'll tell you about the tumour. It's a brainstem glioma, malignant. He was offered experimental therapies as there's nothing else the doctors can do. He refused. The headaches and fits will get worse. He has only a few months to live.'

'He explained that to me, Lily.' Vera filled her glass with the champagne and offered to top up Lily's. Lily shook her head.

'I admire his guts. It's not everyone who could be as brave living with a death sentence,' said Vera.

'He'll be dead by Christmas.'

Vera took a mouthful, swallowed and said, 'Thank you for putting it so delicately. I'd like to believe Richard cares for me.' She paused. 'And a blind man could see there's something going on between you and Marcus. But this revelation of Richard's is all a bit sudden and I've been hurt many times by men and their lies.'

'Well, he doesn't want you for your professional wiles, does he? And he certainly hasn't the time to spend ages courting you.'

'So he's telling the truth when he says he likes me?'

'I'd stake my life on it, Vera. And it's a lot more than like. You could make his last months happy. He could restore your faith in men. And, yes, Marcus and I are close. Close enough for him to have asked me to marry him.'

Vera gasped. 'I wasn't expecting that.' Lily held out her hand and Vera saw the ring that glinted in the sunlight. 'Oh, Lily, you should have told me before. I'm so happy for you.' Vera threw her arms around her friend.

'It was practically love at first sight for both of us,' said Lily, her hands now holding Vera's and her eyes searching her face. 'But I knew I had to tell him about my past. I put it off as long as possible, terrified he'd leave me. Then, one night, I plucked up the courage to tell him I'd been a prostitute since the age of fifteen, and gave it up when I bought the hotel.'

'What did he do?' Vera's heart was beating fast.

'He said, "I love you today and I'll love you tomorrow. The past is gone."' Vera felt her eyes fill with tears.

Lily extricated herself from Vera's grasp. 'I never thought in a million years that a man would love me for myself,' she said.

'I don't see why not,' Vera replied. 'You're beautiful, sexy and kind. And you listen to men, really listen when they talk.'

Lily began to laugh. 'And that's precisely why men like you, you daft cow!'

'Here we are,' Marcus said, clicking the brake on the wheel-chair. He took the bottle that Richard handed him.

Just then a mighty cheer rent the air and the smell of petrol fumes filled the circuit. Richard was staring intently at the cars racing around the track.

'Go on,' he shouted. 'Six main corners and a couple of straights, then the chicane.' Vera saw him look at Marcus but his friend's eyes were fixed on the track. 'Madgwick, the first hurdle. Don't let the car go out too far after the first apex. Ford-water coming up, then St Mary's, a sharp left-hand corner.'

Vera realised he was acting out in his mind then voicing the perils of the circuit. She thought how brave he was to be at the track when he could no longer drive a racing car. Driving had obviously been a big part of his life.

'Don't mess it up at the chicane,' Richard shouted. 'Brake, man, brake. That's it! Catapult out, control the power. He's done it! He's bloody done it! Paul Pycroft in his Jag is the winner of the first race!'

Marcus was jumping up and down and Richard was clapping his hands.

Lily exchanged glances with Vera and they smiled happily at each other.

Vera walked along Fort Road. Christmas was fast approaching and the ground was frosty beneath her feet. In the distance the sea was grey. The bare trees smelled fresh and clean like they'd been newly washed. The past couple of months had sped by in a whirl of trips, parties and outings. Always the four of them, and unless, like now, she visited Richard at his home, she seldom saw him alone. Even then she was likely to encounter his doctor, or the housekeeper who had been his nurse as a child.

Badger's Holt was set back from the road. It was a large, imposing house in the sought-after area of Alverstoke, with a mature garden surrounding it. She reached the mighty oak door and rang the bell and waited for Mrs Summer to let her in.

'He's upstairs,' said the housekeeper. Vera liked the no-nonsense woman with the short grey hair and kindly eyes. Sometimes Mrs Summer would shake her head and Vera would go away, her spirits low, for she'd quickly learned to trust Mrs Summers' judgement as to whether Richard could cope that day or needed to stay medicated in a darkened room. Vera realised that the tumour set the pace on their relationship and Richard didn't want her to see him when he was in severe pain.

Vera climbed the curving stairs and knocked on Richard's bedroom door. Without waiting for a reply she went in to find him asleep in the four-poster bed.

'Wake up, sleepy head,' she said, ruffling his hair. He opened one eye and smiled at her.

'That's a lovely surprise to wake and find you here,' he said. 'Lie down beside me.'

'For a while,' Vera said, climbing on to the high mattress. 'Don't forget we're going to Chichester today, the three of us, to look at wedding dresses for Lily.'

Vera knew the last thing Richard wanted was for her to think he couldn't tackle an ordinary day, no matter what the night terrors had wrought.

'Do I have to go?'

'Yes, then Lily gets a male point of view. She can hardly ask Marcus what he thinks, can she? Her dress is supposed to be a surprise and it's unlucky for the groom to catch a glimpse of it.' Vera snuggled up against him. 'And anyway, Mrs Summer wants to get this bedroom cleaned and you out from under her feet.'

'Ah, Mrs Summer, my housekeeper, my nurse. You could have that job if you wanted, Vera. In fact, we could get married. We could have a double wedding with Lily and Marcus.'

Vera pulled away. 'Sometimes,' she said, 'you make jokes that aren't even a bit funny. It's a bloody good job I know you don't mean it.'

'It's not a joke, Vera. It's a safety measure. If you marry me, you'll inherit my money—'

'I'm not here with you because I want anything from you,' she said angrily. 'And I told you I don't want to be beholden to any man ever again.'

He stared at her. 'Not even me?' he asked quietly.

'Especially not you. I am who I am,' said Vera. 'In the short time I've known you I've come to love you, but it doesn't mean I'm going to give up my way of life. I simply want to make you happy for the time we have left together.'

Richard kissed her. 'Make me happy, then,' he said.

Vera wasn't afraid of the kiss but she was scared of the fire that was spreading through her body. She reached into his pyjama jacket and felt his heart beating beneath her hand. Vera undressed and slipped into bed beside him.

'Do what you want with me,' he said, kissing her again.

He was slender and taut-bodied and marred by the scars of war. Vera ran her hands over his muscles and all that mattered to her was the way he tasted, the way he smelled.

After a long time Richard wiped the tears from his eyes. 'You can't leave me now,' he said. 'And I wish I didn't have to leave you.'

'It's all right, Richard,' Vera said, pressing herself as close to him as she could. 'It really, really is all right.'

The week before Christmas Richard was taken into hospital. He died on the twenty-first of December. His body was taken home to Gilmore Hall to be buried in the family plot.

Vera, at the funeral, stood between Lily and Marcus. She shivered and turned up the collar of her black coat against the rain. She could see Richard's mother standing rigid and alone, a small figure wearing pearls, glossy white against her black apparel. She was huddled beneath a large umbrella. Every so often the older woman looked towards Vera then away again. Her face was like parchment and wet with tears. As with Richard those memorable blue eyes dominated her face.

When the mourners dispersed the woman walked towards Vera. She clasped Vera's hands. 'My dear, I want to thank you for the joy you brought to Richard during the last months of his life.'

Vera tried and failed to hold back the tears. 'He was a good man,' she mumbled. 'He restored my faith in the kindness of men.'

Richard's mother dabbed at her eyes with a lace handkerchief. 'That was because he loved you, my dear.' She moved the umbrella so Vera too was sheltered from the worst of the downpour. 'We didn't meet while my son was alive. Living in Gloucester I never was one for travelling far from home but he contacted me when he could.' The woman leaned closer to Vera. 'The reading of the will takes place next Wednesday. I'd like you to be at my house. I know he's left you something.'

Vera shook her head. Wasn't that just like the man to do the opposite of what she wanted? 'I told Richard I wanted nothing from him.' Richard's mother looked alarmed. 'I don't want what we had together to be spoiled by money. I'm sorry. I can't accept anything. My conscience wouldn't let me.'

Vera stepped back and clutched at Lily's hand, then she turned back to Richard's mother. 'I'm sorry for your loss,' Vera said. 'I didn't know what I had until I lost Richard. He loved me unreservedly.'

A tall man stepped between the two women. 'Come on, Mother, it won't do you any good to stand here in this awful weather.' He nodded at Vera first and then shook Marcus' hand. 'Come back to the hall,' he said kindly. 'Cook's put on a good spread.'

Marcus looked at Vera for affirmation. 'I want to go back to Gosport, to the café,' she said, through her tears.

Chapter 31

1962

'Jesus, you startled me,' Vera said.

Bert handed her a plate of eggs, bacon and chips. Out of his pocket he took salt and pepper canisters as well as a plastic mock tomato filled with ketchup.

'Daydreaming?'

'I was,' Vera said. 'Of the past. Where's your food?'

'I'm not hungry,' he said.

'Well, I bloody am; you make the best chips in Gosport,' she said, spearing a golden-brown morsel.

'Have you thought any more about Alfred Lovell?'

'I have, and I want you to do something for me. Will you?'

'Anything.'

'I'm going to write a note that I'd like you to give him when he calls back.'

'So you reckon he will return?'

'Oh, he'll come back,' said Vera, cutting the bacon.

'What are you going to say?'

'I'll leave it unsealed so you can read it. I got no secrets from you, Bert.'

Vera finished her meal and Bert took the plate, winked at her and carried the dirty crockery through to the caff's sink.

She began the long climb to her top room.

Kibbles was asleep on the bed. Vera smiled fondly at him. He didn't move so quickly nowadays but Vera refused to think about him dying. He was her boy, her love. His throaty purring started up and she bent down and put her face in his fur.

Then, from the bottom drawer of her dressing table, she took a shoe box and began sifting through the photographs. The pictures told James' life story and she selected the one of him in cap and gown at his graduation. The photograph was old and well handled. There were seldom letters between her and Petal. But every now and then a photograph would arrive and Vera would pore over it for hours, days, months.

He was a handsome young man with dark curly hair like hers. You could see he was her boy. He had the same pointed chin and dark eyes.

Vera found her notepad and began to write.

This is your son. I don't know why you came to see me but I don't ever want to see or hear from you again. Return to Australia and have a happy life.
Vera.

Vera tucked the note in an envelope with the photograph.

She wrote 'Alfred Lovell' on the front and went downstairs.

The radio was playing softly. Vera handed Bert the envelope and he slipped it in his top pocket.

'Thank you for listening to me. I've been a right barrel of laughs, haven't I?'

Bert picked up a tea towel and began polishing glasses.

'Vera, you've made a lot of friends, especially in high places. You've sent your boy through school and university. You've bought premises in the High Street and soon your massage parlour will open. You'll have money to retire on. You are a respected member of the community. Don't let the appearance of this man undermine all you've achieved.'

Vera listened carefully to his words. Then she said, 'So you think I did the best I could?'

Bert put his hand on her arm. 'Of course you did. Times are changing and in another few years no one'll be pointing their fingers at unmarried girls who keep their babies. You, Vera, fell back on the oldest profession in the world to give your lad a chance in life and to pay for his education.'

'Too bloody right,' she said. 'Though I'm certainly not sayin' it's the right job for all women.'

'Course not,' Bert said. 'But do *you* think you did the best you could?'

'Did I do the best I could with the life I had?' Vera's voice was calm. 'I think my heart had its reasons.'

Bert's eyes never left hers. 'If that's so, for such a strong woman why are you taking the coward's way out?'

Vera frowned. 'What do you mean?'

Bert shook his head. 'Don't you think it would be better for you to face Alfred Lovell? Give him this letter yourself?'

'Wait a minute,' said Vera. 'I don't want to see the bugger!'

'You have to face your demons, Vera. Then, and only then, can you be free of them.'

For a moment Vera was silent, digesting his words. Then she reached forward and removed the envelope from Bert's pocket.

'You're right,' she said. She looked Bert in the eye and repeated, 'You're right.'

A light wind was tossing leaves along the pavement of The Crescent, a semi-circle of tall white colonnaded houses set back from the sea. Vera stared at the exotic buildings that she knew had been completed in 1830 and were the brainchild of local entrepreneur Robert Cruickshank. Once the houses had been family dwellings. Now some had been turned into flats and apartments that cost the earth to buy or rent.

She had memorised the address and when she reached the gate she opened it and began the walk up the long well-tended garden. Vera looked down at herself. High-heeled shoes, a neat black suit, and a frilled black blouse beneath. She'd taken special care with her hair and make-up and wore her trademark Californian Poppy perfume. She was far removed from the fourteen-year-old girl Alfred Lovell had raped in the scullery of Alma Street.

It was dusk. As Vera pulled the chain to a bell that seemed to clatter for ever, she was seized with panic. Why was she putting herself through this pain?

There were ghosts that needed to be laid to rest. Finally, she would have a voice and no longer be at Alfred Lovell's mercy. Perhaps after today this man would cease to darken her dreams.

Vera heard footsteps echoing. Her heart was beating loudly. The front door slowly opened. He was older than she expected, but still good-looking in an outdoorsy way. He was, Vera saw, just an ordinary man. She began to relax. She could deal with this.

His eyes widened in surprise and for a moment Vera was certain she would have to speak first as it seemed he was struck dumb at the sight of her. Or had she changed so much he no longer recognised her?

At last he spoke. 'Vera?' There was wonder in his voice.

'Are you asking me in or shall we discuss our business on this doorstep?' That's it, girl, she thought, take control.

And now he was flustered. 'Yes, yes, come in.' He stepped aside and Vera went in. The door closed behind her. Alfred moved ahead of her saying, 'Come through.'

Vera was led down a long corridor that emerged into a tasteful kitchen. Her heels clattered on the parquet flooring. It smelled newly decorated. As though reading her mind, Alfred said, 'I rent this flat. Upstairs is another flat.'

'Must cost you,' Vera said, pulling out a chair and sitting down. The chair scraped on the wooden floor.

'I can afford it,' he replied, sitting down across the table from her.

Vera looked at him. 'I'm not here to talk about your finances,' she said. 'I want to know what you want.'

He sighed, made a line with his lips, then spoke. 'I've come back to England to clear up a few loose ends.'

'Was that what I was, a loose end?'

He bowed his head. 'I wasn't proud of what happened.'

'I got through it,' she said quietly.

'I can help, Vera. I have money now. Jennifer died last year and her estate has just been wound up.' He was bright-eyed now. 'I'm rich.'

'So you thought you'd throw a copper or two my way? Thought it might make up for me losing my child?'

'Lost? Vera, you mean the child's dead?'

'Of course he's not dead.' Vera opened her clutch bag, took out her letter and thrust it into his hands. 'I did the best I could for him.'

Alfred was studying the photograph. 'He's like you.' He passed a hand across his eyes and then was silent.

'James is the reason I live,' Vera whispered. 'I had to give him up. But I work so he has a good education. He knows nothing about me, or you, and I'd like it kept that way. He has excellent parents.'

Alfred read the letter she'd written. He sighed and slid his hand across the table, but before it reached hers, Vera said, 'Don't touch me. I only came to see you because I didn't want to be a coward, unlike you.' She looked into his face and was glad he wasn't the man her boy called Father. She thought then of Richard Merryweather and how for a short time she had loved him. Sometimes it's the last love that hurts the most, she thought.

Alfred moved his hand away. 'I'm so sorry, Vera.'

'Sorry is only a word.'

He cleared his throat. 'I made a few enquiries about you before I left Australia.'

Vera knew what was coming. This man had raked up her past and knew how she earned her money.

'Then you know I'm a businesswoman about to open a High Street business—'

'You're a prostitute!'

'I don't need to apologise to you.' And suddenly Vera realised she didn't need to apologise to anyone for the way she made her living and had sent her child through university. The last time she had heard from Petal, she'd been told her boy had embarked on a law degree.

'No, you don't,' Alfred said. 'So it was a choice, not a necessity?'

Vera shook her head. 'You think after you raped me I would ever do anything again that I didn't want to do? If so you're more stupid than I thought you were.'

Vera almost felt sorry for him when she saw the brightness of a tear glisten in his eye.

'So you don't need help from me?' Alfred said, as he wiped his hand across his eye.

'No. I'm an independent woman. But there is something I would ask.'

'Anything.'

'Angela? How is she?'

'Twisting the knife in the wound, are you?' Alfred's eyes were downcast.

'What do you mean?' Vera asked.

From his wallet he took some dog-eared photographs and handed them to her. 'Angela nursed Jen until the end. Unfortunately Jen decided it was time to tell her the truth about my affairs, all of them. At the funeral, Angela said she didn't have to pretend any more. I was to remove myself from her life. I haven't seen her since that day.'

The snapshots showed a blonde Angela cuddling two children.

'Grandchildren?'

Alfred nodded.

Vera wanted to say something. Instead, she shrugged and thought about how life came full circle. She slid the photo back across the table.

'I'm sorry,' he said again.

Vera got up to leave. 'You're only sorry because life's just done a U-turn and bitten you on the arse.'

Out on the road, the wind had dropped. The air smelled fresh and clean. Tonight she knew she would sleep well. Memories were like ferocious animals, ready to tear her apart, but now there would be no more dreams of the past. Life goes on, thought Vera, a smile touching her lips. Thank God, life goes on.

Chapter 32

1970

Vera slipped the last daffodil bud into the water and then carried the vase through to the waiting room of her massage parlour. Setting the flowers down on the glass table next to the blue leather sofa, she stepped back and, smiling, admired the bright yellow blooms. Vera liked Heavenly Bodies to be welcoming, both for the clients and her girls.

A draught of cold air came through the High Street door along with Bert, who said, 'I was coming into town so I brought this letter the postman left earlier at the caff.'

'Shut the damn door then, it might be spring but it's enough to freeze the brass balls off.' Vera's voice tailed away. 'Who's sendin' me letters to the caff?'

She looked at Bert, who shrugged and said, 'I'll go down and put the kettle on. Your girls'll appreciate a cuppa on a brisk morning like this.'

Bert stepped smartly along to the kitchen area and Vera watched him shake the kettle to see how much water was in it. She turned her attention to the envelope, tore it open and took out the single sheet of paper.

Dear Mother

My name is James and I wonder if you would consider a meeting with me?

Recently my parents were killed in a car crash. While clearing their home I came upon a tin box containing my original birth certificate, a bank-book and a letter from them written some years ago telling of my birth mother's sacrifice ...

'Bert!' shouted Vera. She could read no further for tears had filled her eyes and obliterated the writing. *My son's writing,* she thought. *My son, after all these years, has contacted me.*

Bert's face was full of worry as he reached her side. Vera handed him the letter and watched as he read. Finally his eyes strayed from the paper and a smile touched his lips.

Vera looked into his face.

'It's from my boy,' she whispered.

About the Author

June Hampson was born in Gosport, Hampshire, where she still lives. She has had a variety of jobs including: waitress, fruit picker, barmaid, shop assistant and market trader selling secondhand books. June has had many short stories published in women's magazines and is the author of the popular Daisy Lane series.